A STAR TREK® NOVEL

DREAMS OF THE RAVEN

CARMEN CARTER

POCKET BOOKS

New York   London   Toronto   Sydney   Tokyo   Singapore

An *Original* Publication of POCKET BOOKS

POCKET BOOKS, a division of Simon & Schuster Inc.
1230 Avenue of the Americas, New York, NY 10020

STAR TREK is a Registered Trademark of Paramount Pictures.

This book is published by Pocket Books, a division of Simon & Schuster Inc., under exclusive license from Paramount Pictures.

ISBN: 0-671-74356-2

First Pocket Books printing June 1987

10   9   8   7   6

Printed in the U.S.A.

A Nasty Tingle Crept up
the Base of Kirk's Neck . . .

Spock's voice rang out. "Captain, bio-scan readings are inconsistent with our profiles of the Frenni race."

Instinct, rather than thought, moved Kirk to action. His voice rang out to Engineering. "Mr. Scott, recall the shuttlecraft." He edged forward on his seat. "Mr. Sulu, prepare to raise shields as soon as those ships are back aboard."

"Kirk, what hass happened?" came the bewildered voice of the alien as the shuttlecraft turned back towards the *Enterprise.*

Kirk hesitated.

"Captain, why thees gamess with uss? Pleasse hurry, we hass injured needssing medical care."

"Captain," Spock said. "Energy output levels in their engine room are increasing." On the viewscreen, the cruiser began to turn slowly.

Jim felt the soft snap of a trap springing shut. "Scotty, get those shuttles landed! We need to raise shields!"

"Five seconds, Captain."

Kirk chanted the count to himself. "Now, Sulu!"

But even as the helmsman moved to obey, the Frenni craft burst into motion, racing straight for *Enterprise.*

Look for STAR TREK Fiction from Pocket Books

Star Trek: The Original Series

Star Trek: The Next Generation

Dedicated to my mother and father

Prologue

KYRON GENTAI-HANN, nephew by marriage to the Exalted House of Kotzher, and captain of the *IKF Falchion*, was bored and angry. He had been in a perpetual state of boredom and anger for an entire year, ever since the Klingon Military Council had "honored" him with a posting to the Belennii star system, a worthless holding of the Empire set in a position of supreme strategic unimportance in a far-distant corner of undisputed space.

That Kyron, a warrior of acknowledged skill and long years of service to the Empire, should have received such an assignment was directly attributable to his alliance to the Exalted House of Kotzher, now exalted in name only. This last year had given Kyron sufficient leisure in which to regret, with increasing bitterness, his marriage into a family which had fallen into imperial disfavor. Of his wife he thought nothing at all, confident that she returned his lack of interest.

Being a Klingon, Kyron did not feel compelled to keep his growing resentments to himself. On the contrary, the privilege of bullying the crew of the *Falchion* was one of the few meagre compensations still left to him. His subordinates—no less bored or angry, but perhaps even more resentful since they had less scope for bad temper—had spent the first months of the long voyage to Belennii engaging in frequent bouts of petty

7

bickering which inevitably culminated in physical violence. The resulting fatalities reduced the somewhat crowded conditions of the crew quarters, thus easing the most unbearable of the tensions. By the end of the first year of their tour of duty, the remaining crew members had settled into a sullen acceptance of the tedium of routine patrol over a quadrant of space that contained one white dwarf; two yellow stars without planets; 4,020 asteroids of sufficient size to merit a star-chart notation; and a periodic comet which would reappear in their area in 845 years.

On the 451st day of that patrol, Captain Kyron was expatiating at great length on the cowardice of the Imperial Ministry in advising the Emperor to accept a truce with the Federation. Such criticism bordered on treason; however, if the captain cherished any hopeful fantasies of being recalled to Klinzhai in order to stand trial, he was greatly deluded. His crew had long since ceased to hear his words, despite the loud and bellicose manner in which they were delivered.

"Peace is for the soft worms of the decadent Federation dung-heaps!" screamed the captain from his command throne. Beads of sweat gathered on his bronze-dark skin; his forked eyebrows bristled stiffly with rage while his moustache drooped damply from the exhalations of his oratory. "Peace is the corpse that feeds their maggot growth!" He had reached a fever pitch of invective against his own government and was now marching into a denunciation of its former enemies.

As he peered down into the red shadows of the crew pit, his voice dropped in pitch. "Do not be fooled by their treachery," he warned his listless navigator. "They are weak but they are also cunning . . ."

"Commander," called out the communications officer. "I am receiving a transmission."

8

". . . and should be killed outright like defective newborns." Kyron paused for breath, and only then did he realize that one of his crew had spoken. In the last 451 days he had never been interrupted in the midst of his diatribes; he was unprepared for such a novelty.

"It isn't time for a scheduled communication, Kath," he barked angrily at the offending officer. Having built up a storm of temper, it made little difference to him where it was directed.

"No, my lord," agreed Kath with proper subservience. He, too, seemed rather stunned by the occurrence. "But it is not a message from Command Base; it is from an alien craft."

At those words, a hunched figure in a dim corner of the bridge came to life with a guttural curse. The sound of frantic, if somewhat belated, computer activity followed soon after. "Scanners reveal an unregistered scoutship at 457 kilometers, approaching on an intercept course, rendezvous at 94-mark-12," announced the negligent science officer as calmly as his anxiety allowed.

Kyron gave an exultant howl of glee. "Imbecile! Eye of a rotting cadaver!" He pulled a disrupter from his belt and stunned his science officer into unconsciousness. Thus appeased, the captain turned his attention to the intruding alien.

"Raise shields," he ordered with a spreading grin. "Lock phasers on target." An unregistered craft was fair game for his battlecruiser. He cared little whether it posed any real danger; the *Falchion* was long overdue for battle maneuvers. Almost as an afterthought, he inquired of Kath, "Who are they?"

Kath released the broadcast from the alien. ". . . *your Imperial Servant, most unworthy of attention, beseeches most humbly . . .*" came the bleating voice from the communications translator.

"Gleaners!" spat out Kyron with disgust. He had little use for this race of scavengers that eked out a subsistence living from the leavings of the Klingon Empire. "Prepare to fire."

"We bring you great wealth and power," continued the voice from the scoutship.

Kyron stayed his next command. "What trickery does this scum propose?"

"A wreck, such salvage we have found," whined the Gleaner. *"We can offer information . . ."*

The captain of the *Falchion* ordered Kath to open communication channels. "Where?" he demanded of the alien. "Where is this wreckage?"

"Ah, worthy ship chief," answered the Gleaner with humble solicitude. *"We would be only too glad to share this knowledge with you in the privacy of your vessel . . ."*

And for a percentage of the haul, thought Kyron with a touch of pragmatism. He loosed a savage kick at his stunned science officer, urging him to regain consciousness with greater haste; Jaeger was quite adept with the mind-scanner and would be needed soon.

"Very well," Kyron said grudgingly. "I will discuss terms with you. Prepare to beam aboard." His toothy grin returned. He would have plenty of opportunity to destroy the Gleaners later, after they had given him the information he wanted.

Chapter One

CAPTAIN JAMES T. KIRK of the U.S.S. *Enterprise* stopped dead in his tracks at the sight of the phaser rifle aimed at his chest. His two companions followed his example. The weapon was impressive: its polished metal surfaces were studded with jewel-like power settings which pulsed with a hypnotic rhythm. The face behind the gun was impassive.

"We come in peace," declared the starship captain calmly. He was shorter and stockier than the men who flanked him, yet he possessed an air of command that owed more to force of personality than to his gold tunic and braid. Kirk smiled his most winning smile and turned his hands palm up in a gesture of friendship, but the sturdy form which stood in their path showed no signs of giving way. The round face of the rifle-bearer twisted into a scowl and his hands gripped the stock more tightly. Passage through the narrow corridor remained blocked.

"Try 'Take us to your leader,'" suggested the first of Kirk's companions, an older man dressed in science blue.

"Hardly original, Bones."

"To old troopers like us, perhaps, but *he* may never have heard it before."

The second of Kirk's companions tried his own

approach. "We require immediate access to the next area. Let us pass." The Vulcan's tone was decidedly more emphatic than that of his captain, but just as ineffectual. More so—the whine of the phaser's power pack grew in volume.

McCoy snorted. "Well done, Spock. Your diplomatic powers are astounding. If you're not careful, you'll get us shot. And a loose phaser bolt could pierce the hull and destroy this entire section of the trading post." The broad wave of his arm included the corridor in which they stood and a generous amount of the metal structure to which it belonged. "I, for one, do not want to eat vacuum for breakfast."

The science officer stared coldly at the doctor. "The illogic of this situation is not fascinating—it is tedious." He took a step forward.

"Steady, Mr. Spock," cautioned the captain, holding him back. "We mustn't alarm the native population." He continued smiling down the gun barrel. "In fact, I'm sure we'll all be friends before too long." This time Kirk took the step forward.

The phaser burst into fire and bright bolts of red light rained over the bodies of the three officers.

"Die, Klingon pigs!" yelled their assailant. Loosing another salvo from his gun, he turned and ran down the corridor.

"Am I expected to fall to the floor, wounded and dying?" asked Spock archly as the young boy disappeared around a corner.

"You're no fun at all," complained McCoy. The three men continued their walk away from the outer docking ring of the station and headed for its center hub. "See if I ever ask you to play cops and robbers." The Vulcan could think of no reply to this reference to traditions of Human childhood. The doctor took advantage of Spock's silence to turn his attention to Kirk. "Better not let Star Fleet hear of this fiasco, Jim. It could ruin an otherwise sterling military career."

"You win some; you lose some," said Kirk philosophically, smiling at the memory of the freckled face which reminded him of his own nephew, Peter, at that age.

When their corridor reached an intersection with the station's third ring, Kirk looked to the left and right along the curving walls, searching for another glimpse of the boy, but the small form had disappeared amidst the adult crowds. Purple-suited station personnel—mostly Human and Andorian—strode briskly about their duties; merchants and traders of various species moved with more leisure, passing in and out of the small shops that lined the ring. A group of Tellarites waddled across the path of the two Humans and their Vulcan friend; a single Crysallid sprinted jerkily ahead of them.

"That young child," said Spock, recovering the conversational initiative, "is a prime example of the difficulties inherent in implementing a truce with the Klingons on a sustained basis."

"You mean to say that you found him hostile to the initiatives of peace?" asked McCoy solemnly, lifting a rounded eyebrow to match the cant of Spock's slanted one. Kirk noted that the doctor's impersonation of the Vulcan was improving.

" 'Die, Klingon pigs,' does lack a spirit of reconciliation," said Spock with equal solemnity. If he was aware of McCoy's mimicry, he chose to ignore it. "That such attitudes are to be found in one so young presages obstacles to extending amicable relations with the Klingon Empire through the next generation."

"The truce didn't maintain that we had to like

13

Klingons, Spock," countered McCoy. "It just said we had to stop killing them. And, more to the point, that they had to stop killing us."

From long experience, Kirk sensed that his two officers were laying the groundwork for an extended argument, although the actual terms of their conflict had not been settled yet. He launched a tactical diversion.

"I've always wanted one of those." Spock and McCoy followed the line of their captain's outstretched arm and its pointing finger to the window of a small tradegoods shop which specialized in used equipment for asteroid-miners. The display held a familiar array of battered environment suit accessories, solar cookpots, and out-of-date entertainment tapes.

From amidst the clutter, McCoy's eyes picked out the one small item that had drawn Kirk's attention. "The knife."

"A Tyrellian blade, Bones. Fifth Dynasty."

Spock contemplated the long thin blade and its squat handle. "More likely Fourth."

"Whoa, Jim." McCoy grabbed Kirk's arm and pulled him back. "If that trader gets one look at your face, he's going to double the price." He waited until the eagerness in Kirk's eyes was properly subdued. "Okay, now we can give it a try."

As they crossed the threshold of the store, the doctor looked back over his shoulder at Spock. "And you, don't say a word."

The Vulcan stood silent as his Human companions were greeted by a short, plump man draped in the flowing robes of the local Trade Alliance Guild. They exchanged meaningless pleasantries and engaged in the ritual discussion of merchandise which was of no interest to either side. At the first mention of the knife, however, the trader quickly pulled the weapon out of the display window.

"A beautiful artifact, one that I am not often privileged to handle. Tyrellian blades are prized for . . ."

McCoy cut the speech short. "How much?"

The trader pressed the blade into Kirk's hands. "Feel the weight and balance of a knife made by a true craftsman. You won't find its like in the whole sector."

"How much?" insisted the doctor.

Kirk was too obviously entranced with the weapon. The trader paused for a quick assessment of his customer, then named a price.

"Two hundred credits?" McCoy gave a soft hoot of derision. "Jim, this man heah thinks we're tourists."

"Gentlemen, please." The trader shook his head forlornly. "Two hundred credits is a bargain for this item. Planetside, this would cost close to three hundred. It's your good fortune that this station is a backwater and demand for antiques is low."

Spock reached out to inspect the blade but McCoy had already taken it from Kirk's hand.

The trader donned a well-practiced expression of sincerity. "Of course, I'm always willing to give Federation officers a special discount."

McCoy and Kirk smiled back as if they believed him.

"Just how much of a discount are these stripes worth?" Kirk flashed the cuff of his sleeve over the counter.

"For you, Captain, at least twenty-five credits."

Spock opened his mouth, then quickly closed it as McCoy shot him a warning glance. The doctor turned the knife around and around, peering critically at its surface. "The handle is cracked."

"It's very old," said the trader, jerking it out of McCoy's hands. "Age leaves its traces." He proffered it to Kirk again. "One hundred and fifty credits."

"And the blade's edge is dull," pointed out McCoy. A swift kick to Kirk's shin cued the captain to lose interest.

The man behind the counter studied the effect of McCoy's comments on his customer. "The edge is worn because the knife has been used, Captain. This was a working weapon, not a decorative toy." Kirk's interest appeared to revive somewhat, but his enthusiasm was not high. The trader's show of exasperation approached a genuine emotion. "One hundred and twenty-five credits, and that's my final offer."

This time the Vulcan first officer spoke aloud before McCoy could stop him. "If that price is acceptable, the item is either a forgery or illegally obtained."

At those words, the trader whisked the knife out of Kirk's grasp and under the counter. "I'm so sorry. This item is not for sale after all." He removed his smile as well.

"Jim, it wasn't a forgery," declared McCoy as the three of them left the shop and resumed their walk down the corridor.

"No, it wasn't."

Spock could not confirm their judgement since McCoy had not given him an opportunity to study the weapon. "Doctor, if it was indeed a genuine Tyrellian blade, then it was certainly smuggled out of the Tyrelli System."

"We're starship officers, not Interstellar Customs."

The Vulcan was unmoved. "There is little satisfaction to be gained in the possession of an artifact which has been removed from its planet of origin against the wishes of its native population."

"No, I suppose not," said Kirk in what he hoped was a convincing tone.

"It would have been one helluva bargain," muttered McCoy with regret.

Kirk saw that the lines of battle were now clearly established, but there was no time left for McCoy and Spock to indulge themselves in verbal sparring. The long corridor came to an end in an arched portal. Beyond the portal lay a large domed area, the center hub for the wheel-shaped Wagner Trading Post. The eyes of the starship officers were drawn to the spectacular view provided by the room's construction. Both the deck and the dome itself were formed of faceted clearsteel which allowed the rich inky-black texture of space to spread over, around, and beneath them.

Above the dome, gleaming softly like a small moon, the U.S.S. *Enterprise* hung motionless on the dark velvet backdrop of space. Walking across the transparent floor to the railing which marked the curving wall, Kirk feigned a casual interest in the sight of his ship, but deep within he felt the same knot of excitement he experienced each time he saw her from a distance. His eyes eagerly traced the familiar lines of the disk-shaped primary hull and the slim nacelles which powered it.

Spock, too, walked up to the dome's edge, but he looked out, not up, to inspect the four concentric circles of the space station structure. "Wagner Post was designed by T'rall of Vulcan, though admittedly in her youth, before the full scope of her engineering powers was developed."

Kirk beckoned to McCoy to join him, but the doctor stood rooted in the center of the circular deck, his eyes calculating the distance to the nearest exit. "I don't mind being in space so long as it keeps a low profile." He pointed an accusing finger at the invisible surface beneath his feet. "This is definitely letting it get out of hand."

Spock looked up from his inspection. "True, there is no functional necessity for this architectural feature. However, it shows evidence of the aesthetic influence

17

of her Andorian training. Andorians are susceptible to claustrophobia."

The soft chiming of a chronometer rang through the air, bringing Kirk's attention back to duty. If he didn't hurry, he would be late for his meeting with the station manager, a lapse which might be viewed as a sign of military arrogance. Small space stations such as this one, so often ignored by a distant central government, were quick to take offense when they were noticed. He reluctantly turned his back on the *Enterprise*. Motioning to Spock, Kirk returned to the center of the room. "Why, doctor, you look as green as my first officer."

"I'm not fond of heights," said McCoy irritably. "In the future I'll know to avoid Andorian architecture. Hortas have the right idea—they dig tunnels through solid rock."

Spock pointedly ignored the doctor's grumbling criticism. "Captain, we are due to meet Post Manager Friel in eight point six minutes." He pointed confidently to one of the eight portals, all seemingly identical, that opened into the dome. "That way."

"Coming, doctor?" asked Kirk, his legs straining to match his first officer's long strides.

"No way," stated McCoy emphatically. He ducked his head as they passed under three Pegasi hovering gracefully in the air. "I'm off-duty, which means I can forgo official calls. This is a trading post, and I have every intention of promoting interstellar commerce to the limits of my credit line."

"Just stay out of trouble," called out Kirk as the doctor veered off in another direction.

Led by Spock's unerring sense of direction, the two officers actually arrived early. Unfortunately, they weren't early enough to suit Manager Friel. "It's about time you got here," stormed a large, imposing woman as they walked through the doors of her office.

Kirk suppressed a sigh of exasperation and prepared himself for an hour or two of tiresome diplomacy. He feigned a smile and cast it in the manager's direction. However, Friel made it immediately clear that her impatience was not an expression of temperament, despite the reddish glints in her hair and the fair Irish features of her face. "We're receiving a Priority One distress call from an incoming freighter. Captain claims they were attacked by a Klingon battleship."

Spock's eyebrows flew upwards. The corners of Kirk's mouth flew downwards. "In Federation space?"

"I don't have the details," said Friel, sweeping a mountain of tape cassettes and paper printouts from her desk onto the deck in order to reach her computer terminal. She flicked a combination of switches that brought forth the image of a slender cobalt-blue Andorian. "Timmo, have you re-established contact with the *Saucy Lady?*"

"No," he whispered in the reedy tones of his race. Friel snapped off the terminal with a moderately good rendition of an especially vile Orion expletive.

"I couldn't agree more," said Kirk. He ignored Spock's obvious curiosity concerning the translation. "What have you heard so far?"

"Static mostly. Timmo picked up the distress call fifteen minutes ago. The priority code was clear enough, but the explanations were too fragmented to get a full account of what happened. There was definitely an attack," she insisted angrily, seeing the skepticism lurking in Kirk's eyes. "Neil's an old spacedog. He's been on the Wagner run for seven years and he doesn't get hysterical over an occasional sighting of a Klingon battleship."

"An occasional sighting?" A slow burn worked its way up from Kirk's collar to his face. "Just how often have Klingons crossed over into this sector?"

Friel developed a rather unconvincing cough, but the delay was good for only a few seconds. "Oh, well, now and again."

"When was the last time?"

Her attention was suddenly riveted by the tapes and papers scattered across the floor. "Eight, maybe nine months ago."

"The truce negotiations were completed only last month," noted Spock.

The station manager addressed her reply to the impassive Vulcan rather than face Kirk's stony rage directly. "We're all a long way from home out here. Klingon, Human, Andorian. After a few years of routine patrol, a crew gets sick and tired of living on a ship. They need shore leave."

"And they're willing to pay top dollar for new provisions," said Kirk.

Friel shrugged. "I'm not a military post or a military target. I don't shoot them and they don't shoot me. So what's the harm . . ."

Her defense was cut short by the bleep of her intercom. The communications tech appeared back on the screen, his delicate antennae quivering with agitation. "Yes, Timmo?"

"Captain Neil on communication band 12," he announced. Simultaneously, the broadcast from the freighter echoed into the office.

". . . they need help in a bad way. One ship blasted—the other badly crippled and leaking its guts out all over the sector. Need medical assistance for heavy casualties and techies for engine repair. If it can be repaired."

"Who needs help?" shouted Friel into the intercom.

"Frenni merchant caravan. Except it's not a caravan anymore. The Verella *was destroyed and the* Selessan *won't be going anywhere without help."*

Kirk drew a sharp breath when he heard the ships

named. He moved to the terminal. "Who attacked them?"

"Klingons." The man's bitterness cut through the crackling of static. *"The caravan had established subspace contact—they were expecting trade negotiations for ship's stores—but the battlecruiser attacked instead. No explanation, no warning."*

The captain whisked out his communicator. "Kirk to *Enterprise,"* he called in a low voice, still keeping one ear tuned to the report from the *Saucy Lady.*

". . . and we picked up their distress call ten hours ago. I volunteered to change course and pick up survivors, but they advised me to leave the sector fast and send back armed rescue. So I got the hell outta there."

Kirk's communicator beeped in reply to his call. "Enterprise *here, Captain."*

"Cancel shoreleave, Lt. Uhura," he announced grimly. "Recall all personnel to the ship and inform Mr. Scott that we'll be warping out of orbit within the hour."

Chapter Two

Captain's Log, Stardate 5302.1:
    Despite a recent truce which has suspended formal hostilities and military engagements between the Empire and the Federation, the *Enterprise* is responding to a report of Klingon aggression . . .

JIM KIRK BROKE off his narrative at the approach of his first officer.

"Strictly speaking," said the Vulcan, moving to one side of the command chair on the bridge, "Frenni space is not Federation territory."

"A civilian ship and its crew have been blasted to smithereens and you're arguing the subtleties of diplomatic law," snapped McCoy from Kirk's other side.

"The distinction is hardly irrelevant, doctor," insisted Spock. "An attack against a neutral ship—in that ship's territory—does not constitute an attack against the Federation."

"He's right, Bones," said Kirk, stemming any more of McCoy's comments. The captain amended his log entry accordingly.

"By custom, the ancient space routes of the Frenni race are invested with the rights of a planetary system. These corridors of travel tunnel through both Federation and Klingon space. The nomadic merchants have maintained a strong neutral relationship with both sides, a

relationship based on commerce and trade. Now, for reasons unknown, a Frenni merchant fleet has been attacked by the Klingons."

He paused to take a breath.

"It's crazy," said Lt. Sulu heatedly. His eyes were riveted to the helm, his slim, muscular frame tensed with the effort of guiding a starship at faster-than-light speed. The captain had ordered maximum warp speed, which made piloting trickier but more fun. "The Klingons have an import-dependent economy, which makes it suicide to endanger relations with a primary trade source."

Ensign Chekov brushed ineffectually at the mop of unruly brown hair which threatened to blind him. "The Klingons don't reason—they're Cossacks," muttered the young Russian as he double-checked his computed navigation coordinates for the starship.

Kirk raised his voice to override any more interjections.

"Nevertheless, such an attack raises concern for Federation security in this part of the galaxy. As the only starship available within this quadrant the Enterprise *is responding to the distress call from the* Selessan, *Merchant Esserass commanding. Estimated time of rendezvous is 1.5 hours."*

This time when he paused there was an expectant silence from the bridge crew. Kirk logged the entry with a jab at the panel on his armrest. "Thank you, gentlemen. You may continue your discussion now."

The junior officers looked abashed, but Spock took the statement at face value. "Current knowledge would support Mr. Sulu's contention that an attack on the merchant caravan is indeed detrimental to Klingon self-interest. Therefore, it is possible that the attack was that of an individual acting without official approval."

"A rogue warship?" asked McCoy with surprise. "That's a rather fanciful notion."

"It is merely one hypothesis," said Spock, quick to dispel the idea that he possessed an over-active imagination. "An alternative hypothesis would be that the Klingons have gained another source of trade, one which has severed their reliance on the Frenni."

"That possibility would imply a new, and powerful, alliance for the Empire," said Kirk uneasily.

War. The word seemed to hover in the air, unspoken yet reverberating. A shift in the balance of power could tempt the Klingons to shatter the uneasy truce, or at least see how far they could stretch its boundaries.

Lt. Uhura was the first to break the silence. She flashed a brilliant smile. "It's so entertaining to be on the cutting edge of diplomacy." Her exaggerated enthusiasm raised an appreciative round of laughter from the bridge crew.

Kirk grinned ruefully. "Yes, we do seem to pull more than our share of galactic quarrels." A small light on his armrest came to life. "And domestic quarrels, as well," he sighed, flicking a switch. "Yes, Scotty?" he asked, knowing full well what was on his engineer's mind.

"Maximum warp . . ." The Scotsman sighed. *"Ah, well, I dinna need t' repeat myself—you've heard it all before. Just consider it said again. If you'll be wantin' me I'm in the main engine room."*

"Having a fit," added McCoy. He cast a challenging glance at Spock.

"Really, doctor," said Spock. "Your habit of exaggeration is most inappropriate. Mr. Scott is not throwing a tantrum—he is simply showing his professional concern for the proper functioning of this vessel."

"He's spitting tacks," insisted McCoy.

This time Spock's face froze in concentration as he

tried to make sense of the unfamiliar idiom. McCoy was searching for yet another colorful phrase with which to confound the Vulcan when Kirk returned the conversation to factual matters. "Mr. Spock, would you please continue the briefing."

"Certainly, Captain." Spock returned to his computer station and directed the crew's attention to a side viewscreen. Three dim stars dotted the image; the rest was black. "The *Selessan* is currently adrift on the perimeter of the Belennii star system, a small, undistinguished holding of the Klingon Empire. It is an unstable trinary composed of one white dwarf and two yellow stars. Despite its proximity to Federation outposts and minor trade routes, the system has never supported a Klingon military base. It is too far removed from the core of the Empire to insure an uninterrupted supply line. Neither are there targets which would justify the large expenditure of resources necessary to invade this sector."

Spock turned back to the captain. "There is no logical basis for a single ship to mount an attack. It is an exceptionally aggressive action with no readily discernible benefit. One vessel, while capable of causing considerable disruption of local commerce and transportation, would still stand little chance of challenging Federation military forces. It would be a senseless suicide mission."

"It could start an intergalactic war," argued Kirk. "Ships from every planetary system in the Federation pass through those shipping lanes. Random attacks could antagonize a sufficient number of voting Council members to authorize a retaliation on the Empire. The truce would be destroyed."

"It's barely gotten started," said McCoy. "And you're saying it's already over?"

"Hardly an unexpected development," said Spock with clinical interest. "Numerous factions in the military have strongly opposed the truce from its first proposal. The success of the initiative is due largely to recent strains in the Klingon alliance with the Romulans; the current government wishes to avoid a battle on two fronts. However, they lost a great deal of political favor in the process of accepting the truce agreements."

"You mean they might not be able to stop a war?" asked McCoy with a growing sense of horror. "Good Lord! The lives of millions of people could be put in jeopardy!"

"It is only a hypothesis," said Spock blandly.

"Why you cold-blooded . . ."

Uhura's voice overrode McCoy's. "Captain, I'm receiving faint transmissions from the *Selessan.* We should be in hailing range shortly."

"Thank you, Lieutenant." Kirk forestalled his first officer from demanding an exact time estimate from the communications officer by announcing, "I've met Captain Esserass, of the *Selessan.*"

"Indeed, Captain." Spock allowed himself to be deflected from the reprimand. McCoy was still fuming over the Vulcan's professed callousness, but he also accepted the change in conversation.

"Many years ago," admitted Kirk, "when I was a lieutenant aboard the U.S.S. *Farragut.* Our galley refrigeration units malfunctioned and we were forced to trade for ship's stores. Unfortunately, all they had were several tons of Orion *demma.*"

Rumors and innuendo about the nature of *demma,* both its source and its effect on those who ate it, were common folklore throughout the galaxy. An accomplished storyteller, Kirk let his statement hang in the air until the full implications of the situation were absorbed. A few anticipatory chuckles dotted the room. McCoy grinned broadly. Even Spock took on a speculative air.

"By the time we arrived at Star Base 7, sick bay had run out of fertility control ampules and . . ." The rest of the somewhat raunchy tale was cut short by a loud burst of static from communications. Uhura dutifully tuned the frequency.

"*Pleasss to hurry, we haff much need of assisstance.*"

Kirk recognized the soft slurring voice of a Frenni. Casting aside his jovial air, he ordered Uhura to open a channel to the merchant ship. "*Selessan,* this is Captain Kirk of the U.S.S. *Enterprise.* We are due to drop out of warp speed in one hour." He waved aside Spock's attempts to reply with greater precision.

"*Much gratitude, Captain. We await your arrival with much happinesss.*" A long pause ensued. "*Kirrk . . . Ah, yess, it does recall. Did you enjoy the* demma?"

To Kirk's discomfort the memory of that trip turned the tips of his ears fiery pink. "*Yes,*" he laughed self-consciously. "*I did indeed, Captain Esserass.*"

"*For our rescue I will introduce you to other delicassies. Those that can be salvaged,*" sighed the weary merchant. "*Good trading, Kirrk.*" The contact was severed.

Despite his gentle banter, the alien's voice had been ragged and weak. McCoy scowled in Spock's direction. "Casualties. That's what war is all about."

Spock sighed at the note of challenge in the doctor's comment. "And in such circumstances your duty post is in sick bay."

"Don't you dare lecture me on duty!" flared McCoy bitterly. "I'm the one who has to patch together the living and autopsy the dead." He turned on his heel and stalked off the bridge.

"He knows you didn't mean it that way," said Kirk to his first officer.

The Vulcan did not reply. He walked back to his computer station and took his seat before the panel. "We will rendezvous with the *Selessan* in 1.2 hours."

During that time the *Enterprise* crew prepared for the forthcoming rescue operations by handing Kirk a staggering number of data tablets which required his signature. When he wasn't juggling red tape, he was dealing with Scotty's increasing concern for his engines. After an hour's silence, a querulous McCoy began calling the bridge with flimsy excuses in order to check on its activity. And alert status was a constant reminder to everyone of the possibility of an encounter with the marauding battlecruiser.

"Sensor sweeps reveal no Klingon presence," announced the first officer as the starship dropped to sub-warp speed. "We will reach the *Selessan* in 23.4 minutes."

"Can we use transporters for the rescue?" asked Kirk anxiously.

"Negative. As I surmised, radiation residue from the *Verella*'s destruction will render the transporters inoperative. Trace ionized particles have already begun to affect instrument functions."

Kirk brooded on the risks created by that restriction. Using the shuttlecraft to evacuate the Frenni crew meant a minimum of several hours with shields dropped. The operation must be carried out as swiftly as possible. "Uhura, notify sick bay that paramedic teams should report to the hangar deck." Together they dispersed orders throughout the ship as the *Enterprise* coasted towards its rendezvous.

"Approaching the *Selessan*, Captain." Sulu's hands danced rapidly over the helm. The faint outlines of the merchant ship appeared on the main viewscreen. At the same time navigational deflectors set off a barrage of sparks in the darkness.

"That is what is left of the *Verella*," explained Spock as the debris in their path was vaporized. The remaining ship grew larger on the screen. It was an ungainly agglomeration of oddly-shaped cabins welded together in a haphazard pattern. Perhaps the single engine nacelle had once possessed sleeker lines, but now its metal surface was roughened and scored by phaser fire.

Spock huddled in communion with his computers. "Sensor readings are degenerating. However, the *Selessan* registers as having suffered significant impairment of ship's systems. Life support systems are barely functional; engines are idle; weapon power is depleted."

"Welcome, Kirrk. Are we not a ssory ssight?"

Kirk had to agree. "We'll have you out of there in no time," he said reassuringly. He thumbed his intercom switch. "Bones . . ."

"Paramedic Team C has boarded the *Galileo*," came McCoy's crisp reply. "Sick bay surgical teams are on standby."

Kirk switched channels. "Shuttle bay, prepare for launch." Out of the corner of his eye he could see the launching sequence flicker across the engineering station computerboard even as Scotty's voice acknowledged the command.

Sitting back in his chair, Kirk frowned at the image of the *Selessan* on the viewscreen before him. "No visual from the interior, Lt. Uhura?"

"None, Captain. I can't trace the source of the trouble. Audio frequencies are working with intermittent static, but the rest of the signal transmission is dead."

He motioned her to engage ship-to-ship communications again. "Captain Esserass, we are not receiving a visual signal from your ship."

"Not surprissing. My communicationss operator iss dead. I triess to work the equipmenss, but there iss much damage."

"Understood." Kirk turned to his first officer and spoke quietly. "Spock, can you run a bio-check for Klingons on that ship?"

Spock frowned. "The energy debris makes readings unreliable . . ."

"Do the best you can. I don't want my crew boarding that ship blind."

"Captain Kirk, technical and medical teams boarded. All shuttlecraft ready for launching."

"On my command." The captain turned to the helm. "Lt. Sulu, prepare to lower shields." Still he held off his final order. "Well, Mr. Spock?"

"There is considerable distortion, however bio-scan readings are inconsistent with Klingon anatomy and physiology."

"Shields down, Sulu." Kirk returned to the intercom. "Launch shuttlecraft, Mr. Scott." A red light flashed on the engineering board, confirming the launch. Kirk followed the action in his mind's eye. The shuttle bay doors of the secondary hull would yawn open, baring the hangar deck to the vacuum of space. One by one the shuttlecraft would lift off the deck. Any moment now they would appear on the main viewscreen as they headed for the . . .

Spock's voice rang out. "Captain, bio-scan readings are still fluctuating, but the life-form readings are also inconsistent with our profiles of the Frenni race."

A nasty tingle crept up the base of Kirk's neck. "Instrument error?"

"Possibly," conceded Spock returning to his board. "I will need more time to re-check calibrations."

Kirk gnawed at his thumbnail. "Not Klingons, but not Frenni either." Instinct rather than thought moved him to action. His voice rang out to engineering. "Mr. Scott, recall the shuttlecraft." He edged forward on his seat. "Sulu, prepare to raise shields as soon as they hit the deck."

"Kirrk, what hass happened?" came the bewildered voice of the alien as the shuttlecraft turned back towards the *Enterprise.*

Kirk hesitated. *"Selessan,* identify your crew."

"But Capsain, we hass idensified oursselvess," responded the merchant with an overtone of anger. *"Pleasse hurry, we hass injured needssing medical care."*

The distinctive sibilant voice was that of a Frenni; the merchant captain had remembered Kirk from their past encounter. "Spock?"

The Vulcan stood firm. "Systems checks maintain sensors are operational. The readings are not those of the Frenni race."

And the shuttlecraft were still outside the ship.

Kirk kept his voice calm and played for time. "Esserass, we're experiencing systems malfunctions due to the radiation debris in this sector. There will be a slight delay . . ."

"Capsain, why thees gamess with uss? We are friends of the Federasion and muss be helped. We canss do no harm with thiss sship."

Kirk turned to his first officer. "Weapons?"

"Still no functional weaponry detected." Spock's brows quirked in puzzlement. "But energy output levels in their engine room are increasing." On the screen, the cruiser began to turn slowly.

The captain of the *Enterprise* felt the soft snap of a trap springing shut. "Scotty, get those shuttlecraft landed! We need to raise shields."

"Five seconds, Captain."

Kirk chanted the count to himself. "Now, Sulu!"

But even as the helmsman moved to obey, the Frenni craft burst into motion, racing straight toward the ship.

Chapter Three

McCoy PULLED AWKWARDLY at his surgical gown, the tabs and clips eluding his fumbling fingers. Only minutes ago his hands had been sure and steady, nimbly weaving a tangle of severed nerves into a functioning spinal cord. Now surgery was over after fifteen grueling hours of human cut and paste, tedious and dangerous work even with the aid of the best medical technology Star Fleet could offer. Freed from the demands of operating he felt exhaustion overtake him with numbing rapidity. The loose gown dangled in his hands, then dropped to the floor. How many times had he, as chief surgeon, lambasted any doctor or nurse for just such a lapse?

There's no excuse for messy medical practice. Messy habits have a way of staying with you.

He still made no move to pick the garment up. Instead he slumped down onto an equipment locker. If it hadn't been there he would probably have collapsed to the floor, next to his discarded gown.

The surgical washroom was a peaceful eye between the two storms which had buffeted him relentlessly for nearly two days. Behind him, for the moment, the operating room was empty, while the sounds of the recovery ward ahead were muted by closed doors. The only voices were those of the ship's intercom droning an interminable list of damage reports and status updates. Scotty was busy with his own particular surgery.

"Doctor." Nurse Chapel was standing by his side. He realized that she had been standing there for a while, but the fact of her presence had barely registered.

"Who's next?" he asked automatically. He had started receiving patients within minutes of the first impact against the hull. Now, over a day later, he was still at work treating the lesser injuries that had lost priority to those courting death. Two crewmen were in bio-stasis, so badly injured that only a starbase, a very modern starbase, could put them back together in a form resembling the human body. Sixteen others would never wake up. The ship had not suffered such heavy casualties in a long time.

"That's all, doctor. Your shift is over for the day." Chapel began to rattle off the duty roster for the medical personnel in a no-nonsense tone that implied that any objection on his part would be a professional insult to the capabilities of his department. Four names were missing from the list; a team of paramedics had been killed on the hangar deck. He had hand-picked each of its members . . .

McCoy listened wearily, half admitting to himself that his supervision would be useless even if he stayed. His head was throbbing, his eyes were unfocused, and his response time was barely beyond catatonia. Then he stopped short, mentally stifling a groan of irritation. "I can't leave yet." He leaned forward with effort. "There's Benson, the chest injury from Engineering. Those lacerations were only stapled together until he stabilized."

Chapel hesitated, then reluctantly spoke. "That won't be necessary."

McCoy's head snapped up. "Dammit, Christine, don't coddle me! What's happened to Benson?"

She turned coldly matter-of-fact. "He's dead. Vital signs were low but stable when he entered op-prep, but then . . ."

A burst of fury propelled the surgeon to his feet. "Why wasn't I called? Where is he now?" *Enough death, dear God. Please, no more.*

Chapel blocked his steps bodily, forcing him to a halt. "Doctor McCoy, crewman Benson is dead. You know as well as I do that our staff took every possible action to save his life, but it simply wasn't possible."

The spurt of adrenalin gave out, leaving him drained. "Of course. I'm sorry, I didn't mean . . . I just . . ." He trailed off in confusion. What had he thought he could do—catch the Angel of Death on his way and wrestle him to the ground? "Thank you, Nurse Chapel." He looked into her face and saw the fatigue that blurred the strong lines of her features. "I guess it's time for me to go away."

"Yes, it is." She still looked stern, but her voice had regained an edge of tolerance.

"How the hell do you put up with me?" he muttered as he stumbled out of the room.

Walking down the corridor revived McCoy somewhat, at least sufficiently to enable him to dodge the scurrying work crews and skirt the obstacle course of conduits, uncrated spare parts, and the occasional body half submerged in the floor or ceiling or wall. Though it was early morning by ship's time, the corridors were lit at daylight intensity to accommodate repairs. The concept of morning and evening in space was wholly artificial, but he hated such a blatant reminder of that fact.

"Gravity crews t'Deck Seven . . . gravity crews t'Deck Seven. Prepare for adjustment procedures in 4.5 hours. Repeat . . ." Scotty's voice sounded hoarse even through the filtered intercom.

McCoy idly wondered just how much damage the *Enterprise* had sustained. As a doctor he was most concerned with the human wreckage, yet he had been unusually alarmed by the gyrations of the deck during the attack. With what little attention he could spare from his medical duties, he had gathered that the identity of their assailants was still to be determined. Pieces of the Frenni ship were stored in the shuttle bay; pieces of strange bodies, salvaged from amidst that space debris, were in stasis next to Ellison and Takeoka. With luck, the latter might defrost in slightly better condition than the aliens. McCoy shook his head as if to dislodge the relentless stream of sick bay concerns that trailed after him. There wasn't much sense in dwelling on their chances now—the ship wouldn't reach a sizable starbase for several weeks.

Uhura's voice rang out of the intercom. *"Captain Kirk, to the bridge."* Then Scotty's voice sounded out. *"Captain Kirk, come to phaser control."*

"Kirk here. I'll be there when I get there."

McCoy chuckled over the conflicting demands and wondered how soon it would be before Kirk headed for sick bay. The frustration in the captain's voice was the first step to a tension headache.

These musings kept the morbid ghosts at bay until McCoy reached his cabin. Once inside he headed straight for the sonic shower, stripping off his soiled clothes along the way. *Sweat feels like blood,* he thought and shuddered at the persistence of dark thoughts. Even the blast of cleansing vibrations failed to clear his mind.

Out of the shower, McCoy caught sight of his face in the mirror. It was the same face he stared at unthinkingly, every morning. This time he studied it carefully. The broad, regular features implied a stockiness that he did not possess. Fatigue accentuated the lines around his mouth and forehead. The blue of his eyes was dulled to grey, the whites veined with red. Above them his brown hair had not thinned, but it was lightly flecked with white.

I look more like my father every day.

Pushing away from the mirror, he wrapped himself in a robe and turned to survey a room littered with crumpled clothes and towels which he hadn't bothered to stuff in the cycle bin. His plants looked wilted. Unread medical tapes lay scattered over his desk, along with a pile of printouts from the last batch of correspondence that had come with sub-space communications from Star Fleet. Uhura had a way of wheedling personal mail deliveries onto every official communications exchange. He hadn't had time to read any of it yet, but a few more hours' delay would hardly matter, since the messages had probably taken several weeks to work their way across space channels. The doctor also resisted the impulse to start cleaning up. He needed sleep desperately, yet had reached that stage of nervous exhaustion that left him restless and slightly nauseous. It was a familiar sensation, first encountered during the grueling routine of a first-year resident.

I'm too old for this.

He threw himself down on the bed and tried unsuccessfully to empty his mind. Twice he sprang up to call sick bay as one question after another invaded his thoughts. Had he actually entered the new dosages on Vergalen's chart or only made a mental note that it had to be done? Then he had a sudden sick feeling that he had failed to alert Dr. Cortejo about the need for follow-up surgery on Galloway's abdominal wound. No, Chapel would have passed that information on to the other surgeon anyway. Dammit, he trusted her wits more than his own at times. Oddly reassured by this, he finally drifted into sleep.

The shrill whistle of shipboard communications dragged McCoy out of unconsciousness. He awoke slowly, the tendrils of a nightmare blending with reality, drowning out the meaning of the words blaring out through the room. His fingers were actually twitching in response to the dream, in which he had been knitting together yards of nerves that lay scattered about the command deck.

". . . commences in approximately 30 minutes."

Blast Montgomery Scott. Couldn't he fix this ship without creating such a public ruckus? A glance at the chronometer showed the passage of only four hours, but McCoy felt no desire to fall asleep again. A return to nightmares wasn't all that inviting. As long as he was awake he might as well get some work done. Jim had asked for a report on the alien tissue fragments as soon as possible, and while the autopsy had been handled by Frazer, the xenobiologist, it wouldn't hurt to translate the man's obsessive technical jargon into a language somewhat more accessible to the captain. Besides, McCoy was curious to see just what kind of life form had wreaked such havoc in sick bay.

He pulled himself out of bed, donned his last batch of fresh clothes, then stumbled to his desk. Rubbing bleary eyes into focus, he logged on to the computer system and called up the autopsy file.

The report opened with photos of the fragments—a gory beginning but useful for a sense of the aliens' morphology. The first two shots were practically meaningless, just chunks of orange pulp that could as easily have been anything from vegetable matter to foam insulation. They were followed by a startling close-up of a massive head covered with steel-blue skin, its round red eyes open and staring with a look of almost human malevolence. A blue-black crest of brushy hair ran from the forehead back over the skull; a chitinous beak gaped open at the center of its face.

McCoy felt the hairs on the back of his neck stand on end. What the hell . . . He stared at the image in surprise. Though somewhat grotesque in its decapitated state, there was nothing inherently frightening about the alien's appearance, certainly nothing to justify the tingle of apprehension that was tickling his spine. Yet, he sensed a shroud of menace in the features of this unidentified being. He continued to stare at the head for several minutes, but no further chills developed, and Frazer's technical discourse failed to loose any more impressions.

"*. . . morphological structures evidence no congruency with established configurations . . . DNA molecular sequences of amino acids reveal origins considerably divergent from biochemical evolution of known alien species.*"

McCoy snorted. "In other words, you've never seen anything like it and you don't know what it is." Picking his way through a few of the most convoluted of the xenobiologist's sentences, McCoy amended a less abstruse version to the explanatory text. He made no mention of his own reaction to the alien; Spock would flaunt an intolerable condescension if McCoy reported "vague terror" with no apparent basis to support his uneasiness. The association, if indeed there was one, would come in its own time.

Still restless, McCoy snapped off the terminal and turned to rifle through the printouts. Despite Spock's disapproval, the doctor's professional correspondence was automatically printed by the computer system. McCoy liked the feel of paper and the rustle of pages: a flat screen filled with type was not a proper manuscript.

The first few packets were journal reprints and an unpublished report from the ship's surgeon of the U.S.S. *Welborne*. These were tossed aside for more careful perusal in the future; a long, limping voyage home had certain advantages. Then, unexpectedly, he saw the single page of a letter. Most of his personal correspondence came on tape, from a small circle of people who were willing to pay the extra cost of transmission. Here was an exception.

Puzzled, he glanced down at the signature. The name unleashed a sudden flood of memories that left him weak with the pain of their return. After the memories, he absorbed the meaning of the words written in the terse, brief paragraph.

He crumpled the sheet convulsively. After all this time, it shouldn't matter so much. Hell, it shouldn't matter at all. Yet his hands trembled. One corner of his mind retained a clinical detachment, noting that he had entered into a mild state of shock. The rest of him just felt sick. For a moment, he considered calling Jim Kirk. But no, that would mean talking, explaining, more remembering. And to what purpose? He had talked himself out years ago and failed to . . . Well, he had just failed.

McCoy stared at the wad of paper resting in his palm and fought against a tide of bitterness.

God, I'm too old and too tired to start this battle again.

Pulling himself upright, he carried the letter into his bedroom and placed it in the center of a decorated metal tray that lay on his dresser. From the drawer beneath, he pulled out a worn travel pouch. His fingers withdrew a small probe and deftly flicked a switch that lighted the tip with a pinprick glow. At its touch, a small spot on the paper began to darken, then smoke. In seconds the paper was engulfed in flames.

"Alert, alert! There is fire in this room."

"That, my dear shipboard computer, is the smoke of a funeral pyre. It is definitely against regulations." However, the brief burst on the tray was over and the computer fell silent.

Sleep was out of the question now, but McCoy was too shaken to do anything else. If he stayed awake, the recriminations would start creeping in, a litany of anger and regrets that were almost like old friends. With unsteady steps the doctor made his way to a small cabinet and opened its door. Riskelian mescal should do the trick just fine. Using both hands to steady the shaking bottle, he soon filled a squat glass to its rim with a pale red liquid.

"To the waters of Lethe!" Half the drink was quaffed in one gulp. His body convulsed for a second at the jolt of hot fire that ran down his throat. The Red Nova brand-label wasn't kidding. Before the remaining contents could be downed, the door buzzer announced a visitor. Good, the more distractions the better. "Come in."

Spock entered the room. The first officer's hands were full of memory chip packs and data tablets. He was wearing the look of self-absorbed concentration that accompanied every ship refitting. He launched into a stream of technical jargon without any preamble; at times like these he tended to forget Human social conventions.

"Hold on there," interrupted McCoy with a wave of his hand. With effort, he could keep his voice steady. "I didn't hear, much less understand, a word you said. I was prepared for a 'Good morning, how are you?' or at least a simple 'Hello, Doctor'."

Spock did not argue the issue. "Hello, Doctor," he said flatly and began to repeat his statements. "The electromagnetic pulse dampeners failed to fully protect the circuit backup for the MedQuiz PF-3500 internal systems file . . ."

"And I don't want to understand a word," McCoy said emphatically. He took another, tidier, swallow of his drink. "I'm off duty."

The first officer still could not be sidetracked. "I require your permission for a systems adjustment to the medical department computers. It will in no way interfere with patient care."

"Well, why didn't you say so in the first place. I thought you were in a hurry to get these things done." McCoy grinned maliciously as the Vulcan's mouth tightened. Baiting Spock was the best restorative to be found on board the ship.

"Sign here." A data tablet was stiffly proferred.

McCoy drained the last of the Red Nova before putting his glass down. His hand was still shaking as he reached for the tablet, a fact which did not escape Spock's notice. "Don't look so disapproving, Mr. Spock." The doctor scrawled a hasty initial on the form and returned it. "I'm not drunk. At least not yet. Care to join me for a drink before you disappear into your computerized briar-patch?"

An arched eyebrow flew up. "Your species' preoccupation with ingesting large quantities of alcohol-based compounds . . ."

Gotcha, McCoy exulted and poured himself another glassfull.

". . . is a constant source of puzzlement. Despite its known poisonous qualities, you persist in this custom."

"Not despite, Mr. Spock. *Because* of its poisonous qualities." He swallowed another mouthful of the fiery liquid.

The first officer frowned, suddenly aware that once again he had been maneuvered into an argument that he couldn't win because his logic wasn't part of the game. "I must attend to my duties." He ignored the smirk on McCoy's face and turned to leave.

"All hands alert. Gravity adjustment in 10 seconds."

"Oh, Spock," called out McCoy, reluctant to let his prey escape so soon. "I've been meaning to talk to you about that little transaction you botched for Jim at the trading post . . ."

When the deck tremors began, the first officer was already braced for the movement but McCoy immediately lost his balance. Above the whine of the ship's engines came the shatter of glass hitting a far wall and the crack of bone against metal.

"McCoy!" Spock fell to his hands and knees to crawl across the floor as it heaved and buckled. By the time he reached the crumpled form there was already a small pool of blood forming under the head.

"Gravity adjustment complete. Repeat, gravity adjustment complete."

Chapter Four

Captain's Log, Stardate 5308.5:
   The *Enterprise* lies dead in space, seriously damaged by an attack we still cannot explain . . .

KIRK STARED AT the crumpled pylon of the *Enterprise* nacelle with a horrified fascination. Its once elegant lines were twisted and bent, destroying the parallel symmetry of the ship's profile. Its cracked and pitted surface was encrusted with dark splotches, like the oozing blood of a wound, for the impact of the alien craft had fused the Frenni metal into the very fabric of the pylon even as it destroyed it.

Around the deck the bridge crew had lapsed into silence when the probe camera began transmission. Scotty's first damage report had detailed the effect of the alien attack within hours of the encounter, yet no verbal descriptions could have prepared them for the sight. No miracle slight of hand by the chief engineer could repair this structural collapse.

"If we hadna been stopped for th' rescue, we'd be stardust now. Th' engines would have imploded," said Scotty. They stood side by side at the engineering station on the bridge. Unlike Kirk the chief engineer avoided looking at the scene framed by the viewscreen. He had already inspected the damage by shuttlecraft; a far more detailed image was burned into his mind.

44

"If we hadn't stopped for the rescue, we wouldn't have been attacked," answered the captain bitterly. Yet, no matter how many times he went over the events, he had to admit that he would have acted in the same manner. It had been the wrong action, but there was no way he could have known that. *I should have known it anyway . . .*

Slowly, the camera panned down the pylon to the secondary engine hull. Its rounded sides were dotted with debris, as if a careless cosmic hand had sprinkled them with grains of pepper.

"The last of th' breaches are bein' sealed now. We should have restored hull integrity within five hours, but we havna the resources to repressurize all the decks. Two work crews will stay suited t' staff life support systems and ship's services." Scotty's long face was grey with fatigue, but even more, with grief. The devastation which had been wreaked on the *Enterprise* was weighing heavily upon him.

"How soon before we can get out of here?" Still mesmerized by the panorama before him, Kirk was amazed that the ship could travel without disintegrating. Nevertheless, Scotty reassured him that it was possible to return to the trading post dockyard.

"The nacelle itself is fairly much intact, but if we tried moving now, even at sub-warp speed, th' strain of th' forward momentum would shear it loose. Once most of the decks are repressurized, maintenance crews can start shoring the juncture t' th' hull. It won't be functional, but at least it'll stay with us." The chief engineer fought off a slight shiver. The temperature on the bridge had dropped several degrees as the brittle cold of deep space gnawed at the ship's weakened energy reserves. "We willna recover warp drive until we hit dry dock and replace the pylon entirely, but th' impulse engines are sound enough."

The viewscreen filled with the length of the right nacelle, undamaged, pristine, useless without its twin. The bridge personnel resumed their duties. A soft chorus of voices blanketed the deck.

"Time estimate, Mr. Scott?"

The Scotsman sighed heavily. Kirk always wanted predictions of the unpredictable. "At least 48 hours, maybe more. Dependin'." He was too tired to elaborate on the plethora of factors which could further complicate an already immeasureably messy situation.

Kirk let it pass. "Weapons?"

"Phasers are operational, but power levels are low. We cracked a dilithium crystal when th' deflectors hit the cruiser." Bad timing. The Frenni cruiser had been crushed between the expanding shields, exploding into the deadly spray of metal which had hit the *Enterprise*'s engine hull and propulsion unit with such destructive force.

What would have happened if our shields hadn't stopped them? wondered Kirk. There was no way to know whether the approaching alien craft had intended to bring its crew aboard the *Enterprise* by force or whether it had been bent on annihilation of the starship.

"Deflectors?" Kirk had saved his worst fear for last. Scotty confirmed his pessimism.

"Like a leaky sieve. A handphaser could drill right through to the ship's hull."

"At least we're alive," said Kirk, searching for some comfort.

"Aye, I suppose we are." Scotty's weariness was sufficiently deep to dampen his enthusiasm about the prospect of existence. "Though we're sittin' ducks for any other ship that feels like takin' a shot at us."

Kirk was all too aware of that fact. "That's my

department, Scotty. You worry about getting us out of here. In fourty-eight hours."

"Aye." The chief engineer looked very worried indeed.

The captain continued his rounds. "Lt. Uhura, are you sure space communications are operational?"

"Yes, Captain. I'm receiving sector buoy signals on navigation frequencies and normal static levels on hailing frequencies. We're a little out of the way of local space broadcasts, but I've picked up some faint transmissions from the trading post, apparently routine communications. No more distress calls and no coded signals."

Which could mean the Klingons had left Federation territory. Or maybe not. Regardless, the *Enterprise* was maintaining strict communications silence on the assumption that either Klingons, or hostile aliens, were somewhere in the sector. In its present state, the starship couldn't risk betraying its location by using space communications channels. Two messenger drones had been sent out instead: the first warned the trading post to take precautions against attack, while the second sent a full report of the incident to Star Fleet Command. Despite its miniaturized warp drive the unit would take a full two weeks to reach the nearest Starbase.

Kirk gritted his teeth at the memory of his request for assistance. He disliked asking for help; he hated needing it even more. Still, given the time and distances involved, the chances were that there would be no reinforcements available for quite some time. Time enough to get his ship out of trouble, or beyond help.

Uhura continued her report. "Ship communications are another story altogether, Captain. Chekov is disrupting the intercom system with his repair work on the computers. I lose a different deck every hour."

As she talked, Kirk heard the soft sigh of the turbo-lift doors parting, and felt, rather than saw, the quiet approach of his first officer. "Mr. Spock, I'll need a status report on sensors . . ." Kirk's voice trailed off as he turned around. The dark oil stains on Spock's tunic looked distressingly like blood, but Human blood, not Vulcan.

"Captain, your presence is required in sick bay."

"Problems with the medical bank computers?" Yet he knew that wasn't the case. There were subtleties in all of Spock's impassive masks, and this particular look was grimmer than most.

"Dr. McCoy has suffered an accident. He's in surgery now . . ."

Human blood after all.

By the time he reached sick bay, Kirk had prepared himself for the critical care area. He hated entering it, an aversion that in no way deterred him from doing so when necessary, but for him this room was a symbol of failure, his failure to keep his crew alive and well. The sight of so many quiet forms made him ache inside. If he had detected the Frenni trap, if he had reacted just a few seconds faster, this room would be empty.

"Captain." Christine Chapel was waiting for him. "Dr. Cortejo has completed the surgery. Dr. McCoy is still unconscious, but vital signs are stable." Her professional manner was on full force, a shield against the emotional toll of her work. Kirk would have felt better about McCoy's condition if she had betrayed more of her anxiety.

"I want to see him." The memory of Spock's blood-soaked shirt was still too fresh in his mind.

The nurse nodded. "He's in the resonance chamber. Dr. Cortejo can fill you in on the details while they run the scan. Now, if you'll excuse me, I have to get back to my patients."

She's got to get some rest, thought Kirk as Christine Chapel left his side. But then everyone on board, himself included, could use a good night's sleep. Which didn't mean they were going to get it any time soon.

The captain worked his way deeper into the labyrinth of medical sections until he heard the precisely enunciated accents of the man who was now acting chief medical officer. Eduardo Cortejo Alvarez was not a popular man on board ship. His somewhat portly figure was held rigidly upright by an air of arrogance. The impatient disdain with which he treated non-medical personnel, especially his patients, was a discordant contrast to McCoy's warmer style. Since the chief medical officer set the tone for sick bay, Cortejo's imperious manner was a constant source of irritation to the medical staff. Only a mutual respect for each other's surgical talents kept the two surgeons from open warfare. McCoy wasn't going to like having Cortejo in charge for the next few days.

However, when Kirk turned a corner and came face to face with the contents of the resonance chamber, he realized fully that his chief medical officer was in no position to care who was running sick bay. Even in sleep the human body displays subtle signs of movement, but McCoy's form was utterly still, devoid of consciousness. His face was almost white, with the skin stretching tightly over the bones beneath. Ironically, the head injury was marked only by a small medpatch behind his right ear.

"What's his condition?" demanded Kirk of the two doctors standing outside the chamber.

"He's in a coma, Captain." It was not the surgeon who answered. Kirk vaguely remembered that the young doctor who faced him was a Star Fleet resident finishing a training tour. He tried to recall a name but failed; trainees came and went too fast for him to keep track of them all.

"Dr. Dyson, attend to the scan," snapped Cortejo. "I will not waste my time pushing buttons." The resident flushed at the reprimand, but with a hastily stifled scowl that betrayed anger rather than embarassment. She returned to the control panel.

Kirk watched as McCoy's body passed back and forth within the scanning rings of the resonance chamber. A narrow platform moved him in slow increments through the rays so that the computer could capture a series of images, atom-thin slices from a phantom dissecting knife. Dyson's fingers skimmed over the controls transforming this information into a holographic recreation of his body, a ghostly twin, which formed outside the chamber. The head area was alive with colors from the dense accumulation of scan slices.

After ordering some adjustments to the resolution, Cortejo began a monologue. "The injuries are the result of a number of factors in the fall. The immediate impact with the edge of the desk created a superficial scalp wound and a linear skull fracture." His index finger traced a bright purple line on an orange skull. "Fortunately, the blood loss from the laceration was not excessive and the occipital bone is intact. There were no bone fragments to penetrate the brain matter below. Thus, from a surgical point of view, the damage was minimal and easily repaired.

"However, the impact to the free-moving head caused a rotational movement which resulted in an acceleration concussion. The effects of this trauma could be serious, though I'm more inclined to be optimistic from what we've observed so far. Dr. Dyson is the real expert in neurological examination." The surgeon relinquished center stage to the slight, dark-featured woman at his side.

Though somewhat discomfited by the sudden attention Kirk focused on her, Dyson spoke concisely. "The major mechanism of primary diffuse brain injury after blunt head trauma is the mechanical shearing and tearing of nerve fibers and blood vessels. An examination of Dr. McCoy's brain scans shows no discernible lesions or shearing of tissue. However, there's no way we can detect whether the nerve fibers have been stretched. The only indicator is neurologic function—and that can't be determined until he wakes up.

"As for secondary mechanisms, there was a brief increase in intra-cranial pressure, but probably not sufficient to damage the brain. No signs of brain shift, edema, or hemorrhage. It's fortunate that Mr. Spock was present to summon the medic team. Complications could have developed if there had been any delay in entering surgery."

"Speaking of surgery," broke in Cortejo, "I must get back to my work. This is no longer my field." He gave the captain a grudging nod of acknowledgement but left without any further notice of the resident.

Kirk began to appreciate the depths of McCoy's exasperation with this man, but the matter at hand overshadowed Cortejo's shortcomings. "This stretching of the nerve fibers—what would be the result?"

Dyson gave a frustrated shrug. "Dysfunctions ranging from mild confusion to deficits of memory, recognition, word association, motor coordination, any of which could require months or even years of regenerative therapy. There's no further way to measure the severity of the injury until he's conscious. Usually, the longer the coma lasts, the greater the likelihood of neurological impairment, but in this case it's difficult to judge the source of unconsciousness. Dr. McCoy had just gone off duty from a rather grueling stint in surgery. Nurse Chapel says he was exhausted when he left. Also," there was the slightest trace of hesitation, "his blood alcohol level was elevated. Not to toxic levels, but certainly combined with the fatigue, and the blood loss, and the blunt trauma . . . Well, he's certainly earned a spell of unconsciousness," she finished with a wry smile.

Irritation at her gallows humor cut through Kirk's worry. Perhaps that was the point. Beneath the usual timidity of a junior officer dealing with a commander he caught a glimpse of a keen medical mind at work. He wondered what McCoy's professional assessment of Dr. Dyson had been.

The scan was over. Two nurses gently rolled McCoy's still body onto a grav-stretcher and whisked him away under Dyson's supervision. Kirk could do nothing more. *What a stupid accident,* the captain thought as he made his way to a turbo-lift. After all the wars and murderous aliens and insane careening about the galaxy, his chief medical officer had been injured during a gravity adjustment. When McCoy recovered from this Kirk would make sure he received a ship deck-klutz award. The doctor had been only too willing to pass them out to the parade of crewmen that collected scrapes and bruises and broken bones by tuning out the general ship communications.

The turbo whined to a halt and disgorged the captain onto the bridge. At his entrance, the crew looked up expectantly. Somehow, despite his medical duties, McCoy had become an unofficial member of the bridge personnel, always lurking on the fringes of its action. "He's unconscious, but stable," announced Kirk, then turned to Uhura. "Dr. Dyson will be sending continual reports. Alert me the moment his condition changes."

He circled over to the computer station. "Mr. Spock." His first officer had practically disappeared into the circuitry beneath his panel, leaving only two booted feet behind, feet which flayed about at erratic intervals. A muffled Vulcan phrase seeped its way up through the metal. "If I didn't know better, I'd think you were swearing."

"Curse words do not exist in the Vulcan language," said Spock somewhat more distinctly as he heaved himself back out onto the deck. One hand held a frame of circuit chips. Kirk was relieved to see him wearing a clean tunic. "Unfavorable circumstances are changed by action, not by symbolic verbalization of emotion."

"So what action are you taking?" Under better circumstances, Kirk would have been asking these questions in the comfort of the briefing room, with his officers grouped around him, answering in turn.

Spock's fingers skipped nimbly over the frame, jabbing here and there to dislodge particular wafers from their place in the frame. He made no attempt to maintain eye contact with the captain; only his responses indicated he was even aware of the man's presence. "Pulse dampeners have been repaired. Damage to computer circuitry was sporadic, but all damaged systems have been identified." He worked his way down a mental list of priorities. "Mr. Chekov is leading a work crew in the installation of back-up memory units in all areas essential to ship's operation or defense."

These last words seemed especially emphasized. Kirk guessed that the rumor of lost drama tapes was true. Well, no one would have much time for recreation anyway.

"Short-range sensors will be operational in seven

minutes." Spock stopped his poking and began to snap new chips back into the holes. "Rough calibration will take an additional hour."

No longer blind, but still fuzzy. "What about long-range sensors?" Spock had already ducked back inside the computer's entrails, but his acute hearing had discerned the question. Kirk, whose ears were not so sensitive, was forced to bend down to catch the reply.

"That will take longer since they sustained direct physical damage. Mr. Scott's repair estimate for the equipment is twelve hours. Calibration will take another four from that time."

Sixteen hours. "Spock, we still haven't figured out who attacked us, or why. There could be a whole battalion of those aliens staring us right in the face, and we wouldn't know it."

"A somewhat disconcerting image, Captain." Above their heads a portion of the computer station came to life with a series of self-satisfied clicks and whirrs. "But essentially correct."

As he straightened up, the captain muttered some especially strong emotive symbols under his breath. Not only had the alien kamikaze attack been completely unexpected, the reasons behind it were still clouded. Kirk was a master tactician, but even he needed some knowledge of the nature of his adversary on which to base strategy. The bodies found in the wreckage were not of any known Federation race or its allies. Neither were they any of the Federation's known enemies. Yet, this alien's enmity was unquestioned: Frazer, the xeno-biologist, estimated that some twenty individuals had annihilated themselves in an attempt to cripple the *Enterprise.* This latter action held the strong implication of more forces in the area. Forces which could be lurking just outside scanning range . . .

"Captain." Spock broke through Kirk's reveries.

"Short-range sensors are about to become operational." The first officer had risen from the floor and was hunched over his terminal. His fingers flicked a rapid combination of switches. "Right . . . now."

At his words, yellow alert sirens began to whoop across the bridge.

Chapter Five

THE SLOW, STEADY blink of the bridge's yellow alert was starting to grate on Kirk's nerves. After ten hours there still wasn't more than a faint shimmer of matter on the edge of sensor range; just enough disturbance to warrant caution, but not enough for action. Not that there was much action the *Enterprise* could take in her present condition. Then again, there might in fact be no substance to the shadow; it could be a relic of battle damage to the delicate equipment. Certainly the viewscreen revealed no alien craft, only the faint glow of stars.

Drawing his eyes away from a futile search of the screen, the captain slumped in his command chair, fighting the impulse to gather yet another round of status reports from the bridge crew. If he stayed in one place much longer his yeoman would load him with a stack of data tablets needing signatures. Kirk got to his feet. He feigned a fascination with the unchanging viewscreen, moved closer to study its image, then veered off. He walked slowly behind the duty stations, nodding absently at the crewmen as they worked, until he reached Communications.

"No change in audio reception, Captain." Uhura's bright, hard tone signaled, to those who knew her well, a tightly checked anger. "Communications sweeps are still negative." Just as they had been ten minutes ago.

Kirk assumed a look of innocence which did not convince the lieutenant of his good intentions. He eyed the computer station as his next target, but his courage failed him. Spock was obviously pained at his inability to provide reliable data from the impaired sensors and any interruption would only deepen the Vulcan's chagrin and delay repairs.

Perhaps his crew was too good, reflected Kirk sourly. A less efficient performance would give him a legitimate reason to harass the officers and thus absorb his restlessness in overseeing their duties. As it was, everyone on the bridge was competently engaged in repairs or surveillance, providing him with no distraction from the nagging desire for some sort of resolution. What the hell could he do *now?*

As if on cue, Lt. Uhura looked up from her station and smiled, genuinely, at Kirk. "Captain, Dr. Dyson requests your presence in sick bay. It seems Dr. McCoy is waking up." The bridge crew kept working without pause, but an unvoiced cheer ghosted across the deck.

"Thank you, Lieutenant." Kirk breathed a silent sigh of relief. His one brief glimpse of the doctor, pale and gaunt, had been unexpectedly unnerving. "Mr. Spock, you have the conn," he announced, heading for the turbo-lift.

"Yes, Captain." The first officer straightened up from the circuit panel beneath the science station. The inevitable litter of discarded chips lay scattered on the floor beneath him and the desk surface above. "And Captain . . ."

Kirk paused, looking back at the Vulcan. "Mr. Spock?"

"When Dr. McCoy regains consciousness he should be informed that the medical systems computers are fully operational."

"Of course, understood." And he did understand.

Spock was incapable of voicing his concern for McCoy across the length of the bridge, but it existed nevertheless.

Enterprise medical personnel were too professional to betray a personal interest in any one patient over another, yet coincidentally a large proportion of them discovered duties that brought them into the vicinity of the intensive care unit. Kirk marveled at the vigor with which they ignored one particular corner of the room, yet hovered on its perimeter.

Dr. Dyson and Nurse Chapel were flanking the chief surgeon's body, intently scrutinizing the vital signs monitor on the wall. In contrast to other panels in the room, this one was approaching a normal configuration. Kirk might not be a doctor, but through the years he had become familiar with the medical equipment. A cautious smile on Chapel's face was a confirmation of his diagnosis. "He's coming out of the coma, Captain," she explained in a low voice, her eyes switching rapidly between the panel, Dyson's actions, and the unconscious form of Dr. McCoy.

"What about brain damage?"

"Too early to say yet," muttered Dyson absently. "The brain is a tricky organ and the monitor hasn't been built yet that can track all its subtleties." Her head was nodding in concert with the jerky progress of one particular indicator. "We'll get a rough idea when he wakes up, which should be soon."

She bent down and took hold of McCoy's shoulders. "Dr. McCoy, can you hear me? You've been asleep long enough." This was followed by a very gentle shake. "You must wake up now. Answer me, Dr. McCoy."

The slightest flutter of eyelashes betrayed a response. "Bones, wake up!" Kirk tried to make his words an order; they came out more like a plea.

The limp body began to transform with the tension of consciousness. "Thatta boy," crowed Dyson and began to slap at his cheeks. "Wake up and give me hell for beating up on a patient."

The flutter increased in intensity, then the lids snapped open. McCoy groaned but his eyes were clear and focused. "What happened?" His voice was little more than a croak.

"Can you tell me?" asked Dyson. "What do you remember?"

Dark eyebrows furrowed in thought. "I fell. Hit my head. And it hurts," he added.

"I'll bet it does. You gave yourself quite a fracture. Now tell me who you are."

Only the slightest hesitation preceded his answer. "Dr. Leonard H. McCoy." Already the voice had gained strength.

"And where are you now?"

Kirk smiled at her pedantic tone. If McCoy weren't so groggy, he'd have balked at being put through his paces.

Propping himself up on one elbow, the doctor looked up at the three people grouped around him, then at the room in which they all stood. "Well, it's got to be a hospital, but I'll be damned if I've ever seen one like this before. How far are we from the ranch?"

"Ranch?" Dyson kept her tone neutral, but her body tensed.

"Yeah, the Black Spur. I know breaking horses may not be the safest way to spend a vacation, but I didn't think this area rated a high-tech ward just to treat broken bones . . ." His voice trailed off in confusion as he took in more details around him. His gaze stopped short at the sight of Kirk's uniform. "I'm not in Waco, am I?"

"No, you're not," Dr. Dyson said genially. Her eyes

flashed a warning at the captain to remain silent. "Tell me more about the accident."

McCoy lay back down on the bed, gingerly resting his head on the pillow. His voice took on a slight Southern drawl. "I don't really remember the fall itself—not unusual for a head injury—but I can't have lost more than a couple of minutes . . ." He raised his head for another vague look at the area around the bed. "Anyway, I was riding this chestnut gelding with a bad disposition and an iron mouth. We had a slight disagreement about jumping barbwire fences. He wanted to, and I didn't. Somehow, I'm the only one that ended up going over." His hand described a lofty arc. "Just as well to forget what that landing must have been like.

"Say, I must have knocked myself silly 'cause I don't remember getting here." An edge of worry crept into his voice. "How long have I been out?"

"You were unconscious for a few hours," Dyson said easily. "And now it's time for you to get some more sleep, real sleep." She looked up at Chapel. "Nurse, prepare a sedative."

"I don't need a sedative!" The querulous tone was fully in character.

"I'm the attending physician here, and I say you do." This was clearly a non-negotiable issue. She was a small woman in stature, but her strength of will was a good seven feet tall.

"Well, as a sign of professional courtesy," said McCoy reluctantly, "I'll agree to the treatment."

Chapel placed a hypo against his arm and released the medicine with a soft hiss. "You're going to be just fine."

"Thank you, nurse." His eyes closed slowly. After his inspection of the service uniform, McCoy had never looked at Kirk.

Dyson began a soft rapid patter of instructions as she

scratched notes on a data tablet. "Chris, arrange to get a private room set up, even if it's just a supply closet. I know it's not going to be easy with sick bay as crowded as it is, but we can't afford to have the crew around him when he wakes up. I'll need a monitor but otherwise try to keep the room as spare as possible—it'll lessen his disorientation when he starts to take a good look around. And get the shipboard speaker turned off in there so he doesn't hear any announcements."

That's what got him in trouble in the first place, thought Kirk.

"Where's Dr. Cortejo?" asked Dyson.

The nurse paused a moment to check her mental calendar. "Surgery. He won't be out for at least another hour."

"Mmm. Well, there's nothing he can do now, but see if you can catch him when he's out so he knows what's going on. It seems he'll be acting chief for a while yet."

Kirk was impatient with questions but held himself in check. The effort must have showed on his face. Dyson gave him a quick glance. "Just a few minutes more, Captain, then we can talk." She signaled him to follow her out of the ward, still writing as she walked. By the time they reached her office the data tablet was completely filled.

Dyson pitched her voice for the medical log. "Computer, enter the following update on patient Leonard McCoy." She inserted the tablet into a slot on her desk.

"Reading."

Only then did the woman turn and face the Captain. "Aside from the memory loss, Dr. McCoy showed no signs of verbal aphasia or speech disorders. Motor coordination appeared normal, though there was limited time for observation. We'll have an exact determination of any subtle disability when we can run some in-depth performance tests. As for the rest, I won't pretend to be able to give you any definite information; amnesia is one of the least understood of brain disorders. It could be temporary—lasting only until he wakes up again—or it could last for some months. Or he might never recover his recent memory."

"That's not a very satisfactory answer." Kirk's statement was an acknowledgement of frustration rather than a reproach. "He's obviously forgotten the last several years of his life. He didn't recognize me or the ship; I'm not even certain he recognized the Star Fleet uniforms. Just how far back does this amnesia reach?"

"Well, that's one piece of information we may be able to determine now. I want to have a good idea of just where in time he thinks he is before explaining the situation to him.

"Computer, pull a complete medical history on patient Leonard McCoy."

"Acknowledged. Record on visual."

"From his description, that fall may have been serious enough to be in his records." Dyson peered intently at the screen and began to scroll the document backwards. Starting at the present, McCoy's life was unraveled line by line. After what seemed a very long time, the screen stopped. "This is probably it: 'Slight concussion and a bruised rib.' Hospitalized overnight at a clinic in Waco, Texas and released after routine observations indicated no complications."

She looked up at the captain. "Twenty-five years ago."

Chapter Six

THE ODORS THAT permeated the autopsy lab made Kirk's stomach roil in protest. The sights which the room offered only made his nausea worse. He didn't mind the chunks of tissue floating in specimen bottles—these were mangled beyond recognition—but the dismembered body which was spread out on the slab before him was a definite source of discomfort. The captain forced himself to concentrate on the scientific interest of the display.

"Of course, this is just a reconstruction of what they look like," explained Lt. Steven Frazer as he placed the last of the pieces, a severed foot, onto the table surface. "There were no whole bodies available."

Little wonder. The merchant ship had been reduced to twisted fragments and molten slag.

"But no Frenni or Klingons?" Kirk asked insistently.

"Nope." The xenobiologist was surprisingly colloquial in his speech. It was only on paper that he became a stupefying bore. A typical product of the Martian Colony school system, according to McCoy. At the thought of his chief surgeon, Kirk's stomach gave another ominous lurch. Steadfastly ignoring his body's traitorous behavior, he moved closer to the table to better examine its contents.

The decapitated head was the largest, and most intact, piece in the anatomical puzzle. It had survived the vacuum of space with surprisingly little disruption. Whereas a humanoid would have shown extensive hemorrhaging of its skin, this creature's outer surface was protected by a rubbery layer of steel-blue skin. The large, liquid eyes were shielded by a clear lid. Frazer believed that their venomous red color was probably natural. The black fibers of the skullcrest bristled stiffly even in death. The only concession to mortality was the open, gaping beak.

The massive head implied an equally massive chest, yet there were only a few pieces of oozing orange tissue arranged haphazardly in the center area. Sections of limbs were laid out on either side of them to suggest an upright, bipedal figure with two arms. Only one clawed foot and one taloned hand were present.

"How accurate is this 'reconstruction'?"

"Not very, as far as the internal organs are concerned," admitted Frazer, cheerfully rearranging the parts in question. He was tall and attenuated, with ruddy skin and an unruly shock of black hair. "But the basic shape is right. I haven't missed any extra legs, or the presence of a tail."

"Mean looking," muttered Kirk. Normally, he could not be tempted into such a xenophobic reaction, but dammit, these creatures had tried to destroy his ship.

"Mr. Spock entered a provisional taxonomic name into the computer log," said Frazer, "but the crew has already dubbed them 'Ravens'."

The word brought back the sharp scent of Iowa farmland in the harvest season, and the shadowy memory of a spare, stooped old woman. Kirk's grandmother had called ravens the harbingers of death, and as a young child he had felt his pulse quicken at their harsh caws. The trees near home had often harbored the sleek, blue-black birds whose cunning, aggressive natures and rapacious appetites brought them into conflict with farmers. The name was well chosen. Another connection formed in Kirk's mind. Ravens could also be taught to speak, to mimic sounds. Before the rescue attempt, Kirk had been convinced he was speaking to Captain Esserass, and only a very strong faith in the abilities of his first officer had shaken this certainty. How had they known so much? Enough to trick him into lowering the ship's shields?

"Are these aliens telepathic?" he asked. Such an ability could account for the accuracy of the impersonation—the "Raven" could have picked it directly from the mind of the gentle Frenni merchant, or possibly even from Kirk's mind as they talked . . .

"Probably not," said Frazer. "Recent studies have pinpointed the biochemical markers present in most telepathic species. I didn't find any evidence of those properties in these aliens."

Kirk's cheek twitched in anger. Then Esserass had probably been tortured for his knowledge. Mind-probers were quite effective, but one of the common side-effects of the procedure was death.

"But they have a fascinating nervous system," continued the xenobiologist with boyish enthusiasm. "I've never seen anything like it and Dyson says it has 'journal article' written all over it." He snatched up the alien head and flipped it over to reveal the back of the skull. One hand parted the fibers of the crest. "Look at this!"

Swallowing an upsurge of bile, Kirk did as he was told. Underneath the crest was a deep groove which bisected the skull neatly in half. "Yes?" he prompted Frazer for the significance of what he saw.

"The skull is divided into two lobes, but I mean *really* divided," the lieutenant explained. "Each side is a fully developed brain, with no neural connections between them. Each side has its own brain stem as well, but these don't join until this knot on the spinal cord." His fingers traced a line down the nape of the neck, stopping at a slight bulge perilously near the point at which the head had left its torso.

"Cases of double-brained development are very rare in higher species. And even then one brain has marked dominance, while the other is simply an especially dense cluster of neurons controlling select functions of the involuntary nervous system."

"A mutant?" suggested Kirk.

"No. From what we can make out of the tissue fragments it seems to have been a common feature of the Ravens." The young man shrugged. "But we haven't figured out what purpose it serves to have two brains. Under most evolutionary pressures it would be a fatal handicap. We'll need a live specimen before we can learn any more."

Kirk winced. "The last thing I want to see right now is a live version of this." He gestured at the lumps on the table.

Frazer grinned. "Yeah, I guess so. I certainly wouldn't want to face one without a phaser." He set down the head and reached for the one hand. Grabbing the limp appendage by the wrist, he waved it in Kirk's direction, oblivious to the man's pale complexion. "These talons are not only razor-sharp, they're also poisoned. Here, under each nail, is a venom-producing gland that packs enough wallop to paralyze a horse."

Kirk felt greatly in need of just such a numbing tonic, but Frazer seemed immune to the stench arising from the dismembered Raven.

"The venom is composed of various body fluids and a complex organic compound. The medical department thinks it may have potential as a new anesthetic. Of course, it won't be much use until we can counteract the effect. Once the structural analysis of the venom is finished, I'll have a pretty good chance of developing an antidote."

"Anything else of interest?" Kirk asked with an attempt at sincerity. He regretted having eaten lunch before entering this room, and his body threatened to redress that offense at any moment.

"Naw, that's pretty much it," finished Frazer, letting the hand drop back onto the countertop with a soggy thud.

Kirk made his exit as quickly as dignity would allow. Possibly quicker.

By the time he reached the shuttle bay hangar, Kirk's lungs had cleared themselves of the obnoxious odors of the autopsy room and his queasy stomach had settled somewhat. He walked carefully over the uneven deck and reflected on the significance of the torn and gouged surface. One shuttlecraft, the one carrying a paramedic team, had been the closest to the *Selessan* when the recall order was issued and thus the last to reach the *Enterprise*. The pilot had known the starship was defenseless without shields; she had also known Kirk would not raise shields until the last shuttlecraft landed. So Prusinowski hit full speed on her return flight. She won the race to reach the ship but miscalculated the approach deceleration. All aboard were killed when the shuttle crashed into the deck. Another two crewmen had been crushed as it skidded across the length of the hangar and slammed into the back wall.

The worst of that damage had been patched, but the crumpled shell of the craft was still lodged in its final resting place. Not too far from there was another high jumbled pile of wreckage. Tractor beams had recovered portions of the Frenni merchant ship from space; Scotty's repair teams had pried more from the hull of the *Enterprise* where the pieces had been imbedded. For the last five hours, Lt. Sulu had been searching the remains for any insight into the nature of the alien attackers.

"What have you found so far?" asked Kirk as he threaded his way between rows of misshapen fragments that littered the hangar deck.

"I'm still working on the initial organization, Captain." Sulu waved at the minefield he had created. "It's a complicated puzzle."

Kirk nodded vague approval at Sulu's vague report. Privately he suspected that the search was futile, but he needed more information about the Ravens. Sulu, whose usual duty as helmsman was rendered irrelevant by the ship's current condition, could be spared on the off chance that some clue existed. "Carry on, Mr. Sulu."

"Aye, sir." Sulu gazed intently at the mangled piece of metal in his hand until the captain was out of sight. Once the coast was clear, he seriously considered flinging the chunk across the deck, but ultimately decided there would be no gratification in the gesture. Sulu turned to his right and carefully laid the piece down in a pile of others just like it.

A groan issued from the depths of the debris, as if the ghosts of the defeated aliens were mourning their lost ship. "This is useless," wailed the phantom.

"Well, it was a good idea . . . in theory," said Sulu evenly. Since it had been his idea, he felt constrained from voicing his regret.

"Perhaps." A tousled thatch of brown hair materialized on the other side of the mountain of space flotsam. "But, in practice it is not so good an idea." Chekov worked his way around to Sulu's side. "Ve vill never find any useful information in this junk."

The helmsman sighed in agreement. He pulled a cracked ventplate from the heap and held it up to the light. It was the most recognizable object he had found so far. The Frenni ship had been twisted and torn by its impact with the pylon and partially vaporized by the raising of the shields, a somewhat belated response which had done little to save the *Enterprise* from damage and much to erase any evidence of the attacker's origin.

"And now the captain will expect answers." Chekov continued his list of grievances against Sulu's proposal to inspect the wreckage. "Worse, Mr. Spock will expect answers. I do not like to disappoint Mr. Spock." A good portion of the ensign's waking hours were spent in gathering and analyzing data for the science officer. Chekov viewed the effort as a daily sacrificial offering to appease a particularly demanding demi-god.

Sulu turned the ventplate upside down. "This reminds me of free-form sculpture from Benega IV. My academy roommate was Benegan and he showed me how to work the metal . . ."

Chekov drowned out the rest of the explication with an extremely loud and guttural stream of Russian.

As soon as Kirk stepped out of the turbo-lift Spock rose smoothly from the captain's chair. The Vulcan was never reluctant to exchange the duties of command for those of science.

"Have you read Frazer's report?" asked Kirk, settling into the vacated seat.

"Yes, Captain. Most interesting." Spock's tolerance for teasing was high, but Kirk suspected he had approached his limit in one area—lately Spock tended to avoid the word "fascinating."

"I suppose you even understood it," sighed Kirk. Not even McCoy's emendations had rendered the report comprehensible to him, thus necessitating a personal acquaintanceship with its subject matter. "It doesn't answer our most pressing question—why were we attacked? Why were these Ravens trying to destroy this ship? And at the cost of their own lives."

Spock did not challenge Kirk's designation of the aliens as "Ravens." The term had entrenched itself too quickly among the science staff. "They do exhibit extremely aggressive tendencies," admitted Spock. "Their motivations, unfortunately, are not subject to autopsy."

"Greed and lust for power are the most common excuses for fighting," mused Kirk.

The Vulcan offered another. "Territorial defense is also a frequent basis for warfare."

"Not this time. This wasn't their territory."

"Perhaps they believed it was," argued Spock impartially.

"Or they don't care who it belonged to, they simply want to take it over. Territorial expansion is another popular attraction for slaughter, right up there with greed and desire for power."

Spock grew impatient with this undirected speculation. "Alien minds and alien cultures are often possessed of motives beyond our comprehension."

Kirk groaned and laid his head in his hands. "Do Vulcans suffer from tension headaches, Mr. Spock?"

"No," said the first officer. "But my Human half has proved troublesome at times."

"Well, at least the truce is still intact." Kirk kneaded his temples to ease the pain that was taking root. "That tale of a Klingon attack was faked—simply a ruse to draw us into their trap."

Spock arched an eyebrow. "That certainly is the most attractive interpretation, Captain." He registered Kirk's annoyance and relented. "However, even in the cold light of objectivity, it is also the most probable."

Kirk observed that the pounding in his skull had

fallen into sync with the yellow alert lights which had flashed with monotonous regularity for the last fifteen hours.

Spock followed his gaze. "One hour and twenty-two minutes until long-range sensors are operational."

And what will we find then? Kirk wondered wearily.

Chapter Seven

THE SECOND TIME Leonard McCoy awoke he was alone in a small featureless room of metallic grey walls and a ceiling obscured by deep shadow. The only light was a faint glow that came from the monitor above him; the only sound was its soft hum.

At first he was content to lie still and let his thoughts wander idly over landscapes of scrub grass and mesquite bush, to recall the sting of dust carried by a dry wind and the baking glare of a summer sun overhead. Inevitably, these thoughts led to the memory of his fall, which led him back to the bed on which he lay. Ironically, this vacation had been an attempt to escape as far as possible from the reminders of daily rounds and night shifts in ER. At least he wasn't working, but McCoy wasn't sure he liked this side of hospital life any better.

Still, he shouldn't be here long, since only his head seemed to have suffered from contact with the ground; the rest of him felt remarkably whole. Starting at his toes and working his way up, McCoy wiggled and tensed each muscle of his legs, arms, and chest without experiencing a twinge. No broken bones, no wrenched tendons, no bruises. This latter fact began to nag at him. He might not have picked up any bruises from this last fall, but he certainly had the day before when the gelding had unexpectedly bolted, leaving McCoy hanging in air. Yet no amount of prodding or pinching could produce the expected tender spots. This puzzlement served to direct his attention back to the scene in the hospital ward. As a result his puzzlement deepened. He had the vague recollection that the place had not looked like an ordinary hospital. Yet no one had actually said where he was. They had been full of questions, not answers.

They. There had been the doctor who talked with him and the nurse who gave him the sedative. But the third, who was he? The image of the man's uniform was blurred, his face indistinct.

Where am I? wondered McCoy with an edge of annoyance.

He sat up in bed to inspect the monitor. Its basic shape and function were certainly familiar, but this was the most sophisticated model he had ever encountered. Numerous indicators were newly configured and their markings only cryptic letters and numbers. *Could they have sent me all the way to Dallas?* The desire to find out where he was grew very strong.

McCoy flipped on a low room light and saw nothing around him that would yield information. The small space was depressingly functional and antiseptic. He swung his feet over the edge of the bed and stood up, waited patiently for a wave of nausea and dizziness to pass, which it did, then took an experimental step forward. Balance and muscular reflexes undamaged, he noted with satisfaction.

Then he took notice of the black t-shirt and blue robe he was wearing; getting dressed was his next priority. With increasing confidence he began a search of the room, only to find no sign of his clothes, indeed no store of any personal effects. However, tucked in a small shelf by the bed were a pair of soft-soled shoes and a folded jumpsuit, all of which fit him comfortably. He headed for the doorway.

The trip was short-lived. Before he had taken more than five steps, the door swept open to admit the tall, blonde nurse he remembered from the ward. "You're going in the wrong direction," she said genially, and pointed to a back corner of the room. "It's that way."

McCoy flushed. "I was headed for the hallway."

"There's no need. Just use the call button under the monitor and I'll come in."

Somehow McCoy found himself being led back to bed as she talked on. "My name's Nurse Chapel. I'm here pretty much all of the time, so don't worry about not being able to reach me. I realize you're a little too big to need tucking in bed," she said doing just that, "but if there's anything else you want, just ask." As if from nowhere she presented him with a small capsule. "I'm sorry you're having trouble sleeping but this should help you . . ."

"I *want* to be awake," replied McCoy warily. "I also want to know just where I am and how long I've been here. That doctor said I was unconscious for hours—how many hours?"

"Are you always this energetic at three in the morning?" asked the nurse in a conversational tone.

Despite her pleasant manner, McCoy recognized the evasiveness of the response and felt his puzzlement turn into uneasiness. "I'd like to see my medical chart."

Chapel considered. "You were in a coma for twelve hours, Dr. McCoy. Dr. Dyson is concerned that you not overstress yourself early into recovery. Now you, as a medical man, should recognize the advisability of getting some more rest. You can read your medical chart in the morning with your attending physician, and the two of you can argue treatments together to your heart's content." With a smile, she again proferred the capsule.

Her performance was convincing, yet somehow the doctor sensed that it was just that—a performance—and not the reasonable statement of fact it appeared to be. "At the risk of being a difficult and demanding patient, I'd like to see it now."

Her pleasant facade held steady. "And I haven't the authority to give it to you. What would you say to any nurse of yours who gave a patient their medical chart?"

He chuckled despite himself. "Fine, you win. Just tell me what hospital I'm in and I'll go to bed like a good little boy."

"Why, it's called Enterprise General." The hesitation had been slight, almost imperceptible, but Chapel was better at evasion and diversion than she was at outright lies.

She was almost out the door when McCoy spoke again. "I don't believe a word you've said, Nurse Chapel." He stared straight into her startled face. "Now why would you lie to me?" The words drawled out a challenge.

Sighing heavily, she punched a button on the intercom panel. "Dr. Dyson to sick bay."

They spent the time waiting in guarded silence, staring awkwardly about the room. Chapel welcomed the entrance of the doctor with palpable relief. "Your patient has some questions. It seems they can't wait until morning."

"Thank you," the woman answered with a sleepy yawn. Her long brown hair straggled untidily out of a hastily tied bun; her blue science tunic was rumpled in a manner familiar to all on-call doctors. "You can get back to the ward now. Don't worry, I'll call you if I need you."

Once the nurse had left, McCoy burst out with

impatience. "What's going on here? I want to know where I am and why I can't get any answers about my condition." Beneath the anger was fear.

"You'll get answers." Dyson did not make the mistake of adopting a soothing manner. "But until you hear everything I have to say, you'll get the answers in the order I choose to give them." She waited until McCoy gave a reluctant nod before continuing.

"As the result of a fall, you sustained a linear fracture in the occipital region of your skull. Due to the resulting concussion you were in a coma for just over twelve hours. Based on informal observation I can say that organic damage does not seem extensive." She gave him a disgruntled look. "Your verbal abilities certainly haven't suffered. But you haven't escaped without effect."

She paused to search for the right approach. "Think very carefully. What do you remember from after your fall at the ranch?"

McCoy's brows furrowed together. "Waking up here, wherever I am." A ball of tension began to form in his gut.

"Well, more than twelve hours have passed between your vacation and now. The fall you remember, the one from a horse, is not the accident from which you are recovering. At that time you received a slight concussion, and a body bruising, but nothing serious. You've awakened from a coma that was the result of a second, later, fall. You've lost the memory of the intervening time."

"How much time? Weeks, months?" Then he looked up at the monitor, one he had never seen before. "Not years?" he asked with disbelief.

"Yes, years," came the reply. "You don't recognize

me or Christine Chapel, but you'll remember us again, probably soon. Alarming as your state may feel, bear in mind that your recovery has barely begun."

McCoy listened in silence. He recognized the careful words of a physician trying not to alarm a patient. "Or I might never recover."

"That is a possibility," sighed Dyson in reluctant agreement. "But I wouldn't get my hopes up. Despite the dramatic appeal, extended amnesia is fairly rare. It's much more likely that you'll start remembering bits and pieces, until the whole picture, or most of it, returns."

"Well, I certainly hope I remember you," he said with a spark of humor. "You have me at a disadvantage." She clearly knew the right tone to strike with him, one that would deflate his self-pity before it had a chance to take root. "Now where am I? And how long have I been here?"

"I think we've talked enough for tonight."

"Is it that bad?" McCoy asked, suddenly grim again. "So bad that I need to get my news spoon-fed in small doses?"

"You've had a shock, more of one than you realize. If you just . . ."

"You don't give me much credit, do you, Dr. Dyson? Well, I'll have you know that I'm getting mighty tired of this white-gloves treatment. A little shock is nothing compared to the holy hell I'm going to raise if I don't get some answers soon."

"Damn! You're a worse terror as a patient than you are as a doctor." Dyson weighed the determination in his voice. "All right," she relented, "you get the whole load of news in one session. At present you are on board the U.S.S. *Enterprise,* a Federation starship assigned to exploratory duty on the edges of mapped space. The man in uniform who was with us when you woke up is James Kirk, the captain of this ship."

"What!" McCoy's voice held more than disbelief: he looked aghast at her words. "But I'm a doctor, not some star-happy spacerat."

"You are indeed a doctor. In fact, you're chief surgeon of the *Enterprise*."

McCoy snorted. "Then the Federation must be pretty hard up for help. I'm a family doctor, not a surgeon. Hell, I've never been beyond the Moon and you're asking me to believe . . ." He ran down and began to look confused. "Why, reaching that rank would take . . . years. And you did say it had been years." His face paled. "How many?"

This time Dyson answered him. "It's been twenty-five years since you were on that ranch."

"Sweet Georgia," he said in awe. "That makes me an old man now. Half a lifetime and I don't remember any of it." He sank back into the bed. "What have I been doing in all that time?"

"I can't fill you in on the details, Doctor," said Dyson. "But Captain Kirk knows you well and he'll be able to give you a better idea . . ." She was cut off by the blaring of a klaxon. An emergency alert was overriding the room's intercom silence.

"Red Alert—Red Alert. All hands to battle stations."

"Not again," Dyson groaned.

"Again?" McCoy demanded. "What in hell is going on?" His words were addressed to her back. The doctor was already at the door.

"Sorry, I've got to go," she yelled over her shoulder. "We're under attack. Stay here."

"Dammit, where is here?" But she was gone. As the klaxon continued its wail, the lights dimmed briefly. Through the walls came the sounds of running feet and shouting voices. "Under attack! I must have been insane to join Star Fleet."

The lights went off completely. He waited, but they did not return. "I resign," he muttered into the darkness, and began a groping journey to the door.

Chapter Eight

AFTER HOURS OF meaningless sensory gibberish, the input from long-range scanners sorted itself into coherence. The image which appeared then on the main viewscreen escalated the yellow alert to red.

Of all the scenarios which had filled Jim Kirk's mind in the last 24 hours, this was definitely his least favorite: to be face to face with a Klingon warship while the *Enterprise* had buckled shields and no warp drive. He settled back into the command chair as if bracing himself for the combat to come. "Can you get us out of here, Mr. Sulu?"

The helmsman shook his head decisively. "The nacelle is still unsteady. If I try to move the ship now, we'll go into a spin. And even if it were anchored, we can't outrun a battlecruiser with impulse engines." His voice was still ragged from his frantic dash from the hangar deck to the bridge.

"Chekov, what kind of damage can our weapons do?"

"Not much, Keptin." The ensign wiped sweat off his forehead. He had kept up with Sulu all the way but the run had cost him as well. "Phasers are at thirty-three percent capacity. Even with a solid hit, that von't break their shields."

Kirk's fist hit a communications switch. "Scotty, I need power!"

"There's no more t' give," came the frantic voice from the speaker. *"Ship's systems are pared t' th' bone, and we've lowered life-support t' a barely sustainable level. We can't fight, we can't run, we can't defend ourselves . . . I need a miracle."*

"Then get ready to cut life-support systems completely at my signal. All power to phasers."

"What?"

"You heard me, Scotty. We can last at least fifteen minutes from shut-off. If we get through that time, then we can worry about breathing."

"Captain." Spock's imperturbable voice cut through Scotty's protests. "That may not be necessary. Sensors indicate minimal radiant energy from the Klingon vessel—its engines are cold."

"But it's moving."

"At an extremely leisurely, decelerating pace, consistent with that of a drifting ship propelled only by inertia."

"Like our Frenni cruiser," said Kirk bitterly. The ploy had tricked him once. Now, though forewarned, he had no defense against another attempt. "And what are the bio-readings this time?"

"None." Spock seemed as surprised as his captain at the answer. "There are no signs of living beings aboard, Klingon or otherwise."

"That would mean an entire crew dead . . . Could the scanners still be dysfunctional?"

"Unlikely. All other indicators are recording normal conditions." Spock continued his observations, his tall form hunched over the science station. "At present rate of drift, the warship will not be within phaser range for at least five hours."

"My miracle," whispered Kirk to himself. Aloud, he said, "Uhura, secure from general quarters, but monitor all hailing frequencies. If you hear the slightest squeak from that ship, I want to know."

"Yes, Captain." As the call went over the ship's intercom, dimmed lights began to brighten and the bridge air lost its edge of stale mustiness. Then a *beep* from her communications panel called Uhura's attention. She listened intently to the silent message, her hand pressed to the metal spiral in her ear. "Captain, medical section reports a missing patient—Dr. McCoy."

"Missing? What do you mean missing?"

"He seems to have wandered away from his room during the alert, and no one has seen him since. He's nowhere in the medical section."

"Issue a ship-wide call for Dr. McCoy to report to sick bay, then alert security to begin a deck-by-deck search." As if there weren't enough problems.

"Mr. Spock, our puzzle seems to be growing more complex. We now have a battle-damaged Frenni ship, but no Frenni; several unidentified alien corpses; and a drifting Klingon warship, but no Klingons."

"Indeed, Captain. A most intriguing set of variables with which to deal. It reintroduces the problem of Klingon intrusion into Federation space."

"Yes, it seems our bogus 'Merchant Esserass' wasn't lying about Klingon involvement. But *how* are they involved? Who attacked the Frenni caravan? Where did the Ravens come from? Why is the battle cruiser adrift?" Kirk looked to his first officer. "Answers, Mr. Spock?"

"You have enumerated the questions fairly comprehensively, Captain. Unfortunately, delineating a problem does not automatically illuminate the solution. I need more data."

"Keptin, Mr. Spock!" Chekov had finished a series

of navigation calculations and the results were causing him great agitation. "I've traced back the course of the warship. Its path intercepts that of the *Selessan*."

Kirk blinked in surprise. "But it's moving *toward* us, and it certainly wasn't within sensor range when we first arrived here."

Spock stepped down to the helm and studied the instrument array. "Interesting," he said evenly. His fingers touched the panel, transferring a star-chart to the main viewscreen. "According to Chekov's vector analysis, the Klingon ship and the Frenni caravan were probably in close proximity at this point." Two ship icons rested side by side on the map surface. "Ion particle residue indicates this as the site of a battle, one which destroyed the *Verella*. Both remaining ships lost engine power but continued to drift apart from the momentum of their earlier flight." The icons moved several inches apart.

"We encountered the *Selessan* here." A starship icon appeared. "While the Klingon cruiser was still moving out of sensor range. However, as its deceleration continued, the gravitational forces of the Belennii system exerted sufficient effect to pull it off course." The solitary icon began to arc back toward the *Enterprise*.

"Its heading is 83-mark-4, though, so it vill not come closer than 8.5 kilometers," said Chekov. The map wavered and was replaced by a panorama of untroubled stars amidst the void.

"There's your additional data, Spock. What do you make of it?"

The science officer balked. "At this point, Captain, any extrapolations of that occurence would more closely resemble fiction than reality. I still need . . ."

". . . need more data," echoed Kirk sympathetically. "Very well, Mr. Spock." It was best not to push Spock too far. Extended speculation without hard facts tended to leave the Vulcan in a decidedly cranky mood.

The captain turned back to the helm. "Lt. Sulu, we hardly need a helmsman on duty, since this ship isn't going anywhere. You'll be more useful preparing a boarding party for that cruiser."

"Yes, sir!" The young man's face split into an excited grin. Aside from the lure of a new ship, this assignment would put a quiet end to his fruitless search through the Frenni ship wreckage.

Kirk did not fail to catch a look of envy on the navigator's face. "You, too, Chekov. I want every inch of that ship checked out; let's get Mr. Spock that extra data he needs."

Chekov offered a silent prayer to the patron saint of down-trodden ensigns for this chance to appease the Vulcan. Surely an intact Klingon battlecruiser would provide a satisfactory quota of answers.

"Captain," called out Uhura, "Security reports no sign of Dr. McCoy."

"Damn. It can't be that hard to find a dazed and wounded man. How far can he have gotten?"

The doors of the turbo-lift snapped open. With a muttered curse, McCoy jumped through the portal and glared back at the doors as they snapped shut. He was far from dazed.

"Bones!"

There was no reaction from the doctor. He turned around slowly, eyes widening in surprise as they wandered over the glittering, humming instrument panels that lined the bridge. When they reached the viewscreen he gave a visible start and remained riveted in place.

"I'll be damned," he exclaimed softly. "I really am in space."

Kirk rose from the command chair and crossed over to him. "Dr. McCoy?"

McCoy pulled his attention away from the vision of deep space and found himself the center of attention on the deck. He flushed. "Sorry to intrude, but I've been trying to find 'sick bay.' If someone could give me some directions . . ."

"Don't worry, I'll have a security guard show you the way." Kirk kept his voice deliberately matter-of-fact. Off to his side, Uhura began to whisper quietly into the intercom.

"Thanks very much." McCoy's attention sharpened on Kirk's face. "I remember you."

The look of anticipation on Kirk's face faded as McCoy continued. "You were there in the hospital ward when I woke up. You must be Captain Kirk." He held out his hand in greeting.

Solemnly, the captain shook hands with his chief medical officer.

Still conscious of the crew watching him, McCoy glanced nervously around the room, his gaze sliding quickly over the unfamiliar faces. "I didn't mean to cause any trouble. Actually, I just got lost trying to stay out of the way during this red alert commotion."

"You haven't caused any trouble," said Kirk. "We were simply concerned when you didn't answer the ship's intercom."

"I heard the orders—I just couldn't figure out how to talk back." McCoy gave another baleful glance at the turbo-lift doors. "Or how to get that blasted contraption to work."

Despite himself, Kirk smiled. "I'll see to it that you get a thorough orientation to the *Enterprise* so you don't get lost again." He watched as McCoy's eyes drifted back to the view screen, mesmerized by the black velvet surface. "Would you care for a tour of the bridge, doctor?"

With all due ceremony the captain led a curious McCoy to the communications station and introduced him to Lt. Uhura. "This is the voice that has been ordering you to sick bay."

"Then I came in the right direction after all," said McCoy with a slight courtly bow as he took her hand. She accepted the compliment with a gracious smile, and only Kirk could detect the effort in her pretense of formality.

While Uhura held the doctor's attention with an explanation of the sub-space transmitter, Kirk motioned for Spock to come closer. Until now the first officer had stayed motionless at his station, but at the captain's signal he rose quietly and walked towards the small group. Without words the two officers came to a quick understanding of the situation: the Vulcan's sudden presence might jolt McCoy's memory.

When McCoy turned around there was no doubt that the confrontation was a shock, but the doctor's reaction revealed only amazement, not recognition.

"This is the ship's first officer, Mr. Spock," said Kirk easily, though he couldn't stifle an inward stab of disappointment.

McCoy swallowed his surprise. "How do you do?" His hand made an abortive move upwards, but Spock's stony countenance seemed too alien for such a Human gesture as a handshake. Somewhat at a loss, McCoy clasped his hands behind his back and rocked nervously on his toes. "Forgive me any social blunders, but I've never met a Vulcan before."

Spock nodded impassively. "There is no need for apology. I have learned to accommodate Human social conventions."

"Oh, really," answered McCoy weakly. He glanced sideways at Kirk, as if appealing for help, but the captain only smiled.

The need for further conversation was forestalled by Christine Chapel's sudden emergence from the turbo-lift. "Uh oh," murmured McCoy under his breath. "I'm in for it now."

"Hmm. Perhaps we should continue your tour later," said Kirk as a grim-faced Nurse Chapel swooped towards them. Her worry over the doctor's disappearance was rapidly transforming into anger.

McCoy stepped forward meekly. "Don't shoot. I'll go peaceably." Her expression did not lighten, but she came to a halt and showed no inclination to drag him bodily off the bridge.

"Well, it's been a pleasure meeting you, Captain." The doctor nodded affably at Spock, smiled at Uhura, and turned to follow Chapel to the exit. After several steps he hesitated; a look of confusion crossed his face. Looking back briefly, he called out, "I guess I'll need to talk to you later about . . ." He broke off and walked quickly through the opening doors.

With Chapel handling the recalcitrant turbo-lift, McCoy was free to sag weakly against a wall. He closed his eyes and fought against a wave of nausea. Throughout the duration of the alert he had been filled with an energizing sense of wonder as he worked his way from corridor to corridor, dodging the self-absorbed crew. In their wake, sliding doors revealed quick glimpses of laboratories and offices all dimly illuminated by the glow of emergency lighting panels. He had pushed aside Dr. Dyson's disturbing words and concentrated on the novelty of his surroundings, letting himself be drawn farther and farther away from his room, until at last he had lost all sense of direction. But finally, as he was leaving the bridge, the knowledge had caught up to him again, bringing a wrenching sense of disorientation.

I'm supposed to know these people, this ship. I've been here for years. I'm never going home again.

He felt as if a chasm had opened beneath his feet, and a glimpse of the depths had left him spinning from vertigo.

"You're tired," said Chapel, not without sympathy.

"I'm old," McCoy responded bitterly, though he still couldn't bring himself to accept that he had aged so much seemingly overnight.

"Forty-eight is hardly doddering," came the acerbic reply. The abrupt change of tone opened McCoy's eyes in surprise. Chapel was studying him with an expression of bemusement. "And you've been sprinting through the *Enterprise* at an alarmingly sprightly pace for an elderly man."

"This isn't funny!" he flared. "What do you care that I've lost half a lifetime? What does anybody care on this tinpot rocket? I don't know you. I've never met you before in my life." Even as the doors of the lift opened he continued shouting. "It's lies, all lies. I've been shanghaied off Earth and I want to go back."

Strong arms were taking hold of him. "Let me go! Let me out of here!" Blind with fury, McCoy began swinging his fists and grappling with the bodies which tried to restrain him.

The unseen forces prevailed, pinning him down to the floor. He heard a soft hiss by his ear and felt a cold spot at the base of his neck. Then he lost consciousness.

Chapter Nine

THE WALK THROUGH the interior of the *Falchion* had a curious dreamlike quality. Red boarding lights posted at irregular intervals created a dim trail that wound its way through narrow shadowy corridors and cramped crew quarters. The basic lines of the ship were familiar, yet form and function were both oddly distorted for alien bodies and minds. An alien ship devoid of alien life: no Klingons were on board.

Spock's summons had pulled Kirk from a deep sleep, moving him to action and the appearance of alertness, but fatigue blurred the distinction between the unconscious realm and his present surroundings. He half-believed himself to be in a mildly disturbing dream. The Vulcan first officer, however, was firmly grounded in the reality of the situation. "The sensor scan readings have been confirmed by a thorough deck search. The boarding party reports there are no living beings aboard the ship. No bodies, either. Yet, the lifeslips are all berthed."

"I don't like the feel of this, Spock."

"The feel, Captain?" The obligatory challenge to Human emotions.

"This situation bears an uncomfortable resemblance to the disappearance of the crew of an Earth ship of the sea, the *Marie Celeste*. She was found adrift with no

89

sign of her crew. The mystery was never solved."
Spock made no reply to this bit of trivia.

"What about the ship's log?" asked Kirk.

"Wiped clean. The complete record of this ship's activities has been erased from the computer system. Therefore, the immediate history of this vessel remains unknown. However, Star Fleet intelligence reports indicate the *Falchion* had been posted on routine border patrol of the Belennii system for nearly two solar years. The commander of the ship was Captain Kryon, a seasoned veteran who should have deserved a better assignment. However, there have been indications of political upheavals in the current Imperial line of succession. He may have incurred political disfavor."

"Or he may have been placed there in preparation for an attack on the Federation," said Kirk thoughtfully. He followed Spock through a narrow doorway and found himself in the command center of the warship, the rendezvous point for the boarding party. The shadowed forms of half a dozen crewmembers, indistinguishable from one another in the dim red light, were scattered about the cockpit, waving tricorders in every direction. Here, more than anywhere else, the lack of power was most evident: equipment panels lay dark and silent and the viewscreen was reduced to a blank wall.

"Captain, this is an unparalleled opportunity to study Klingon technology." The disembodied voice was that of Lt. Aziz. As one of Scotty's disciples, she was enchanted by engineering systems.

"Sorry you won't have more time to check it out," answered Kirk, failing to identify her position in the crowd that milled in the half-light.

"That's all right. I've already got enough information to keep me busy for months, but Sulu's dying to fly a

Klingon warship—he can't be trusted near the controls."

"It's the chance of a lifetime!" the helmsman's voice rang out excitedly. He too was merged among the crew.

"Is it functional?" asked Kirk in surprise.

"As far as we can determine," said Aziz.

Spock picked up the narrative. "All ship's systems are in working order, though power levels are low due to engine shutdown. Presumably, with sufficient time, levels could be restored to normal capacity."

"So where are the Klingons?" It was a rhetorical question, another Human response which Spock ignored.

"It's just like the *Marie Celeste*," said Sulu with relish. This time he made himself known by moving toward the senior officers. "Abandoned at sea in the Bermuda Triangle, crew vanished into thin air."

Spock was pushed to a rebuttal. "I too am familiar with the myths and legends associated with early ship-travel on Earth's oceans. However, I see no need to delve into the realms of the supernatural to explain our current situation. A *rational*"—he stressed the word carefully—"explanation would be that the crew has boarded another vessel."

"Leaving a functional warship behind, adrift in Federation territory?" Kirk countered. "That may indeed be a rational explanation, Mr. Spock, but only of very *irrational* behavior on the part of the Klingons. And since the *Selessan* had no Frenni aboard, we are left with two missing crews to account for. We've faced our share of cosmic mysteries, encountered the unknown, the unexplained, the fantastic. Now we're meeting the known acting out of character. I don't like it."

Spock gave no reply; on general principle he politely ignored the captain's more blatant effusions of emotion.

Kirk's eyes searched the shadow-laden command deck. Where was the shade of its former captain? Surely it lurked just out of sight . . . Sleep was lulling him into fantasy even as he stood.

Chekov's voice echoed weakly over the ship's intercom. "Sir, I've completed an inspection of the outer hull. There are signs of recent phaser damage."

Those words brought Kirk back to attention. "So the *Falchion* did attack the Frenni caravan . . ."

"But, Captain," interrupted Sulu. "Where do the Ravens fit in?"

"It was probably a joint attack," said Kirk grimly. "Chances are the Klingon Empire has found a powerful new ally, and together they've decided to wage war against the Federation."

"And it must have been the Raven ship that carried the Klingon crew off the *Falchion*," said Sulu with noticeable disappointment. This solution was not as appealing as a metaphysical phenomenon.

Kirk knew his science officer was suffering under the weight of this rampant speculation. "Mr. Spock, every new fact we gather seems to compound our difficulties."

"That is the inevitable risk of any scientific endeavor, Captain," replied the Vulcan without apology.

"All theories aside, one fact remains: this ship is functional. In fact, it's in better shape than the *Enterprise*." Kirk chuckled softly. "Lt. Aziz, how long will it take to restore life-support systems and bring the engines back to full power?" The boarding crew came to a standstill at his words.

"No more than four hours," replied the engineer promptly. "Sooner, if Linguistics can decipher certain control designations."

"According to Scotty's last estimate we have another

ten hours before the *Enterprise* is ready to depart. Sulu, that gives you six hours to learn how to fly her."

"Yes, sir!" His assent served for all the boarding party. A furious burst of activity signaled their enthusiasm for the project.

"An armed escort," noted Spock with appreciation. "With fully powered weapons and shields."

"And a cloaking device which will make the *Falchion* our ace in the hole. We'll need that card if there are any Ravens still lurking about this sector." Kirk sent up a small prayer that those aliens had not learned how to detect a shielded vessel. The Empire did not hand out such knowledge freely, not even to its allies. "A small crew should be able to handle this ship. Sulu can double as pilot and commander, with Aziz as engineer . . ."

"I recommend Ensign Chekov as navigator and science officer," added Spock. "Since he has already familiarized himself with the ship, it would save time to use his knowledge." Despite its back-handed delivery, the suggestion was a definite compliment to the junior officer.

"Recommendation accepted," replied Kirk. The ship's speakers reverberated with the effusive thanks of the ensign. Kirk suspected his first officer wished to escape before Chekov lapsed into Russian. "If you're ready to return to the *Enterprise*, Mr. Spock?"

"Quite ready, Captain."

Kirk pulled out a communicator, activating contact with the ship. "Mr. Kyle, two to beam aboard."

When the shimmer of the transporter beam finally faded, Kirk found himself swaying dizzily on the platform. Spock steadied him with a touch. "Sleep is a biological necessity."

"You're the one who woke me up," accused Kirk. He shook off Spock's grip and walked down the steps.

"Besides, I suspect you've been awake for the last three days."

"Four point five to be exact. However, as a Vulcan, I find a short session of meditation sufficiently energizing to forego extended periods of complete unconsciousness."

"I get the same lift from a stimulant. If you need me, I'll be in sick bay."

By the time he reached the medical complex Kirk was racked by yawns, and the presence of so many beds only increased his desire to lie down in a dark corner and sleep for days. Unfortunately the relief he sought proved to be more elusive than he had bargained for.

"You've had two stimulant injections within the last forty-eight hours," said Dr. Cortejo with heavy disapproval. "I can't possibly authorize additional medication for another twelve hours."

"I'll be comatose by then."

"It takes at least ten to twelve hours for the chemicals to dissipate in your system," said the doctor didactically. His thin lips were set quite firmly.

"But I'm the captain," was the only reply Kirk could muster. "There are times when it is necessary for me to remain awake." When this produced no reaction, he continued unwillingly. "As chief medical officer, Dr. McCoy was aware of the need to balance medical judgement with a sense of perspective. The present tactical situation has priority over my optimum biochemistry."

The doctor's face betrayed his affronted pride. "Very well, but I take no responsibility for the consequences of your action." He motioned to Nurse Chapel. "And speaking of chief medical officers, Captain. You should know that Dr. McCoy was carried screaming into this ward after his little side trip to the bridge." With a wave of his hand, Cortejo dismissed himself from the room.

"Another five minutes with that man and I'd need a sedative to keep me from breaking his neck," Kirk said to the nurse as she approached him.

"You'd have to stand in line, Captain." She tripped the plunger of the spray against his arm.

Within seconds a hot fire coursed through Kirk's veins; the creeping fog of unconsciousness receded. "How much truth was there in what he said?"

"I'm afraid that was a fairly accurate description. But it was more of a temper tantrum than the ravings of a lunatic. Check with Dr. Dyson if you're worried." Chapel pointed him toward Medical Records.

Kirk found the neurologist hunched intently over a computer terminal. At his approach, she flicked off the screen and began an unruffled update on her patient. "The results we've received so far are very promising for a rapid physical recovery. But I can't form a final prognosis until we've finished the full battery of tests."

"What about his . . . temper tantrum?" asked Kirk. The description of McCoy's departure from the bridge had been disconcerting.

"The rage was a good sign." She smiled at the captain's dubious look. "Delayed stress. I would have been more worried if he had taken the news calmly. Now he's ready to absorb information about his past. In fact, it's important that he get it soon. The time lapse won't seem real to him until he's learned more about his missing years." She picked a computer tape off the desktop. "Mr. Spock pulled his personnel file. I'd rather that he read it with someone who can fill him in on the personal details."

"That someone being me," agreed Kirk, accepting the tape.

She led the captain to a small alcove where McCoy was running through a series of motor coordination trials. He stood bare-chested in the middle of the area, his lean muscles tensed in concentration, as he faced a panel set into the wall. Flat metal disks dotted the surface of his skin, monitoring his responses. Dyson's assessment of his mood seemed accurate. He was alert and apparently calm, despite the somewhat aggravating task of trying to catch small colored spheres that popped out of the testing apparatus before him. When the final ball had been ejected, and missed, McCoy looked back at his audience.

"What now, Dr. Dyson: jigsaw puzzles, or skipping rope, perhaps?"

"History lessons. Captain Kirk has your records and can answer any questions about what you've been doing for the last two decades." She peeled the sensors off his back. "Don't try to force a recall of the events he describes; you're more likely to jog memories if you're relaxed."

"That's easy for you to say."

"That's why I'm the doctor and you're the patient." McCoy yelped as she plucked a last sensor disk from his ribcage. "Take good care of him, Captain," she advised before she left. "He's medical property."

"I'm beginning to feel like a lab specimen," muttered McCoy, pulling a plain tunic over his head and fumbling with the unfamiliar fasteners. The sleeves were bare of command stripes, a detail that bothered Kirk more than he cared to admit. "Is there some private place where we can dissect my life, Captain Kirk? I promise not to get hysterical or throw fits."

"We'll go to my cabin," suggested Kirk, leading the way out of sick bay. "A little Saurian brandy should steady your nerves."

"Really? I've never tried the stuff," McCoy said innocently.

Kirk whooped loudly, badly startling a crewman in the corridor. By the time they reached a turbo-lift his laughter had subsided sufficiently for him to call out their destination. "Well, your mind may not remember, but I'll bet your body does. Your bloodstream has a long-standing acquaintance with Saurian brandy."

McCoy accepted the teasing in good humor. "How many more vices have I picked up?"

"That's the worst of the lot, doctor. You've lived a clean life despite my best efforts to corrupt you."

"How long have you known me, Captain?" asked McCoy. The seemingly casual question was edged with wariness.

"Many years." Kirk's answer only increased McCoy's tension. The captain moved back to a less personal topic. "Although the *Enterprise* is my first starship command." A brief sketch of the ship's exploratory mission kept McCoy's attention until they reached the senior officers' deck.

The first minutes inside the captain's quarters were comfortably familiar—Kirk poured drinks while McCoy wandered about the cabin—but when Kirk turned, glasses in hand, the resemblance wavered. The man he saw was subtly different in stance and bearing. Ease and assurance had been supplanted by a quick nervous energy.

Kirk proffered a goblet to his guest. "The best brandy this side of Rigel." Regrettably, his own tumbler contained nothing stronger than Altair water. Kirk raised his hand in a toast. "To your health, doctor."

McCoy took a cautious sip of the oily liquid. Then another. "That's one hell of a vice," he gasped, but the liquor had little effect on his restlessness. He paced the

length of the room's low shelves, fingering alien artifacts. "You're a well-traveled man." The inspection of
curios moved him into the bedroom area, but there he
caught sight of himself in a mirror and quickly averted
his eyes. "I'm still not used to that face," he said
apologetically, walking back into the study.

"It's not a bad face," chided Kirk.

"Not for an old man." Setting his drink aside,
McCoy picked up the tape on Kirk's desk. "So this is
the sum total of my last twenty-five years. Freeze-dried.
Add water and walk directly into the future." He
peered suspiciously at the computer terminal. "Well,
let's not put this off any longer. How do you work this
machine?"

Kirk inserted the tape and flipped the necessary
switches to illuminate the first file page. "Personnel
record of Leonard H. McCoy."

McCoy settled himself into the desk chair. He tapped
at the scroll key on the terminal, muttering an impatient commentary as he watched the screen. "Yes,
thank you, I know when I was born and where. No
surprises there." The data unrolled line by line. Suddenly he hit freeze frame.

"Next of kin, Joanna McCoy." His brow creased with
confusion. "Who the hell . . ."

"That's your daughter," interrupted Kirk.

"My daughter?" repeated McCoy. "I have a daughter?"

"Yes. She was only a few years old when you joined
Star Fleet, so she's been raised by your sister Donna,
on Centaurus."

"A daughter. But that means she was born during my
residency . . ." The doctor did some rapid mental
calculation. "Twenty-one! She's almost as old as I
am . . . I mean was . . ."

Kirk sat down across from him. "We've been on this mission for several years, but I know that before this voyage you saw her as often as you could. Since then the two of you have kept in touch through intergalactic communications. Though you once joked that Joanna's at the age now where she's glad to have a parent a few hundred lightyears away."

"If I've got a daughter, then what about a wife? That's the usual package deal, isn't it?" McCoy's eyes searched over the computer screen. He read a name aloud. "Jocelyn? But I don't know this woman." He fought against a return of the vertigo which had attacked him on the bridge. "What happened to her?"

"You were divorced." Kirk pushed past his reluctance to talk about McCoy's marriage. "It didn't last long . . . and the parting was . . . bitter."

"I hope I wasn't romantically sloppy about it. Did I sigh and pine for my lost love, Captain?"

"No," said Kirk tightly. "You never discussed it."

"Well, that's some comfort." He snapped off the computer screen. "I'll bypass the Star Fleet commendations. I've got quite enough to think about for the time being."

"Bones . . ." The captain broke off at the look of inquiry on McCoy's face. "Sorry, it does sound a bit strange. That was my nickname for you."

" 'Bones' as in 'Sawbones'?"

Kirk chuckled. "You often claim you're really a country doctor at heart."

McCoy stiffened at the statement. "Yes, Captain. It seems that my ideals were a casualty of my marriage and divorce. I've never cared much for high-powered, technology-dependent specialists—like surgeons. I had dreams of building a family practice in a rural area where a good doctor can become a part of his patients' lives. It never occurred to me that I might not follow through with those plans."

"Time, and experience, can change a man's perspective." Kirk found himself groping for words to justify his friend's actions. "You never regretted your decision to enter the service."

"Well, I regret it now, Captain Kirk." McCoy's blue eyes darkened with barely concealed anger. "I want to return to Earth as soon as possible."

Kirk choked on his drink. "So do I, doctor, but unfortunately it's not that easy. This isn't a pleasure cruise. We're on a military ship facing combat action. I realize you're not familiar with shipboard routine, but surely you've noticed that we're undergoing battle-damage repairs."

McCoy nodded slowly. "The wounded in sick bay. And all those crewmen running around the corridors. I guess I've been a bit too self-absorbed to draw the obvious conclusions." His anger was replaced by an edge of uneasiness. "It was a serious attack?"

"Extremely. Our shields are badly compromised and phaser power is dangerously reduced. We'll recover impulse engines in another few hours, but warp drive is out of commission until we reach dock facilities . . ." Kirk stopped his narrative at the look of incomprehension on McCoy's face. The words meant little to him. He had no damning criticism or words of encouragement to offer the captain of a crippled starship. Kirk pared his answer down to the basics. "We aren't going home for quite a while."

"Who attacked us?" asked McCoy with growing concern.

The captain started to reply, then gave a tired shrug instead. "It's a complicated situation. And one you don't need to worry about. Worrying is my job."

McCoy's eyes narrowed at the underlying weariness in Kirk's words. "So we may be attacked again?"

"That is a distinct possibility, as Mr. Spock would say." Kirk watched his friend's expression mutate from puzzlement to annoyance to amazement.

"I could die out here," McCoy protested.

"Yes, doctor," said Kirk grimly. "We *all* could."

Chapter Ten

Captain's Log, Stardate 5524.2:

The *Enterprise* is still badly crippled, but we are proceeding under impulse power to Wagner Trading Post. Our weapons power is halved, our shields fragile, and a Klingon battle-cruiser is our unlikely escort.

KIRK LEANED BACK into his command chair. Around him, the bridge presented a satisfying appearance of efficiency. All posts were staffed, indicator lights flicked on and off with pleasing regularity, instruments hummed the melodies appropriate to their duties. "Ahead warp factor two."

"Sir?" came a startled reply from the helm.

The captain sighed. He hadn't meant to verbalize the thought; now he had been caught out at wishful thinking. "Quarter-impulse power, Mr. Leslie."

"Yes, Captain." The helmsman stifled a wry smile of sympathy. His own thoughts were not so far from his commander's. With some trepidation, Leslie tripped the sequence to fire the impulse engines of the *Enterprise*. The starship began its movement slowly, without strain, gliding smoothly forward into space.

Kirk had half expected a creaking and groaning of metal. He let loose the breath he had been holding. "Increase to half-power."

"Half-power initiated."

"Heading fifty-three mark six," intoned the navigator in turn. The interplay of the bridge crew fell into its ingrained pattern.

"Mr. Scott," Kirk called out to the chief engineer. "Can we handle full speed?"

"Aye, Captain. That we ken." Scotty's satisfaction was evident even over the intercom. *"For all the beatin' she's taken, th' bonny lass is hangin' together."* His fond tone might have been directed at a precocious child.

"Ahead full impulse power." With this final prod, the *Enterprise* attained the limits of her speed. Kirk watched the stately progression of stars across his viewscreen with dismay. The ship was crawling.

With unnerving prescience, Spock stated, "At our present rate of speed we will reach Wagner Station in twelve point six days."

This depressing fact was not new to Kirk—he had heard the estimate before—however its implications were just now sinking in. A trip that had lasted a matter of hours under warp drive was now stretched into weeks, a humbling reminder of the vastness of space. Kirk had had his fill of humbling events in the past few days. "Uhura, hail the *Falchion.*"

The lieutenant activated the narrow-band frequency which had been established for communications with the battlecruiser.

"Lt. Sulu to Captain Kirk. The Falchion *is ready for impulse speed. Heading fifty-two mark seven. We await your command."*

"Acknowledged, Commander Sulu." Kirk echoed the young man's formality, remembering his own nervousness as a junior officer faced with heavy responsibility. "You may proceed."

The viewscreen flickered to a shot of the Klingon vessel. The bulging forward hull was pockmarked and its metal wings were scarred with black streaks, but the sleek lines of its design were still evident. For several seconds the battlecruiser remained motionless. A brief shudder rocked its frame, then it jerked forward in a series of uneven bursts of speed.

"Falchion *under way, Captain,*" announced Sulu bravely. Within seconds his words carried more weight: the cruiser settled into an even pace matching course with the *Enterprise.* Sulu's formality gave way to exuberance. *"We're learning fast. I'll have this crate doing spins in no time."* The warship began a lazy roll onto its side. The lieutenant was an irrepressible stunt pilot; this quality had saved the *Enterprise* from certain disaster on more than one occasion.

"Just keep your distance while you practice battle maneuvers, Sulu. I don't want one of your loop-the-loops crashing through our hull."

"Aye, sir. Falchion *out."* Pulling out of the roll, he dipped its wings in a farewell salute.

The viewscreen returned to the panorama of stars lying ahead. Without warp drive distortion their pinpoint lights shone steadily. Kirk studied the pattern of stellar bodies. Their positions would change imperceptibly over the course of the next. . . "Twelve days?"

"Twelve point six," corrected the first officer pedantically. Impatience was not a failing to which he would ever admit.

"You'll have time for sleeping now," said Kirk.

Spock was not so easily tricked into a revelation of his Human heritage. He turned the comment back at the captain. "The effect of your stimulant injection is due to dissipate within the next quarter-hour. You should remove yourself from the duty log before your performance is impaired."

"How could anyone tell?" asked Kirk sourly as the science officer stepped down to the side of the captain's chair. "At this speed I could command while dead asleep." He duly initialed the tablet handed to him. "Who's checking on *your* performance?"

"Dr. Cortejo."

To Kirk's ears this unembroidered remark carried a strong undercurrent of emotion. So Spock's endurance was not limitless after all. "Yes, I agree. I'd like McCoy back at work, too."

Spock raised an eyebrow in token reproof, but he did not refute Kirk's interpretation. "Has Dr. Dyson developed a prognosis?" This was the first direct query Spock had made on McCoy's condition.

"She was waiting for the final results of the neurological testing," answered Kirk. Anyone unfamiliar with the complexities of the half-Vulcan's character might have mistaken his reticence for indifference, but Kirk knew the opposite was more likely. The concern was too deep to voice. He remembered the bloodstains on Spock's tunic and felt a twinge of sympathy for his first officer. "I'm going to sick bay now."

Kirk sensed the tension as soon as he crossed the threshold into the medical research lab. McCoy and Dyson barely acknowledged the captain's entrance. Their attention was focused on the data that filled the computer screen before them. The information meant nothing to Kirk, but its significance to the two doctors was obvious.

"Very interesting." McCoy's gaze locked with the neurologist. "I'm not a fool, Dr. Dyson." He seemed about to go on, but thought better of it after a glance at the captain.

He doesn't trust me, realized Kirk with surprise. "Anything that concerns my crew, concerns me," he stated firmly. "And you are my chief medical officer. You'll have to take my word for it that we also happen to be friends."

"All right, Captain," said McCoy. "Then you should know that your chief medical officer is mentally incompetent. There's no evidence here to suggest sustained physical injury to the brain. Clinical indications are that I've entered an hysterical fugue whose origins are pyschological in nature." He gave a wry grin. "In laymen's terms, I've cracked."

"Dyson, do you concur with this diagnosis?" After all, McCoy was hardly in any shape to be practicing medicine.

She nodded her agreement. "That's the most probable conclusion to be drawn from the data. Posttraumatic amnesia is a prominent feature of closed head injuries, but the extent of his retrograde amnesia would usually be associated with substantial brain damage, certainly at measurable levels. Instead, the response test results are consistent with a very mild concussion—slight reduction of fine motor coordination and word association. These symptoms should disappear within a few days."

She paused. "Actually, I suspected this might be the case after the first session, but I couldn't be sure until I saw these figures."

Kirk considered her statement. "But this means the memory is still there, undamaged. It can be recovered."

"Yes, that's the good news."

"The bad news," interjected McCoy, "is that we still can't predict when, if ever, that event will occur."

Kirk bit back his next thought, then reconsidered. McCoy seemed able to discuss the subject objectively. He released the words. "What if Spock were to . . ."

"That would be very dangerous." Dyson picked up on the idea immediately. "For Dr. McCoy definitely, possibly also for Mr. Spock. If the underlying factor is psychological, there will probably be a very strong resistance to manipulation. The mind protects itself from pain with an amazing store of defenses. Amnesia is a reaction to unbearable stress: remove the memory, and the stress is gone. But if memory is restored before the mind can cope with it, the results could be disastrous."

McCoy pushed down a surge of anger. He was getting tired of not understanding what was going on around him. "What are you two talking about?"

"The Vulcan mind-meld."

"Oh," he said, taken aback. "Thanks, but no thanks. I'd rather keep my psychopathology to myself."

"Isn't there any treatment?" demanded Kirk. "Surely psychiatric counseling . . ."

"*I'm* not the one who needs analysis," said McCoy. "Considering the circumstances, *I* feel just fine. It's the McCoy with the stress who needs help, and he's out to lunch."

Dyson ignored his flippancy. "There has been some success with the use of hypnosis and narcoanalysis, specifically sodium amylobarbitone. However, as a bioneurologist, it's a procedure that is out of my field. Ironically, Dr. McCoy is probably the only doctor on board who would be qualified to conduct such a session. Starship crews rarely need such specialized treatment.

"It's basically a matter of time. Time to reach a starbase, or time for spontaneous recovery. Despite this episode, Dr. McCoy's records show that he has a very high threshold for psychological stress. Somehow he's been pushed over that edge, but it's not unreasonable to suppose that the lapse is temporary, a way of bringing rest to the brain while it marshals more acceptable coping mechanisms."

"An unofficial leave of absence?" McCoy quipped. "I trust it's not a court-martial offense."

"Dammit, Bones, that's enough." Without thinking, Kirk lashed out at his senior officer.

McCoy pulled back as if slapped. "I'm sorry, Captain Kirk," came the reply with all the deference and coldness of a stranger. "I'm not accustomed to dealing with military commanders and military protocol."

"Bones . . ." The name did not fit. The man standing before him would not answer him back in kind with a "Dammit, Jim"; neither could he read the apology in Kirk's voice. "The fault is mine, Dr. McCoy. I forget that you don't really know me."

"Of course, Captain," said McCoy with the polite air of a sane man humoring the mad.

Dyson broke into the uncomfortable silence that ensued. "My official recommendation is for Dr. McCoy to be granted a medical leave of absence until such time as I can verify a full restoration of his memory."

"Recommendation accepted, Dr. Dyson." The captain turned to face his chief medical officer. "Lt. Commander McCoy, you are hereby relieved of all responsibilities associated with your position as senior ship's surgeon of the U.S.S. *Enterprise.*" The words tore at Kirk's throat, but the doctor listened impassively. "You may consider yourself as off-duty personnel until such time as Dr. Dyson and Dr. Cortejo have certified that you are fit to return to your post."

"Or until we reach one of those starbases and get me back to Earth," said McCoy firmly.

Kirk gave a curt bow of his head in assent. He left sick bay without another word.

"I realize that this is a difficult time for you . . ." began Dyson once they were alone.

"Please, spare me the lecture on emotional adjustment," McCoy pleaded. "I'll try to take this whole preposterous situation as seriously as I can, but part of me keeps looking for the stage exit. 'Responsibilities as senior ship's surgeon.' For crying out loud, I just finished my first-year residency."

Dyson gave him a speculative look. "So how did you do?"

He groaned. "I'm lucky I'm still in medicine. According to Andy Gildstrom, I'm the clumsiest, most stupid . . ." He broke off. "What was that look for?"

"What look?" she asked innocently.

His eyes narrowed in suspicion. "When I mentioned Gildstrom, you looked . . . startled."

"Oh, it's just that I've never heard Dr. Anderson J. Gildstrom called 'Andy'."

"You know him? What airs is he putting on now? He is . . . was . . . the most insufferable know-it-all second-year resident in Atlanta."

"He's Surgeon General of the Argelius System," she replied with a strangled gasp of laughter.

This time McCoy looked startled. "Surgeon General. Good God, I wouldn't trust Andy to treat a case of the flu, much less put the medical care of millions in his hands."

"He's probably improved his skills somewhat in the last twenty years," suggested Dyson.

"Yeah, right." He frowned suddenly, looking around the room. "Whereas I can't recognize half the equipment in this department. There are nine patients in intensive care, but I wouldn't trust myself to go near them. With coaching from Nurse Chapel I just might be able to handle a few of the outpatient cases. Hell, the paramedics know more about medicine on this ship than I do. If I ran this facility, that means I've lost over two decades of medical knowledge and experience."

"Let's just say you misplaced it." Christine Chapel had entered the room without their notice. "It's going to come back."

"You sound very sure of that, ma'am."

"I am," said the nurse. "But until that time, I'm going to have to work under the supervision of Acting Chief Cortejo. Dr. McCoy, I'll get you for that someday. And Diana, if you repeat that statement to anybody, you'll also live to regret it. Now, the two of you get out of sick bay. I'm tired of your faces."

"But I live here," protested McCoy.

"Not any more," said Chapel, pointing to the door. "You've been released as of now. You've got your own quarters on this ship, and it's time you went back to them so I can reclaim your bed for someone with serious problems. Go." Her mock glower was directed at McCoy, who remained rooted in place.

Dyson tugged gently at his elbow. "You're not being cast out of the Garden of Eden on your own. I'll show you the way to your cabin. Come on." She led him through the bewildering maze of rooms which formed the medical complex, carefully explaining the design of the ship's layout at each turn.

"Are you listening?" she asked finally. His muttered responses to her instruction had taken on a distracted quality.

McCoy stopped walking and turned to face her. "Did I become a *good* doctor?"

"Yes," she said firmly. "One of the best in Star Fleet."

"Thank God." He slouched back against the wall of the corridor, arms crossed over his chest. "This last year . . . well, I was beginning to wonder if I was cut out for medicine after all. Christ, I felt so stupid at times. I hung on because I couldn't imagine doing anything else with my life. I've always wanted to be a doctor—but it had to be a good doctor."

Dyson smiled. "The first year always makes you feel incompetent. I still do sometimes, when I'm on the receiving end of a blistering lecture from a senior physician. I've had a few of those since I've been on the *Enterprise*."

"*My* lectures?"

"Sometimes," the neurologist admitted. "But they were always deserved, and never vicious."

He grinned suddenly. "Unlike those from a certain acting chief surgeon?"

"Hush! Not so loud," she warned him, but her mouth twitched up at the edges. "Do you want to get me drummed out of Star Fleet?" She hauled at his arm, setting him upright once more. "Onward to Deck Five, Dr. McCoy. I've got rounds in fifteen minutes."

"Forget the guided tour, Dr. Dyson," he said falling into step by her side. "Just tell me how you wound up here."

"Here, the *Enterprise?* Or here, Star Fleet?"

"Both. They seem equally improbable to me," he admitted. "I'd never given much thought to space travel until I woke up on board this ship."

"That's because you're a dirt-walker," she answered without thinking. She caught his look of annoyance. "Sorry, nothing personal. It's just that since I've always lived in space, it's the thought of living on a planet that seems rather exotic to me." They turned a corner into a main corridor, not far from the turbo-lifts. She shepherded her charge through the double doors and ordered their destination.

"Go on," he urged several minutes later when they emerged onto the deck of the officers' quarters.

"Well, I grew up on Lost Acre, a space station not

much bigger than the trading post we're headed for now and just as far out into the fringes of Federation territory. I wanted to study medicine and I wanted to get nearer to civilization. Unless you're very rich, Star Fleet service is the obvious solution. They paid my education expenses in exchange for a ten-year hitch in the medical branch. I consider it a fair bargain."

"Well, you got into medicine," said McCoy. "But you're still pretty far removed from civilization."

"Yeah," she admitted ruefully. "Still, the *Enterprise* has a bigger library than Lost Acre did, so I'm ahead of the game." She waved him to a halt. "Your cabin, sir."

He read the neatly lettered plaque on the door:

Leonard McCoy
M.D.
3F 127

Oddly, this was the most convincing evidence of his lost memory that he had encountered: his name, written on a sign he had never seen before.

Dyson coded the door open, taking time to show him the procedure, and led him inside. The layout was similar to that of the captain's cabin: the outer room served as a study, with a desk, chairs and shelves, while beyond the mesh partitions lay a smaller sleeping area. Unlike Kirk's room, this one was in fair disorder. The floor was strewn with clothes, the desk and shelves were cluttered with paper and tapes, numerous plants were dying.

"Am I always such a slob?," asked McCoy viewing the mess with distaste.

"I wouldn't know," Dyson answered with arch bemusement. "I've never been invited into your cabin before."

McCoy blushed furiously. She, unperturbed, proceeded to demonstrate the operation of the room lights, the intercom, and the sonic shower controls.

"Do I tip you for room service?" He trailed after her as she stepped out into the corridor.

Dyson gave him a gentle push back into the cabin. "No, I'll give you a tip: get some sleep." The door snapped shut in his face and she was gone.

McCoy sighed and manfully turned back to face the waiting emptiness. He wandered from one part of the room to another, playing with the panels Dyson had shown him, but he was soon bored by the limited repertoire of beeps and colored lights. He watered the plants, but couldn't bring himself to touch the soiled clothing. He would have filed the tapes and papers but, having no idea where to put them, he settled for making the piles neater.

When all possible activities had been exhausted, he undressed and lay down gingerly on the unmade bed. Yet, tired as he felt, sleep eluded him. Only sheer force of will kept him from tossing and turning. Instead of becoming more relaxed, he could feel his muscles tighten. He grew uneasy without knowing why.

Finally he identified the feeling. It was a sense of waiting—waiting for the real occupant of this room to return. The feeling wouldn't go away. Each faintly heard sound of footsteps seemed headed straight for the threshold of this room and each creak of metal was the opening of the cabin door. After two hours of lying on another man's bed, McCoy jumped up and put his clothes back on. In the end, there was only one answer. Of all the ship's areas, sick bay was still the least uncomfortable for him.

If Nurse Chapel's given my bed away, I'll sleep on the hospital floor.

With a growing urgency, he escaped from the cabin and paced quickly through the night-dimmed corridors to the turbo-lift. He entered the parted doors to an empty compartment.

"Sick bay," he called out self-consciously. *Damn silly way to run a ship*. But his confidence grew as the machinery obeyed his order.

When he reached the ship's medical complex he gave a sigh of relief. Despite its bewildering technological advances, the basic smells and sounds of medicine were reassuringly familiar. McCoy strolled through the wards, unchallenged by the night duty staff, until he found the small supply room which had been cleared out for his use. The bed was still there.

He threw himself down on its surface. Taut muscles loosened in the impersonal surroundings and fatigue quickly pulled him down into a deep sleep. Hours later his body twitched in a vain attempt to escape the torments of a nightmare, but he did not wake up.

Chapter Eleven

"EETS LIKE SWIMMING through borscht," exclaimed Chekov with disgust. *The Falchion's* navigation panel displayed a swirling cloud of fuzzy magenta particles. In the center of the screen one especially dense clump of particles marked the presence of the *Enterprise.*

"This is an early model cloaking system." Unlike Chekov, Aziz did not take the distortion of the ship's sensors as a personal affront, largely because the engineering section was unaffected. "Probably installed during the first technology exchange with the Romulans."

"Then the Klingons got the short end of the bargain," observed Sulu with amusement.

"Da, and now so do ve." The ensign rubbed his eyes. "Maybe eet is broken after all."

"There's nothing wrong with the cloaking device or the sensors," said Aziz sharply. The unspoken corollary to her statement brought a flush of anger to Chekov's face.

"You are just as new at this as I am. Perhaps the power distribution is not properly adjusted." The accusation was a deliberate red flag.

Sulu uttered a silent groan at the impending quarrel. A direct order to stop arguing would only let their resentments fester. So this was how Kirk felt when

Spock and McCoy . . . The helmsman smiled. He had often noticed the captain's ability to distract his senior officers with a sudden jump from one topic to another. The tactic might work here—with some revision.

"Gentlemen, our mission must not fail," announced Sulu gravely. Chekov and Aziz broke off their exchange in confusion. "The fate of this ship and its crew, the fate of the entire universe, depends on us." He turned to Chekov. "You're my science officer. I don't care how you do it, but make the sensors work!" Sulu set his jaw in a line familiar to them all. Understanding dawned.

"As you wish, Captain," said Chekov, coming to attention. He wiped his round face clean of expression. "Incidentally, the solution will require an increase in ship's power consumption that seriously compromises the safety of this ship and the lives of its crew." He tried, and failed, to raise one eyebrow.

Aziz leapt to her feet, hands beating her chest. "No, no! Not me bairns! Let the crew die but dinna hurt me bairns!"

Sulu opened his mouth to speak, then shook his head and dropped out of character. "We need someone to be McCoy. I can't do my next lines until McCoy gives his 'save the crew' speech."

Chekov nodded in agreement. "Dyson does the best McCoy impersonation. Perhaps ve could dewelop a medical emergency . . ."

"Under the circumstances, it would be in rather poor taste to ask her," said Aziz. She picked up a data tablet and resumed her monitoring of the unwavering engine indicators.

The two men sighed and returned to the controls of the *Falchion*.

"Prepare to disengage cloaking device," ordered Sulu as a chronometer blinked through the last seconds of the test period.

"Cloaking device disengaged." Chekov watched as the dancing snowflakes on his sensor screen melted into a flat, featureless sheet of black.

Uhura's voice echoed through the cockpit. "Enterprise *to* Falchion. *You are back on visual. Maintain present course and speed to Wagner Post.*"

"*Falchion* to *Enterprise.* Acknowledged."

The commander and crew of the battlecruiser stared dutifully at the instrument panels of their respective stations. The equipment, oblivious to the concentrated attention lavished in its direction, operated with unceasing dependability. A half-hour passed before Chekov spoke. "Somehow, I thought having our own ship would be different, but it's just as . . ." He stopped.

"Boring," said Aziz in a flat voice.

Sulu's jaw tightened, but he could not suppress his own feelings, even if he was the ship's commander. "Sub-warp is *always* boring." They lapsed into silence again.

McCoy re-checked the story listing in the entertainment logbook; according to the brief description, he was watching a comedy. A row of stars by the title seemed to indicate that it was quite popular. He looked back to the D-stage in the corner of the rec room. It was bigger than any three-dimensional imager he had ever seen, creating almost life-size human figures. A man and a woman were standing on the projection platform, talking to each other in low voices. The image resolution was so exact that McCoy had mistaken the couple for off-duty crewmembers until he had tried to ask them a question. Luckily, no real crewmembers had been in the room at the time, thus sparing him certain humiliation. The couple continued their desultory conversation. Most of the words they used were familiar, but it must have been the ones McCoy didn't understand that carried the punchlines. He found the dialogue incredibly dull, but continued listening for lack of anything better to do.

The empty time felt unnatural compared to his frantic schedule in the Atlanta emergency room. His first impulse was to eat. There was free food at the crew cafeteria—a ticket to paradise for a poverty-stricken young doctor—but his body was quite happily residing in the present and it rejected the need for a meal. His next thought was that he should sleep while he could . . . but again his body rang a dissenting note.

McCoy finally lost patience with the program. He tried to call up some familiar titles—they were lumped in the classics section—but the computer informed him they were unavailable due to a "backlog in systems adjustments." Resisting the impulse to apologize to the man and woman, McCoy wandered out of the room. Without making any conscious decision to do so, he found himself headed toward sick bay. Though he had no official reason for being there, at least the staff never questioned his presence.

Once on Deck 5, McCoy allowed himself to get lost in the tangled layout of the medical complex. He passed idly through unfamiliar corridors, one looking very much like another, until he spied two cylinders of smoked glass, stretching from deck to ceiling, which stood like sentinels outside a lab door. Curious, he peered into the interior of the units, where blue liquid cycled endlessly through a tangled web of coils. *What is that stuff?* As if outraged at his ignorance, the cylinders erupted with a sudden harsh bleeping. McCoy jumped at the sound; his hands flew to the control panel on the wall, fingers pushing here and there on its buttons. The insistent call was stilled; the cylinder's cycling action slowed.

Seconds later a lab technician bolted out of an adjacent room. He drew an involuntary breath at the sight of McCoy.

"Sorry, sir," he cried. "It won't happen again, honest." McCoy was too startled to make any comment, but his silence only increased the crewman's discomposure. "It never would have happened this time except we're running double shifts and I'm covering for Tajiri . . ." Too late, he realized his betrayal of another technician's negligence.

"It's all right." McCoy tried to muster an illusion of authority over a man not much older than himself . . . than he had been. "We're all overworked. Just do the best you can."

"Yes, sir," said the young man with surprised relief. "Thank you, sir." He bolted back into the lab room.

"Any time." McCoy's sarcasm went unheard.

He turned at the sound of clattering footsteps coming towards him. A disheveled woman in science blue was running down the corridor. One hand held a cluster of data cassettes while the other pulled a comb through her tangled hair. She looked up just in time to avoid a collision. "Oh, damn."

"Tajiri, you're late," said McCoy sternly. "Get to work."

"Yes, Dr. McCoy!" With this single earnest cry, Tajiri disappeared through the same door used by the first lab tech.

McCoy was alone in the corridor once again, listening wistfully to the muffled sound of voices behind the closed door. He knew that if he entered the room the voices would grow still and quiet. The cylinder gurgled its sympathy. McCoy looked back at the mysterious blue liquid. Only then did he realize that his hands had worked the control panel . . .

A nurse's page over the intercom sent Dyson running

to the non-critical care ward. The room was empty except for McCoy, but he was doing his best to fill its space as he paced up and down its length. She quickly assessed McCoy's physical symptoms: pale skin, physical agitation, increased respiration; no obvious injury. "What's wrong?" she demanded.

"I'm starting to remember. At least, I think . . . but, I still don't know how . . ."

Dyson took his announcement calmly. "Don't push —you'll only confuse yourself. I'll get a sedative . . ." His pacing stopped abruptly, as she had known it would at the first mention of medication. "Now, what do you remember?"

"That's just it," he said, throwing up his arms in exasperation. His hands took over now that his legs had stopped. "There's this tall cylinder near one of the research labs . . ." He sketched a vague wave toward the rear wall of the ward.

"The stokaline processor?"

McCoy shrugged. "I don't know what it is, but when it beeped, I reset the controls."

"Ah." Dyson's voice registered disappointment. She remained silent for a moment. "What does this machine do?" She pointed to a gleaming metal box nestled in a corner of the ward room.

He shook his head. "Damned if I know."

"It's a portable regen unit. Can you initiate a tissue regeneration run?"

"Of course not."

"Try it anyway." She urged him to approach the control panel. "Go on."

McCoy edged up to the unit. "If I break this thing, Nurse Chapel will throw me out of sick bay for good." He stared at the tidy rows of switches that covered its side. "Now what?"

"Flip the first switch on the second row."

He followed her order, but then his fingers kept moving, changing the configuration of the entire row. The machine came to life. He snatched his hand back as if it had been burned. "What the hell . . . is that right?"

"Yes," she answered. "But it doesn't mean you're recovering your memory."

"You'll have to explain that statement, Dr. Dyson." McCoy's voice was edged with bitterness. "My medical education is too outdated to make sense of what you just said."

She ignored his anger, trusting that it would disappear as his understanding grew. "Knowledge is stored in different ways and in different sites of the brain. Right now, your conscious mind is blocking declarative memory—the intellectual understanding of a particular task. But you also possess a skill memory. Even without conscious control, your brain can recreate a set of familiar physical motions, actions that have been repeated over and over again. Your body remembers, even if your mind doesn't."

"A false alarm," sighed McCoy. "So how will it happen, how will I remember what I've forgotten?"

"I can't predict 'how' any better than I can predict 'when.' If your memory comes back unassisted . . ."

"You mean before any Star Fleet psych technicians start poking around inside my head."

She didn't let him sidetrack her explication. "Some very trivial incident could serve as a trigger. An object, or place, even a few words could start the return of past memories. At first you may recall only fragments of scenes, faces, conversations, then these isolated incidents gradually will start to link together."

"That sounds like a rather lengthy recovery."

"Possibly," she acknowledged. "Or it could happen in a flash, like a door opening. The time in between is often lost. You just pick up where you left off when the head injury occurred."

"So what happens to me while I wait for that door to open?" asked McCoy. He shifted his weight from foot to foot, a prelude to more pacing. "Captain Kirk said this ship is going to be out in space for a long time."

Dyson looked thoughtfully at the blinking lights of the tissue regenerator. "You could assume light duties as a paramedic."

"Me? A doctor out of the dark ages?"

"You still have the ability to operate current medical equipment. The medical computer provides a training course that would explain what you're doing." She caught his hesitation. "On the other hand, you have a perfectly good excuse to just relax, read novels, hang out in the rec room . . ."

"When do I start?"

"I can set up the course now," she answered, carefully repressing her smile. "After that, it's up to you to set the pace." At his insistence, Dyson took McCoy to the Medical Library and showed him the proper log-on for the training program. "Welcome back to duty, sir."

"No way," said McCoy vehemently. "I consider myself more in the nature of a civilian volunteer." He was well into the first lesson before Dyson had left the room.

The sound and feel of the engine room was all wrong. Kirk walked through the cavernous room listening to the uneven breathing and high whine of the *Enterprise*'s lament. The almost imperceptible shiver of the deck that ordinarily signaled impulse power was now magnified and distorted. It tickled the soles of his feet with the intensity of warp-drive speed. Even the familiar contours of the room were transformed by piles of repair materials awaiting installation. The discarded debris from the damaged sections was shoved aside into any unused space, where it would remain until the ship hit docking facilities. Kirk hardly noticed the sharp smell of burnt insulation and wiring; it had permeated every deck of the ship and the entire crew was used to it by now.

"Becker, where's Scotty?"

The assistant engineer looked up from the circuit diagram laid out on the panel before him. Dark eyes stared blankly into the captain's face; his dark face was slack and without expression.

"Becker?" *Forget Scotty, where are you?*

"Yes, Captain?"

Kirk repeated his question, talking slowly and carefully.

"He's on Deck 17, sir." Becker's answer was slurred and his hands were trembling. He returned the glazed stare to his diagram.

"Uh, that's not exactly correct."

Kirk turned around to find the source of the second voice. A tangle of dark hair and two moss-green eyes peered up at him from behind a teetering stack of flat boxes. Kirk grabbed at the top of the pile before it went crashing to the deck, and uncovered a young woman in engineering red.

"Mr. Scott hasn't been on Deck 17 since yesterday," she said, shifting the remainder of her load to maintain its balance. "I'm delivering these cable connectors to him in Auxiliary Control."

Becker was oblivious to this correction. In fact, Becker seemed oblivious to just about everything.

"Don't worry, sir. He's not on duty right now. I'm not even sure he's awake."

She led Kirk away, stepping carefully over the obstacle course of pipes and tools and repair workers. As she had predicted, they found Scotty in Auxiliary Control.

He was reclining on a massive coil of fiber cables. His head had dropped forward on his chest and he showed no signs of life when Kirk and the young woman dropped the load of boxes by his side. He was unbothered by the clamor made by three crewmen working around and over him. The length of cable which served as his bed was rapidly disappearing into a hole in the deck. This had no effect on him either.

Kirk thought back to Becker's exhaustion and couldn't bring himself to disturb Scotty's sleep. He pitched his voice low. "Lt. Kraft, perhaps you'd better give me the current status report."

"Yes, sir." She didn't share his concern for the fragility of her superior's slumber. Her lengthy report was delivered at a volume that was guaranteed to override the noise of the repair team. Scotty didn't twitch a single muscle. She reached the end of her recitation with "And the oscillator frequency monitor has been recalibrated . . ."

"Nay, lassie, we're still four hours away from finishing th' calibration."

Kirk looked down at the sturdy form of the chief engineer. Scotty's eyes were closed, but it had been his voice which corrected the lieutenant. "I thought you were asleep."

"Go on with yer report, Kraft," Scotty ordered, still unmoving and unseeing. "But tell th' truth. Th' captain won't thank ye for making him feel better if there's nae basis for it."

Kraft finished the report without any more reprimands, or reactions of any kind, from the engineer. With a silent wave, Kirk sent her on her way.

"Scotty?"

"Aye?" The voice was alert enough.

"I came by to issue an invitation to my quarters. I'm having an informal gathering later today."

The engineer's eyes blinked open in surprise. "Begging yer pardon, Captain, but there's nae much time in my repair schedule for social events."

"It's for Dr. McCoy. I'd like to . . . introduce him to my senior officers."

Scotty roused himself to a stand. The last loops of the coiled cable slithered away between his feet. "So it's true he's lost his memory. I'd heard th' stories, but I didn't credit them that far. Introduction, is it. Well, I'll be there."

True to his word, Scotty was the first to arrive at Kirk's cabin; Spock followed immediately after. Only the guest of honor was missing.

"Despite the amnesia, certain of the doctor's personality traits remain consistent," observed Spock as the time set for the gathering came and went without McCoy's arrival.

The science officer sat down at the desk computer and quickly immersed himself in a discussion with the central data bank. Scotty simply stared into space. All he needed was a blank wall and his mind's eye could trace the critical circuitry of the warp engines in preparation for the next stage of repair work. Both men were oblivious to Kirk's growing irritation.

Ten minutes later the doors slid open and McCoy stumbled into the room, obviously propelled forward by a hand planted firmly in his back. The hand quickly withdrew, the doors snapped shut, and he stood unmoving at the portal. Facing the three officers, his body shifted into a posture which bore a vague resemblance to command attention.

"At ease," said Kirk, half in jest. McCoy's back lapsed into a more typical slouch, but his unsmiling face did not relax. For the first time, Kirk realized just how damnably awkward McCoy must be feeling.

"I'm sorry I'm late," mumbled the doctor, but he gave no reason for his delay.

Kirk moved forward to greet him, all former irritation fading, and pulled McCoy into the room.

"You've already met First Officer Spock . . ."

McCoy self-consciously kept his arm by his side as he exchanged nods with the Vulcan.

"And this is Chief Engineer Scott."

McCoy turned to the second man and found himself unprepared for Scotty's outstretched hand. "How do you do, sir."

"Don't ye be callin' me 'sir'," said Scotty sternly. "We've shared too many nights over a bottle of scotch t' stand on formalities, amnesia or no amnesia."

"Anything you say, Mr. Scott."

The chief engineer frowned again. "Scotty."

"Sir?" asked McCoy.

Scotty shook his head sadly. "Ah, never mind."

Once the introductions were over, all conversation bogged down. Scotty was still too preoccupied with his interrupted repair work to maintain polite chatter. Spock's social manners were just this side of rudeness even at the best of times; at the moment he was positively glacial. McCoy remained steadfastly mute. Ordinarily, he would have punctured the uncomfortable silence with an outrageous attack on Spock's dignity or prodded the amiable Scotty into laughter. He had never been speechless and sullen.

Kirk tried to draw the doctor out, to determine how he was adjusting to life aboard a starship, but the effect was more like that of a prosecuting attorney dealing with a hostile witness. McCoy answered each question with a simple yes or no and glared furiously down at his boots.

Kirk took pity on his officers and signaled an end to their ordeal. The alacrity with which both Scotty and

McCoy took their leave was proof of how great a disaster the gathering had been.

"Spock." Kirk's call kept the first officer from leaving with the other two men.

Spock waited politely for Kirk to speak again.

"If McCoy were . . . himself, I think he would understand why I'm telling you this." After a moment's hesitation, Kirk briefly outlined Dr. Dyson's explanation for McCoy's amnesia. "We need to find out what he's trying to escape—to find a way to bring him back out of it—before we reach a starbase."

The Vulcan took a moment to consider the issue. "Captain, logic may be of limited use in this situation."

"I'm not asking for logic," said Kirk. "I'm asking for friendship."

Chapter Twelve

"AM I BORING you, ma'am?"

Uhura's dark eyes widened into the semblance of a waking stare. "Not at all, Dr. McCoy. I heard every word you said."

"Lt. Uhura, I haven't said anything for at least five minutes. I've been waiting for you to topple over into your soup." He smiled at her discomposure. "You'd better finish eating before it gets cold." He took a bite out of his own sandwich. They were alone in their corner of the mess; scattered groups of crewmembers, all wearily subdued, were sitting at other tables.

McCoy watched Uhura's head begin to droop downwards again. "Doesn't anybody on this ship get a chance to sleep?"

"Not lately," said Uhura, planting an elbow on the table and resting her cheek against her hand. "Not since the attack."

"About this war you're fighting . . ." wondered McCoy.

"Oh, it's not really a war." Uhura yawned hugely. "At least, not yet. We're still trying to . . ."

A sudden high whine erupted out of an intercom speaker and reverberated throughout the room. Scattered curses and dispirited grumbles from the crew were drowned out by its growing volume. After several uncomfortable seconds the noise stopped just as abruptly as it began. There was a moment of silence, then the low murmur of conversations returned.

"What are they doing now?" groaned Uhura, eyes cast upward as if searching through the deck levels. "Every time I get my equipment working the repair teams mess me up all over again. The Captain will have my hide if I don't clear up shipboard communications systems, but I could be twins and still not have enough time for all my work."

"Then you shouldn't be wasting your off-duty hours baby-sitting me," said McCoy. "For god's sake, go get some sleep instead."

The lieutenant shook her head. "I promised Diana I'd keep an eye . . ."

"Those blood-shot eyes can't see anything." McCoy waved a hand in front of her face. "How many fingers do you see?"

"Seven," said Uhura laughing.

"Just as I thought: advanced narcoleptic hallucinations. A very serious condition if not corrected immediately. I recommend plenty of rest in the isolation of your own room."

She still hesitated. "I really shouldn't leave you on your own."

McCoy's face reddened. "I promise not to wander into new territory again." That morning he had stepped off the turbo-lift onto a strange deck and taken a short stroll to look around, only to fall down an engineering chute. Anti-grav safety fields had kept him from being injured, but he had remained suspended for nearly an hour before a passing crewmember heard his cries for help. "Besides, I can hardly get into any trouble just sitting here eating a sandwich. If it makes you feel better, I'll call for an armed guard to escort me back to sick bay."

"That won't be necessary," said a clipped voice from

behind him. "I'll assume responsibility for the doctor's welfare." To McCoy's surprise, it was the Vulcan first officer who had approached them.

"Thank you, sir," said Uhura gratefully. With a parting smile at McCoy, she gathered up her tray and rose from the table. Spock, carrying a mountain of green salad, took her place.

"Good day, Mr. Spock. Or should I use a military title?" The officer's upright bearing made McCoy feel that a salute was also in order.

"My posting on the *Enterprise* is that of both first officer and science officer. I am by rank a commander," continued Spock with an air of gravity that increased McCoy's discomfiture. "And have been addressed by that title on occasion, but such usage is usually restricted to impressionable junior officers or to senior officers in a situation of acknowledged formality." The doctor's face expressed a faint look of apprehension. "Mr. Spock is quite appropriate," concluded Spock.

The doctor relaxed somewhat. "I'm having a hard enough time remembering names—the fewer titles the better. This morning I promoted some lowly crewmember to a lieutenant." McCoy paused, amazed at the quantity and diversity of vegetable matter which was rapidly disappearing from Spock's plate. "Actually, I'm going through a bit of culture shock on board this *Enterprise* of yours. My knowledge of Star Fleet is minimal . . . or at least it was twenty-five years ago . . ."

Spock answered evenly. "Indeed. Star Fleet is a world unto itself; it can be bewildering to the uninitiated. I found it so myself upon leaving Vulcan." As the level of greenery on his plate subsided, a squat glass revealed its presence on the tray. Spock took a sip of the muddy orange liquid inside.

"Carrot juice?" hazarded McCoy. "I'm sorry, I didn't mean to pry." He hastily retracted the question in the face of Spock's momentary silence.

"As I said before, I do not take offense at human social discourse." Spock lifted the glass as if it were a specimen under analysis. "Beta-carotene is only one of the components in this formula." He detailed a long list of organic vitamin compounds, not all of which were familiar to the doctor. "I am actually half Human and half Vulcan; this mixture is a necessary supplement to my shipboard diet, since my particular biochemistry is unique in its nutritional requirements." McCoy accepted this revelation with polite interest. Spock continued. "We developed this drink soon after your posting to the *Enterprise*. You dubbed it 'orange sludge' and advised that I drink it at least once a week."

"Oh. Well, I hope it tastes better than it looks," said McCoy sympathetically.

"You considered it a noxious substance, nevertheless after some initial experimentation you achieved a blend that I find quite acceptable." He downed the remainder of the liquid.

McCoy frowned at the remains of his sandwich. "I didn't seem to be as concerned about my own health." His brittle tone raised Spock's eyebrows. "According to my medical records, I ingested a fair amount of another type of 'noxious substance' just before cracking my skull." He looked across the table. "You were there when it happened. I was dead drunk; that's why I fell."

Spock's gaze flickered away. "Yes, you were drinking." He cast his mind back to the scene in McCoy's cabin. "But there was more," he said after a moment's reflection. Slowly he searched through his memories, working past the fog of preoccupation and irritation which had clouded his own perceptions that day.

"Physical exhaustion . . . and a tension." Spock's sensitivity to emotional atmosphere was more pronounced than he cared to admit out loud, but McCoy accepted his observations without pointed jibes.

"You were upset," Spock stated firmly. "That, more than the alcohol, contributed to your inattention. Humans are subject to such emotional distractions; it is endemic in the species."

"Upset enough to misplace an odd twenty years of my life?" asked McCoy ruefully. Spock appeared puzzled by the question.

"I guess you haven't heard. My amnesia is psychological in origin. No damaged brain tissue, just a psyche that's too weak to handle stress. The head injury was simply an escape trigger."

Spock stopped his attack on his food. "An escape from what?"

"Life, I guess. According to Nurse Chapel I was exhausted from long hours in surgery and depressed over the high casualties."

"That is hardly sufficient justification for such an extreme reaction." Spock brought his hands together, fingers lightly touching. "I know your mind quite well, Dr. McCoy, and it would not give way to such routine anxieties. Something out of the ordinary must have affected you."

"There wasn't time. As far as we can tell, I stumbled out of sick bay and went directly to my room."

"Where, by all logical considerations, you should have been sleeping. Instead, when I entered your cabin, you had been awake for some time," said Spock. "The answer to what happened may lie there in your cabin."

Shoving a remaining green leaf into his mouth, the first officer rose from the table and carried his tray to a disposal slot in the wall. McCoy followed suit, then scrambled to match the first officer's brisk pace out of the dining hall, down a corridor and into a turbo-lift.

"Deck Five," said Spock. They stood side by side in silence until the lift came to a stop.

"I don't even know what to look for," said McCoy as they headed toward his quarters.

"Neither do I, doctor. But even your admittedly emotional behavior is based on a personal logic of cause and effect. We know the effect; a reconstruction of your actions at that time may reveal the cause." Spock came to a halt at the doctor's cabin door.

On the third attempt McCoy entered the correct security code. The room was just as he had left it before. "I haven't cleaned up," he muttered apologetically. *Hell, it's not even my mess.*

"That is just as well," said the Vulcan approvingly. "You might have removed valuable clues." He remained at the doorway, studying the room before him.

"You make this sound like a murder mystery, Mr. Spock. Only I'm the corpse."

"A very talkative corpse," observed Spock. He stepped forward, carefully avoiding a heap of clothing on the floor. "Surgical tunic. You usually change in sick bay, but you were probably too tired to do so. After an especially long surgery session, your first action would be to shower. You would then change into clean clothes."

"What color, Mr. Holmes?" asked McCoy under his breath.

"Grey," answered Spock. He stared impassively at McCoy's look of astonishment, then continued. "At least, that was the color you were wearing when I entered. I was standing here." He paced his steps until he stood in the center of the outer room. He looked toward the bedroom section of the cabin. "The bed was unmade and the sheets were still crushed, so you had been sleeping for part of the day, but upon my arrival you were standing by the desk," he waved McCoy into position, "with a drink in hand."

The Vulcan closed his eyes and stood in contemplation. "There was the smell of alcohol . . . and of smoke." His eyelids snapped open. "Yes, smoke. Curious. This deck did not suffer from fire damage in the attack."

"I saw some ashes in the bedroom," recalled McCoy and led the way to a metal tray by the bed.

"Definitely against regulations," said Spock sternly as they inspected the black smudges on its surface.

"Don't look at me," protested McCoy. "I don't live here."

The first officer rubbed the fine ash between two fingers. "Probably data paper. No more than a single sheet." He strode back to the desk and rifled through the manuscripts on its surface. "Despite your illogical insistence on hard-copy printouts, you are normally quite orderly in dealing with your paperwork. You clear your desk often. Therefore, these materials probably represent a recent work session."

McCoy picked up a manuscript and scanned its first page. "They look pretty innocuous to me."

Spock nodded agreement. "They are also intact."

"Well, I seem to have burned my bridges," sighed McCoy. "We may never know what was on that page."

"Not necessarily, Doctor." Spock sat down at the computer. When the screen came to life he bypassed the menu lists and swiftly entered into the operating system. A stream of cryptic symbols responded to his promptings. "Fortunately, computer files leave evidence of their activity. According to these records, your most recent computer activity involved Lt. Frazers's autopsy reports on our attackers. However, there was no printout from that session." His fingers tapped another sequence of keys. "Your most recent printouts were from the last communications contact with Star Base 11."

"And the paper I burned was in that delivery?"

"Possibly," hedged Spock. "Computer, access correspondence files for Dr. Leonard McCoy. Screen all documents from the latest transmission, Stardate 5289.1. Authorization Code 23.10.B" He looked up at McCoy. "Since you have no memory of your computer code, I have taken the liberty of entering it for you. However, ethically I cannot examine the contents of your file."

"You've got my permission," said McCoy. "After all, you know me better than I do."

"Under the circumstances, I'm not convinced that your permission is valid," countered Spock. He crossed his arms across his chest. "You are not in full possession of your mental faculties."

"But I may never recover those faculties unless we find the cause of my fugue."

"An interesting philosophical quandary," said Spock reflectively. For a moment, McCoy feared the Vulcan would continue to ponder the intricacies of this dilemma indefinitely, but the first officer turned back to the computer screen. "Unfortunately, my service experience has seriously eroded my ethical standards. In the interest of expediency, I will accept your authorization."

With McCoy hanging over his shoulder, Spock quickly ran through the file. The single correspondence page, when it appeared, drew their immediate attention.

"Well, Mr. Spock," said McCoy after reading the message. "You were right about unusual events. This is a letter from my ex-wife—announcing her remarriage."

Chapter Thirteen

McCoy TRIED TO remember the source of the buzzing sound which he had just heard. It was either the cabin door or the intercom. He reached a hand out to the controls of the intercom and flicked a switch. He was rewarded by the crackle of an open channel.

"Hydroponics."

"This is Dr. McCoy," he said self-consciously.

"Yes, sir, Nelson here."

The soft buzz repeated again. "Never mind, Nelson." McCoy severed the contact. "Come in!"

The door slid aside for Diana Dyson. The neurologist crossed the threshold, allowing the door to close behind her, then stopped. "It's clean in here," she exclaimed, looking around the cabin. No sign of the room's previous disorder remained, and the dead plants had been removed. Even the desk where McCoy sat was bare of its clutter. A single opened book lay on its surface.

"You don't have to sound so surprised," grumbled McCoy. "I take no responsibility for the messy former occupant. I happen to be a very tidy person."

"You're also a busy person," observed Dyson. The book was a medical text; his desk terminal displayed an anatomical illustration. "I'll come back later." She turned to leave.

"No, wait. Please." McCoy flipped off the computer

screen and shut the textbook. He stretched in place. "I've been at this long enough for one evening—my brain will fry soon. Besides, I've just about finished my paramedic course. Surely that deserves some sort of celebration." He was smiling, but his voice held an edge of bitterness.

"Dr. McCoy . . ."

He didn't let her finish. "Please, could you call me Len, or even Leonard? I'm getting mighty tired of all of this bowing and scraping that goes on whenever I'm around."

"What?" Dyson asked in disbelief.

"Well, it's true," he declared with an exaggerated frown of disgust. "And you're a prime example of a ship-wide syndrome. There you stand, practically at attention, ready to escape my presence just as soon as decently possible, and all because Dr. McCoy is a senior officer. Either that or you just plain don't like me."

"You lead a hard life," she teased back.

"I do indeed. Sit down and join me for a drink while I tell you the sad tale of a senior officer's life as seen through the eyes of a most junior civilian." Despite his light tone there was a genuine appeal in his eyes.

"Very well . . . Leonard." She plopped down on a chair.

He, in turn, rose from the desk and bowed low. "And what will be my lady's pleasure from the bar?"

"Wine," she ordered with an airy wave of the hand. "The best bottle in the house."

"Not only the best," he said making his way to the wall cabinet. "But, the *only* bottle. I haven't had many occasions to entertain in my cabin. As I said, high command is a lonely place."

"You didn't say that."

"Well, I was going to say it in a few minutes." He

picked up the bottle and inspected the label. "I don't happen to remember this particular year, but then most of the ones I do remember are now vintage brews." He set about pulling the cork and pouring the wine. "The elder McCoy's tastes seem to have run more to hard liquor to judge from the contents of this shelf. Perhaps they were for medicinal purposes. I'll give him the benefit of the doubt." McCoy balanced two full glasses on a small tray and carried it deftly over to his guest.

"You keep referring to yourself as if to a third person," remarked Dyson as she took a goblet from his hand.

He nodded and sat down across from her. "When I refer to myself, I'm speaking for Leonard McCoy, first-year medical resident, twenty-three years of age. Due to an unfortunate twist in the space/time continuum, I was catapulted through the future to an unknown place, never to return to the home I love. As for the McCoy who is commissioned in Star Fleet as a surgeon, well, I'm beginning to think of him fondly as a close family member, a favorite uncle."

He lifted his glass in a toast. "To Uncle 'Bones' McCoy, may he rest in peace.

"Damn," he swore seeing a look of pain cross Dyson's face. "No wonder no one wants to keep me company. Really, I wasn't trying to be morbid. In some ways I think this memory loss is harder on other people than it is on me. I feel fine, it's just the world around me that's changed, whereas you keep seeing the difference in me. So, please excuse my attempts at humor—they were in bad taste."

"No apologies necessary." She pulled the tag ends of a smile together. "Except for the wine. It's abysmal." She viewed the contents of her glass with distaste.

McCoy grinned. "Dr. Dyson, you . . ."

She didn't let him finish. "If I have to call you Leonard, then you can't call me Dr. Dyson. It makes me feel like an old lady. My name is Diana."

To her surprise, McCoy flushed. "You are most assuredly not an old lady." He covered his momentary discomposure by whisking away the wine. "Definitely a bad year. Just as well that I missed it."

He opened a drawer near the store of liquor bottles. "I'm not sure what any of this stuff is." He pulled out a silvery pouch and puzzled over the alien characters embossed on its surface.

"That's *stiegel*," said Dyson. "A delicacy from Brellian IV."

McCoy ripped open the seal and peered at the crumbly white crackers. He passed one to Dyson, then took another for himself. "Much as I'd like to believe that you came by simply for the pleasure of my company, I suspect it's actually official medical business." He eyed his cracker warily.

"More like unofficial medical business." She crunched on hers without hesitation. "Your physical condition is excellent, which removes you from my active patient list. As for the amnesia, I'm not a psychologist so I don't know that I can be of much use, but Captain Kirk thinks I have a better bedside manner than Dr. Cortejo."

"Did he actually say that?" asked McCoy, nibbling tentatively at the edge of the wafer.

Dyson grinned. "Not in so many words. After all, it wouldn't be politic to impugn the abilities of the ship's acting chief medical officer."

"Not so different from hospital politics," he sighed. "That's one reason I wanted to get away to my own practice. Bureaucracy brings out the worst in my temper. My supervisor called it 'lack of respect for authority.' I called it . . . Well, never mind what I called it, but it didn't improve our working relationship." He glanced at the neurologist's bemused expression. "I didn't get any better that over the years, did I?"

"No." She licked the crumbs of *stiegel* from her fingers. "You're one of the few people on this ship who isn't in awe of Captain Kirk. You scream and holler when you don't agree with him. You even scream and holler at Mr. Spock, which *nobody* else does."

McCoy stopped in mid-crunch. "You can't be serious?"

"Your fights have assumed mythic proportions on the *Enterprise*," she said mischievously. "The crew keeps a running list of the insults you've thrown at him over the years. No one else would dare use them, but sometimes just reading them can make the science department feel better. Chekov swears by it."

"Chekov?"

Dyson's gaiety faded away. "You still haven't remembered anything, have you?"

"No," he answered evenly, popping the last piece of his *stiegel* into his mouth. "When Mr. Spock and I found that letter, I stood there thinking—'This is it. It'll all come back now.'—but nothing changed." He reached for another wafer. "Say, these are good. What are they made of?"

The doctor shook her head. "Don't ask—you'll enjoy them better that way." McCoy hastily dropped the wafer back into its pouch. He left his chair and rummaged once again inside the drawer.

Dyson pulled his attention back to their discussion. "Still, the news of your wife's remarriage must have been a shock."

"Not really." McCoy found another package and

140

sniffed warily at the seal. "In fact, I don't feel much of anything. I don't know her."

"You seem quite unconcerned about what was obviously very disturbing news."

"Disturbing to your McCoy, but not to me. I can't regret a marriage that I don't even remember. Even if that news was the trigger for my fugue, it certainly wasn't the key to bring me back out." He shook his head in disbelief. "That woman's name meant nothing to me the first time I saw it; her remarriage means just as little. Seems strange that it caused so much trouble." Empty-handed, he dropped back down onto the chair by the desk.

"Look, as far as I'm concerned, I've spent the last year eating, drinking, and sleeping medicine at Atlanta General Hospital."

"So what were you doing in Texas?" Dyson asked.

McCoy's face broke into a wide grin. "That trip was my first vacation in years—for two whole weeks I did nothing but ride horses and muck out stables. I had two more days left, but I could have stayed there . . ." He stopped short.

"Forever?" Dyson finished the sentence for him. "But it didn't last forever. You got thrown off a horse and spent the night in a local clinic. Then you went back to Georgia and . . ." She prompted him to continue.

McCoy shook his head stubbornly. "I woke up here. On the *Enterprise.*"

"Still on vacation," taunted Dyson.

"It's a hell of a vacation," shouted back McCoy, but he didn't let his anger build. He took a deep breath instead. "And I know exactly what you're doing, Diana Dyson."

The sarcasm dropped out of her voice. "I never

claimed to be a psychiatrist, Leonard, but I'm doing my best. God knows, it's not easy trying to turn you into a patient."

"Okay, okay, I won't fight it." He leaned back in his chair, stretching his long legs across the floor, folding his arms across his chest. "But, really, I don't remember anything after that fall."

"You could try some simple extrapolation," she suggested, deliberately leaning forward to close the distance he had created. "What *should* have happened after you woke up in the Waco clinic?"

"Well, I must have returned to Atlanta. Back to the emergency room, and morning rounds, and 36-hour days . . . the usual grind."

"Yet according to your personnel records, you were married within a few months of your return."

"That soon?" he asked sharply.

"I thought you went over your records with Captain Kirk?"

"Not the details . . . I didn't really want to know." He shrugged. "After all, what's the point?"

"Perhaps if you were to learn more now . . ."

"No." He sat up straight, hands clenched. "It doesn't have anything to do with me."

Dyson persisted. "It must have been a whirlwind courtship."

"With all too predictable results," said McCoy grimly. He slumped down into the chair. "Reading my file was like meeting a stranger . . ." Dyson let his silence continue. After several moments, he spoke again, haltingly. "I can't imagine doing the things this 'Bones' McCoy did. What a mess he made of my life. A bad marriage, a bitter divorce, this damn-fool leap into Star Fleet . . ."

"Good came of it also. A daughter, for one."

"Some father he was," said McCoy scornfully.

"Leaving his own kid for years on end. I've played some of their correspondence; she's a nice young woman. But hell, after listening in on those tapes I probably know her about as well as he did, and I've never laid eyes on her. *I* wouldn't do that; I wouldn't slink off and leave my family." His voice hoarsened with anger. "I wouldn't . . . yet, I did."

"You can't pass judgement without knowing the circumstances," argued Dyson.

"I wonder. Your Dr. McCoy seems to have given up his life without much of a struggle." His dark brows knitted together in thought. "Perhaps he agreed with me. That would certainly explain this fugue—it's an escape from failure."

Dyson's response was cut off by the sound of the door chime.

"I'm a popular man today," observed McCoy with a shaky laugh. Their rapport was shattered. "Come in!"

When Kirk ended his shift on the bridge, he had intended to go straight to his own quarters. Instead, he had found himself following the familiar route to McCoy's cabin. As soon as he walked through the door he realized that his old habit had led to bad results.

"Good evening, Dr. Dyson." He greeted the neurologist cheerfully, but fully understood her icy glare and civil nod. He had just interrupted a session with her patient, a session that he had ordered.

McCoy jumped to his feet, unsure as to proper protocol between junior and senior officers, and even more unsure of the responsibilities of his own rank.

Dyson took charge of the situation. "Thank you for your hospitality, Dr. McCoy." She, too, rose from her chair.

"What? Oh, of course, Dr. Dyson," said McCoy, reluctantly escorting her to the door.

Kirk bowed aside to let her pass and winced at the

polite smile that masked her anger. Watching the two doctors exchange their formal goodbyes, he recognized a charade acted out for his benefit. Neither was he fooled when McCoy turned from the door to entertain his new guest. With the ingrained manners of a Southern gentleman, McCoy gave no sign that he preferred the company of Dr. Dyson to that of the captain.

Moving to the desk littered with glasses and opened food pouches, the doctor assumed his duties as host. "Some *stiegel,* Captain?"

"No, thanks," said Kirk, restraining a grimace. "I know what it's made of."

McCoy shoved the package into the flush chute.

Now that he was here, Kirk wasn't sure why he had come. "Bones . . ."

"I'd rather you called me Leonard, Captain Kirk."

"Alright, Leonard. My name is Jim."

McCoy nodded noncommitally. A good host never contradicted his guest's wishes. An awkward silence threatened to engulf them.

Kirk plunged directly into the topic uppermost in his mind. "I heard about Jocelyn's letter. I'm sorry . . ."

"It doesn't really concern me," said McCoy. After a moment's pause, he added, "But I'm sure 'Bones' would appreciate your sympathy."

The captain fought against a surge of emotion that dangerously resembled jealousy. Obviously, Dr. Dyson had been able to draw McCoy out, whereas Kirk could barely talk to the man. He searched for a way to break through the uneasy silence which stretched out between them. Before he could speak, the silence was ended for them.

"Red alert, red alert, all hands to battle stations," the call rang out. A flash of scarlet bathed the room. *"Captain Kirk to the bridge."*

Chapter Fourteen

THE CAPTAIN WAS still in the turbo lift when the first phaser burst hit the *Enterprise*. The deck trembled beneath his feet and the turbo ground to a halt. Pounding his fists against the closed doors, Kirk shouted out a series of blistering oaths. As if in response, the compartment moved again and seconds later he tumbled out of the doors onto the bridge.

His eyes flew immediately to the main viewscreen. The normally static view of dimly glowing stars scattered on black was now a backdrop for frenetic battle action. In the distance, a pack of small sleek ships was whizzing around the *Falchion*, like flies around a dog. Much closer, more silver shapes streaked across the viewscreen as they raced around the *Enterprise*'s hull. One vessel suddenly darted forward to deliver a blow, then flitted away. The *Enterprise* shuddered, nearly throwing Kirk to the deck.

"Fire Number Two phasers." Spock issued the order calmly from his position in the command chair. A wide pattern of glowing rays shot forward, scattering the agile ships without scoring a single hit.

Kirk took advantage of the momentary lull to take command. "Report, Mr. Spock."

"At least fifteen Class Five fighters, constructed for a crew complement of two," said Spock as they exchanged places. "They approached in single-file forma-

145

tion behind an asteroid, eluding our sensors until they were practically upon us." The science officer hastened back to his computer station and began a rapid patter of briefing data. "*Enterprise* phaser power at forty-three percent capacity. Shields are holding, but given our previous damage, we are vulnerable to their low-charged phaser fire."

As if to prove his point, another of the fighters dived straight toward them. "Fire phasers," shouted Kirk. A full two seconds elapsed before the energy bolts were released, then the attacking ship blossomed into a fireball that filled the screen with a blinding glare. Before the explosion had faded another attacker ducked beneath the starship, firing a jolting blast into the *Enterprise*'s midsection. "Evasive action, Mr. De-Paul."

The helmsman obeyed instantly, but the starship was sluggish, moving far more slowly than the small fighters. "They can run rings around us, sir."

Kirk slammed a fist down on the arm of his chair. His eyes flickered over the frantic motion on the viewscreen. "Benus, lay down random phaser fire at ten-second intervals."

"Aye, sir." A scattered stream of light beams spat forward into the frame of the viewscreen. The twins evaded the phaser fire easily, but did not attempt another direct attack.

Spock looked up from his sensors. "Captain, this tactic may keep them at bay for now, but it will seriously deplete our energy levels."

Kirk ignored him. "Uhura, open a scrambled channel to the *Falchion*."

Sulu's voice rang out almost immediately. "*They're all over us, Captain . . . They outmaneuver us at impulse speed. Our shields are holding, but they've moved in so closely that we can't hit them back . . .*"

"Warp out of range, Sulu," ordered Kirk flatly.

"But, Captain . . ."

"Warp out of range," overrode Kirk, then continued his plan. "Engage the cloaking device, then return." Sulu fell silent as the implications of Kirk's idea took hold. "The entire fighter pack will close in on us, leaving themselves vulnerable to your sudden reappearance and attack."

"But we can't fire on them without hitting the Enterprise."

"That's right," admitted Kirk grimly. "But we'll pull full power to shields. If you fire a wide beam, it may disable the fighters without penetrating the *Enterprise* hull."

"Aye, Captain." The prospect of firing on the *Enterprise* did not enthuse the lieutenant, but he accepted Kirk's orders without argument.

Kirk swiveled his chair around to face his first officer. "Spock, compute the time logistics for the *Falchion*'s departure and return." The Vulcan complied with his usual composure, but Kirk detected approval of his plan. If only his chief engineer would react as calmly . . .

A flash of exploding light from the viewscreen interrupted his train of thought. "Got another one!" yelled the ensign at the weapons console.

"Yeah, only thirteen more to go," snapped DePaul, ruthlessly squelching the young woman's excitement.

Kirk opened a channel to the engineering section and quickly outlined his plan to Scotty.

"If that lad's nae got a soft touch, those Klingon phasers will slice through us like butter," warned the engineer. The ship rocked again as a fighter slipped through the phaser barrage and fired into the primary hull's underbelly. *"But we canna take much more o' this poundin' so I reckon we havna any choice."*

"Ready, Captain," announced Spock. "The *Falchion* has been briefed."

Uhura touched a series of switches on her panel. "Frequency open, sir."

"Go, Sulu," ordered Kirk.

The *Falchion* executed a fancy roll to pull free of the fighters for just an instant, then shot forward. Its solid shape transformed into a stream of light, then vanished. Five small ships hung in space, cheated of their prey.

Kirk's face twisted into a feral smile. "Fire phasers."

Three of those ships exploded into fiery fragments, but at the same time four of the eight fighters circling the *Enterprise* sprang forward to deliver their own sting. As the starship bucked under the multiple blows, the remaining two ships which had dogged the *Falchion* promptly joined the main pack.

"Maintain random pattern!" shouted Kirk, arms straining to keep him from being thrown to the deck. "Keep them back!"

"Captain, if we take another of those attacks, we'll not have any shields left that can stand up to the Falchion's *phasers."*

"Understood, Mr. Scott." Kirk wiped his brow. "Benus, don't lock on targets. That's an order." He underscored his command. The ensign's instinct was to try to score hits; so was Kirk's. He had yielded to that temptation in order to destroy three ships, and the *Enterprise* was still reeling from the results of that action.

"Falchion due in six point seven minutes," Spock announced without inflection.

They were very long minutes for the captain and his crew. The ten fighters swarmed around and over them, dodging phaser fire, but drawing closer and closer.

Ship's lights grew dim and the soft hum of life support systems faded to a ragged whisper as Scotty channeled more and more power into the deflector shields.

"One minute," announced Spock after an eternity.

"Mr. Scott, prepare to divert all remaining power to port shields," Kirk warned.

"Ready, Captain."

"Thirty seconds."

"Go, Scotty." The lights of the bridge flickered. The helm lost control of the ship's movement. Phaser fire died. Kirk stopped breathing as the fighter ships hesitated, then dived forward en masse.

"Now," said Spock.

The fabric of space rippled and swam and the *Falchion* erupted from the center of the disturbance. It loosed bolts of flame that raked across the bow of the *Enterprise*. Kirk had no time to count how many of the attacking ships exploded before the *Falchion* rolled under the starship and surged upwards.

"Starboard shields, Scotty," shouted Kirk into the intercom, as the heaving of the deck flung him from side to side.

A second fan of fire swept across the far side of the *Enterprise*. This time Kirk lost his hold and was flung to the deck. The air was thick with smoke, choking his lungs and fogging his eyes.

Spock, who had clung to his science station with amazing tenacity, continued to read his sensors. "Two fighters remain, Captain."

Kirk grasped the side of his command chair and pulled himself upright. Through the haze on the bridge the viewscreen showed two bright silver shapes streaking away into space. A dark shadow lunged down into the frame: the *Falchion* was closing in on the retreating ships.

"Sulu!" yelled Kirk.

Uhura was already back at her station, opening the channel for him.

"I want those fighter pilots alive . . ." Even as Kirk spoke, the two ships flamed into a shower of metal fragments.

"Sorry, Captain. They self-destructed," answered Sulu.

"Damn." Kirk appealed to his first officer. "Mr. Spock?"

The Vulcan re-checked his instruments. "Short-range sensor scan reveals no other space vessels in the immediate vicinity." The recent malfunctions had left him wary of the accuracy of his science data. He was monitoring the readouts with greater attention than usual. "Long-range scans show the ghost of . . . gone. Whatever it might have been, we are moving away from it."

Kirk shrugged philosophically. "Good work, Lt. Sulu." He waved a hand in front of his face. The smoke had not cleared from the bridge. "Secure from general quarters." The flash of the alert lights slowed in tempo then faded. Kirk's fingers flipped a switch on the arm of his command chair. "Engineering, restore power to ship's systems. Scotty, damage report."

His call was met with silence. "Scotty, report!"

"Intercom to Engineering is dead, Captain," said Uhura, frantically punching circuits on her communications panel. The malfunctions in shipboard communications had returned.

Checking a curse, Kirk went to general broadcast channels. "Engineer Scott, damage report to the bridge." Lights brightened and clean air began to circulate, but there was still no answer from the engineer.

Spock's voice began a soft drone of lower deck reports. Uhura relayed a sick bay report of ten casualties and one fatality, then continued her battle with the communications board.

"... *bloody intercom* ... *Aye, Captain, Scott here. We had a momentary hull breach due t' ...*" Silence again.

"... decks seven through ten suffered minor damage," continued Spock.

Then a second voice. "*Paramedic Dorf here, Captain. Mr. Scott is going to sick bay.*" The faint protests in the background implied that the engineer's departure was not entirely voluntary.

"Acknowledged, Engineering. I'll meet you there."

Kirk walked to the science station. "Who attacked us? Ravens or Klingons?"

Spock came very close to frowning. "Unknown at present. Detailed sensor readings were impossible under the circumstances."

The captain heaved a frustrated sigh, then tempered it with a wan smile. "Send a shuttlecraft crew to sift through the fighter wreckage. Let's give Frazer some more bodies to work on." The Vulcan nodded. Kirk took a final look around the bridge. "You have the conn."

When Kirk reached sick bay, Scotty was still blustering at the two paramedics who had carried him in. "Why would ye drag me away for a scratch like this one? I've got work t' do." His environment suit was ripped from knee to mid-thigh and the edges of the fabric were stained deep pink. At the captain's entrance, Scott struggled to a stand, effectively preventing McCoy from tending to the bleeding gash.

"Mr. Scott, sit back down. You're not going anywhere until I get your report," ordered Kirk, thus distracting Scotty sufficiently for the medical aid to continue.

"Captain, we've lost deflector shields in half a dozen sections and an equal number are barely holdin'. One of th' aft shields for th' primary saucer collapsed completely under Sulu's phaser blast. The force of that Klingon beam drilled a hole through th' hull plates and stopped just short of th' impulse engines themselves." He broke off to scold McCoy, who was cutting the fabric away from his wound. "Have a care, mon. Yer ruinin' a perfectly good suit."

"Is the breach sealed?" Kirk insisted.

"Oh, aye, Captain, but there were a few moments of nastiness," admitted Scotty. His injury was proof of that.

"How long to effect repairs?"

"At least fifteen hours, Captain. That's assumin' I can stop wastin' my time down here . . ." But by this time Scotty's limb had been fully uncovered. The engineer's cavalier attitude turned to concerned self-interest at the glimpse of bone beneath the bleeding tissue. "McCoy, what are ye waiting for? A mon could bleed to death in th' time it's taking ye t' move."

"I'm working as fast as I can," said the doctor patiently as he ran a sterilizer over the wound.

Kirk found himself distracted from the damage report he had been prying out of Scotty. "Bones!"

"No, just me, Leonard McCoy," answered the doctor. "Nurse Chapel has certified me for paramedical work." With quick, practiced motions he sealed the edges of Scotty's wound into a single jagged weal. He looked up to see a look of apprehension on the engineer's face. "Don't worry, sir. Basic emergency ward treatments haven't changed that much since I learned them." McCoy aimed the beam of a portable regen unit onto the engineer's injury.

Kirk pulled his thoughts back to the *Enterprise*. "Scotty, I need the ship's shields back as soon as possible. Class Five fighters never travel alone and we can't afford to meet their escort without defenses."

"Even if I get shields up in twelve hours, they'll not hold up t' much of a poundin'," warned Scotty. "We've been through two battles already with hardly time t' pull ourselves together. A third attack could punch holes through the ship that I can't patch."

"Not to mention that you're going to run out of room in here," said McCoy, looking around the crowded confines of sick bay. He turned back to the captain. "Just who are these aliens?"

"That's what I'd . . ." Kirk stopped short at the sound of Spock's voice ringing out over the intercom.

"Bridge to Captain Kirk."

The captain stepped over to the wall unit. "Kirk here."

"Report from the hangar deck, Captain. The shuttle-craft crew has identified the fighter vessels as Tennet Fives. One alien body was recovered from the wreckage." A slight pause was Kirk's only warning of the bad news to follow. *"It appears to be that of a second alien species."*

Chapter Fifteen

Captain's Log, Stardate 5539.4:
   Enterprise shields are operational again after nine hours of repair work. We are still on course for Wagner Post, traveling at impulse speed through a sector swarming with crazed aliens, all bent on destroying my ship and my crew. And if I don't figure out why, they may well succeed.

THE ODOROUS CONFINES of the autopsy room were filled to capacity. Lt. Frazer, as the official expert on xenobiology, held the position of authority at the head of the examining table; Spock and Dyson, his research colleagues, flanked either side; Kirk, observer and layman, stood at the foot. They all studied the prone figure laid out between them. The slight figure on the slab was green in color; its eyes were pale pink and its head was covered with downy white wisps of hair.

"Well, it's related to the Ravens," said Frazer wearily, "but I haven't figured out just how related it is."

The xenobiologist's normally ebullient spirits were noticeably depressed by physical exhaustion. Kirk was in no better mood—he wasn't as tired as the xenobiologist, but he was infinitely more worried by the specimen which now occupied the autopsy slab. His nausea was equal to that he'd felt during the last session in the lab, but he listened intently as Frazer detailed the similarities between the two species.

"Despite the superficial color differences, the skeletal and muscular frames are built along the same lines. This particular specimen is smaller and less developed than the blue-skinned Ravens, but I can't tell if that's typical of the green species or simply a matter of individual variation within the species. Same beak, same claws . . ."

"Same venom," said Dyson, speaking up for the first time. "It affects the central nervous system almost instantaneously, paralyzing motor functions and blocking pain receptors. I'm still exploring the exact chain of chemical action."

"What about an antidote?" asked Kirk.

Frazer waved a hand toward a small beaker on another table. It was filled with a pale rose liquid. "I synthesized a promising batch this morning. Would you like a demonstration, Captain?" He grabbed the alien's hand and laid his wrist bare to its raking claws.

"No, that won't be necessary."

The lieutenant's disappointment was obvious but his mercurial temperament soon found distraction in the alien's peculiar anatomy. "And of course they've both got this crazy double-brained skull."

"So they come from the same planet."

Frazer was about to nod agreement but thought better of it as Spock corrected the captain's hasty conclusion.

"Morphological similarities are not sufficient proof of common origin; equivalent environmental pressures may be conducive to parallel evolutionary development. However, given the duplication in basic amino acid sequences, probabilities are high that they share the same planet of origin." If Spock felt any physical discomfort in the autopsy room, it was well masked, but he was definitely pained by Frazer's lack of verbal precision. "However, the extensive morphological dif-

155

ferences may indicate a separate species—or possibly even genus—classification."

He motioned to the young lieutenant and they rolled the corpse over. The xenobiologist pointed to a large bulbous sac bulging from the back of the neck, near the base of the skull.

"We still haven't figured out what this is, but it's probably related to the nervous system functions. A series of ducts leads up to the left brain chamber. There are traces of a similar organ in the Ravens, but it seems to have atrophied."

"Of course, the differences could be exaggerated sexual dimorphism," noted Dyson speculatively.

"Possible, but unlikely," said Spock. "Cellular analysis reveals considerable biochemical dissimilarities."

"Besides," added Frazer. "I still haven't found any evidence that either species has a sex." He poked a line down the rubbery green body. "Heart, lung, stomach, all have a roughly analogous organ, but so far, no obvious reproductive tract."

"Not a promising candidate for asexual budding," Dyson mused. "Not like the soggy Oozers."

Frazer's red complexion deepened in hue. "Hey, watch it! Some of my best friends are Oosians."

"I was using the term descriptively."

"Their minds are far from soggy." Spock's comment was carefully neutral. "In fact, their language is admirably suited for expressing the basic precepts of the Unified Field Theory."

Kirk—who had never met an Oosian—indulged himself in a display of temper. "I don't give a damn about anything but *this* alien," he shouted at the three scientists. "And I want to know more about *this* alien just as soon as humanly possible." The captain looked over at Spock; his voice dropped back to normal. "No offense intended, Mr. Spock."

"None taken, Captain," said the Vulcan. His somber eyes lit up with a glint of amusement. "However, I have no intention of limiting myself to human standards of performance."

The look of despair which passed between Dyson and Frazer implied that the science officer applied his own exacting standards to his subordinates as well, regardless of their fully human heritage. At the science officer's signal, the junior officers began preparing the alien for the painstaking dissection which would provide more tissue specimens for the science staff.

The clinging vapors of bio-stasis fluid trailed after Kirk and Spock, reluctantly losing their hold in the fresh air of the corridor outside the autopsy lab.

The captain drew a deep breath to clear his lungs. "I've broken radio silence."

Spock immediately abandoned his review of the data tablet he had carried out of the lab. He focused his attention on Kirk, noting the grim set of the captain's jaw.

Kirk continued. "I ordered Uhura to fire a communications burst to Wagner Post requesting a log of registered flight itineraries. I need to know where those attack fighters came from."

Spock nodded thoughtfully. "Agreed. The knowledge may well be worth the risk of detection."

The first officer's comment did nothing to allay Kirk's own uneasiness. "If it's not, I may have set us up for another attack. I've been rolling snake eyes on every round so far."

"The rules which govern craps are not generally applicable to reality." Spock strongly resisted the concept of luck. Not even Kirk's legendary reliance on favorable random factors could shake the Vulcan's firm belief in the laws of probablity.

"Well, there won't be an answer from Manager Friel

for at least a few hours," said Kirk with studied calm. "I'll be in my cabin."

Spock headed in the opposite direction but stopped abruptly when he detected the light steps of a man coming up behind him. He pivoted around and marched back to face the acting chief medical officer. "Dr. Cortejo, I had requested your presence at the autopsy report."

"Ah, yes. Unfortunately, I was detained elsewhere." The doctor turned away, only to be jerked back by Spock's swift retort.

"Perhaps you find your new duties too demanding." The Vulcan's face displayed a deadly calm. "If that is the case, I can arrange for you to resume your former position."

Cortejo's mouth settled into a grim line. "My time is reserved for the living. I have no interest in rotting meat."

"Your personal preferences are irrelevant. They are also misguided. If we do not concentrate sufficient attention on the aliens, this entire ship's crew may be reduced to 'rotting meat.'" Spock rammed a data tablet into Cortejo's hands. "For that reason, I am requesting a temporary reassignment of these members of your medical staff to the alien research project."

"This is a third of my department!" exclaimed Cortejo in amazement as he scanned the list.

"Twenty-seven percent to be exact."

"But . . ."

"You have the option to refuse my request," said the Vulcan, with a steely edge to his voice. When the doctor did not respond, Spock offered him a writing stylus.

Ignoring the gesture, Cortejo produced one of his own. He scrawled a signature on the tablet before tossing it back to the science officer. His look of loathing was more obviously displayed than Spock's disdain. They parted without another word.

Seconds later, the door to the autopsy room slid open, releasing another strong whiff of stasis fluid. Dyson peered out into the passage and watched Spock cross the threshold of the research library two doors down. Cortejo had disappeared. "All clear," she called back to Frazer. "I'll see you later."

Before she had gone more than ten feet, McCoy stepped out of the shadows of a cross-corridor. He grabbed Dyson's elbow and steered her into an alcove. "We have a dinner date, remember?"

She shook her head. "Sorry, Len. I can't get away."

"Diana, you haven't eaten all day," protested McCoy.

She shrugged. "I'm up to my ears in autopsy reports. Spock has both the science and medical departments working overtime."

McCoy gave a sudden grin. "Wait a minute. Aren't you part of *my* department? As chief medical officer I could order you . . ."

"Don't try to pull rank around here," scolded Dyson. "Dr. Cortejo has your authority now." She smiled wickedly. "But unlike you, he doesn't have the guts to cross Spock." She bit her lip and made another quick check of the corridor. To her relief, it was empty.

"They absolutely despise each other," she confided happily in a low voice. "Spock cuts the man's ego into tiny pieces every chance he gets."

"Yeah," said McCoy. "I overheard him do just that a few minutes ago." He thought back to the exchange between the two senior officers. "I'd just as soon stay on that Vulcan's good side."

"So would I," said Dyson emphatically. "Which means I have to get back to work."

McCoy sighed and released his hold on her arm.

"Damn those aliens—they're ruining my social life. Say, can I look over your shoulder while you run through those tests?" he wheedled wistfully. "I could take notes or wash beakers or . . ."

"No," said Dyson emphatically. "I wouldn't get anything done with you breathing down my neck." She choked at McCoy's mock leer. "Go away!" Her eyes searched for a wall chronometer. She read the numbers on its face and uttered a gasp of dismay. "Oh, hell! Spock will fry me in oil . . ."

"Okay, okay, I'll take a rain check," said McCoy, admitting defeat. He laughed at her blank look. "Dirtwalker saying. I'll see you later," he called out after her as she dashed towards the Research section. "If I happen to have a free moment in my busy schedule," he muttered.

He could kill another hour by going to the mess hall alone, but his hunger had ceased abruptly at Dyson's departure. He was weary of the confines of his cabin, and the rec rooms were abandoned. More out of habit than desire, he opted for a study session with current medical texts.

Walking a few steps down the corridor, McCoy peered into the research library. Spock occupied the carrel nearest the door, his alien form hunched intently over the computer terminal. Anxious not to disturb the first officer's concentration, the doctor edged quietly into the room, but the Vulcan's hearing was sharper than he had realized. McCoy stopped, impaled by two dark eyes.

"Excuse me, sir. I didn't mean to interrupt."

"You have not done so. My literature search is finished." Spock turned back to the screen with an upraised brow. "As it happens, I have been consulting your opinion on this matter."

"I beg your pardon?"

"The xenobiological index referred me to one of your journal articles."

"*One* of my articles?" asked McCoy. "How many do I have?"

Spock punched a rapid series of keys and beckoned the doctor to the terminal. To McCoy's surprise, his name ran down the length of the left column and disappeared off the screen. The majority of the visible publication dates fell within the last three years.

"I wrote all of these? Aboard this ship?" asked McCoy.

"Thanks to Star Fleet resources the *Enterprise* research laboratories are equipped with technological equipment that is more sophisticated than that generally available in civilian facilities. And due to the nature of our mission, the exploration of new areas of space, we have encountered many phenomena that offered excellent research opportunities. It is only logical that we should avail ourselves of the data."

McCoy scanned the array of titles. "Well, they certainly look impressive, but then I can't tell if they're worth the chips they're written on." He dismissed the listing with a shrug.

Spock's impassive face hardened at this show of indifference. "Your work is that of a professional: always competent, frequently inspired, and on occasion brilliant. You have achieved a widespread reputation as a physician and a scientist on the basis of these studies."

"Thank you, but it's not my work you're talking about. I'm a small-town boy who was on his way to being a family doctor. The Leonard McCoy who wrote these," he waved his hand at the terminal, "doesn't exist anymore. Maybe he never will again."

"An emotional reaction to traumatic injury is certainly understandable in your species." Spock steepled his fingers in contemplation of Human frailties. "However, you should not let these emotions cloud your perceptions too far. Whether you recover your memory or not, the fact remains that you are Leonard McCoy. These publications are yours."

"I beg to differ, Mr. Spock." McCoy stopped short of his next statement; he thought back to the scene in the corridor. "Perhaps I've said enough. I'm in imminent danger of contradicting a superior officer."

Spock looked somewhat taken aback by this deferral. "I assure you that such considerations have never intruded themselves on any of our previous discussions." After a moment's hesitation, he offered, "I have always valued the free exchange of our ideas."

McCoy looked dubious, but he perched on the edge of the desk and continued talking. "Then maybe you can hear me out with Vulcan objectivity. You're free from any personal interest in the ship's surgeon.

"You say that I'm the same Leonard McCoy who joined Star Fleet twenty years ago. Well, you're partly right." He tapped his chest. "This body is certainly that of an old man. I guess it's not in bad working order, but it feels stiff and sluggish to me. Yet identity is more than corporeal existence. Personality accounts for a great deal of our perception of a human being as a particular individual, and personality is shaped by the accumulation of memory and experience. Wouldn't you agree, Mr. Spock?"

The first officer nodded, but said nothing.

"Well, then it follows that while my body has maintained a continuous existence throughout the last forty-eight years, my mind has jumped the track. When I first awoke on board this ship I had the personality of the young man who would eventually become 'Bones' McCoy, but within seconds of my awakening, I began to accumulate a radically different set of experiences.

We may share a common past, but I've missed the incidents that shaped his final character, replaced them with other events. I'm becoming a different person."

"Very logically argued." Spock leaned back in his chair, arms crossed over his chest. "But what happens when the lost memory, the personality if you will, returns?"

"When?" challenged the doctor. "You mean 'if,' don't you?" He jumped up and paced restlessly across the deck. "According to Dr. Dyson, recall might occur gradually, with bits and pieces of his . . . my . . . past appearing sporadically, in which case the two personalities will eventually assimilate into one." The line between his brows deepened. "But in some cases the response is a sudden total recall, with the intervening time lost in its turn."

"That eventuality seems to displease you," observed the science officer.

McCoy stopped short. With a faint look of surprise, he nodded agreement. "It means *my* death."

"Conversely, if your memory loss is never recovered, it would mean the death of . . . the other Dr. McCoy."

"The perfect murder, Mr. Holmes," said McCoy with a humorless laugh. "No messy body to dispose of, just a non-corporeal psyche that won't be missed."

Spock's eyebrows jerked upwards. "There you are wrong. Dr. McCoy is much respected and esteemed by the crew of the *Enterprise;* Captain Kirk feels his absence most keenly."

"So your captain loses a drinking partner," said McCoy defensively. "When you think about it, that's a small price to pay for getting my life back in order. I'm a lucky man really. A lifetime of mistakes have been wiped clean off my slate."

"As have the maturity and wisdom you gained from those mistakes." Spock's voice was colored by an uncharacteristic intensity. "Mistakes that you will inevitably repeat."

McCoy shook his head. "Not this time," he insisted. "I'll be happy this time around. I realize that such a human goal may seem irrelevant to you, but I have a feeling it meant a lot to 'Bones' McCoy. Enough for him to let go."

"Let go of what?" asked Spock sharply.

"All of this," said McCoy with a wave that took in the whole ship. "After all, we found the trigger for the amnesia, but it didn't restore my memory. The only reason for a continued amnesia is a personal desire for escape."

He reached over and flicked off the computer screen. "I think Bones is gone for good."

Chapter Sixteen

"WAGNER POST REPORTS no authorization records for either planetary or Federation military transport in this sector." Spock stood at attention in the captain's cabin, calmly announcing the bad news to the man seated before him.

"Damn." Kirk's fist clenched tightly around a white rook. The chess game, started several weeks ago, had not progressed since the first Raven attack. In his darkest moods he wondered if it would ever be finished.

The first officer approached the desk and eyed the arrangement of carved figures on their crystal tiers. "Yet Tennet Five fighters are short-distance vessels, incapable of penetrating into deep space under their own power."

"So, record or no record, there's probably a subwarp carrier somewhere nearby. That ghost you caught on the sensor scan . . ." Kirk set the rook down on another level of the board, ousting a black knight from the game. "And thanks to my communications broadcast, it knows we survived the fighter attack." Abandoning the game to Spock's inspection, Kirk moved into his sleeping quarters, perched on the edge of his bed, and tugged a boot off his foot.

Spock stared intently at a black bishop which was now in danger. "The fighters' maximum flight distance would carry just beyond the range of a fully functional sensor scan, but our sensors are operating far below normal levels. This impairment, coupled with our reduced speed, means a carrier could easily escape our detection."

"I hope that carrier *is* trying to escape us, Spock." Bootless, Kirk stood up and stripped off his shirt. "Under the circumstances, I'm more worried about overtaking that ship than losing it."

The science officer considered this statement. "Phaser cannons, triple-field defense shields, photon disrupter buoys . . ."

"Which wouldn't mean a damn thing if we had warp speed," said Kirk, now fully unclothed, as he ducked into the sonic shower.

"However, at impulse speed we are less than evenly matched." Spock weighed the strengths of the two sides as if evaluating another chess game. "Our phasers would be hard pressed to penetrate its defenses. Our shields could not withstand more than one direct hit. The *Falchion* will be at a similar disadvantage. Our combined forces may not be sufficient to counter an attack."

"And these aliens do seem determined to pick a fight," yelled Kirk from inside the cubicle.

"Agreed," said Spock. His fingers lightly touched the bishop, but did not change its position. He studied the board yet again and slowly withdrew his hand.

Kirk stepped back into the room. "It's cold in here," he complained, quickly pulling on a clean set of clothes.

"Yes," replied the Vulcan. "And Mr. Scott is contemplating another five-degree drop to conserve power expenditure."

"Maybe we should meet in your cabin. I promise not to complain about the heat."

"In deference to our weakened power reserves, I have altered my temperature controls to conform with the rest of the ship," explained Spock. "Ship's stores has issued me extra thermal blankets. A primitive but effective device for conserving heat."

Kirk smiled in sympathy, but his thoughts quickly returned to the ship's danger. "I need to know where those fighters came from."

"They are definitely of Federation origin. The Tennet Five design is commonly used in planetary defense systems on the frontier, though strict measures are taken to insure that sales are to Federation planets only."

"The black market in military equipment is very resourceful," said Kirk. He sat down again to pull on his boots. "Tennet Fives have been around for a long time, long enough to change hands several times over until the Federation loses track of them; sales records can be forged, too, so that's no real mystery. What I don't understand is what direction they came from. They didn't follow established travel routes, or Wagner Post would have detected their presence or received notice of their passage from other Federation outposts." He stood up and stamped his feet for a final snug fit. "That leaves Klingon territory or uncharted space."

Spock's eyebrows rose high on his forehead. "Both of which are equally unlikely points of origin for a sub-warp vessel."

"Nothing in this mess makes any sense," said Kirk wearily. "Aliens popping out of nowhere. Klingons and Frenni disappearing just as suddenly." He pounded a fist into the open palm of his other hand. "We go over and over the details and yet we still can't form a picture. There's a missing element somewhere." He looked at his first officer. "Logic doesn't seem to be getting us anywhere, Spock."

Spock bowed his head in silent acknowledgement of the captain's frustration. Kirk paced nervously from the bedroom into the outer study. The quick shower had done nothing to relax the knotted tension in his shoulders.

"Dammit, there has to be an explanation for these attacks. We've got to find it so we know who we're fighting and why. I can't defend this ship, this crew without . . ." The soft clink of bottle against glass stopped him in mid-sentence.

"I believe this is your usual drink, Captain," said Spock, handing Kirk a goblet of dark brandy.

"Why, Bones," laughed Kirk in astonishment. "You've grown pointed ears."

Spock did not allow himself to smile. "Have you spoken to Dr. McCoy lately?" he asked the captain.

Kirk frowned and took a swallow of his drink before answering. "Not really. Not since the last attack." With some reluctance, he admitted, "We don't seem to have much to say to each other."

"Indeed," said Spock neutrally. "I, on the other hand, have just finished a most fascinating conversation with the doctor. We discussed the concept of discontinuous personality formation in a continuous corporeal entity."

Kirk stared blankly at his science officer. "What the hell are you talking about?"

"Dr. McCoy can elucidate," said Spock. "I highly recommend it as a topic of discussion, Captain."

"But . . ."

"You will have to excuse me," said Spock with a note of formal apology. "I'm due on the bridge in two minutes." He left the room without further comment, leaving Kirk to puzzle out his words.

McCoy's cabin had changed. Kirk felt the difference as soon as he crossed over the threshold. His eyes swept over walls that were bare of their usual art hangings. Medical books and tapes were rearranged, spread over the shelves, taking the place of McCoy's collection of personal effects. Kirk walked through to the back section of the cabin. The doctor was in bed, struggling to a sitting position, still half-asleep though he had released the cabin lock to let Kirk into the room.

"I'm sorry, I didn't mean to wake you."

"I'm just as glad you did. Crazy nightmare . . . gone now," McCoy muttered, rubbing the sleep from his eyes. He looked up at the captain. "Let me guess—Mr. Spock sent you."

"Not exactly." Kirk spotted a jumble of stone and wood objects shoved onto a corner shelf of the bedroom. "He simply mentioned that the two of you had had a 'fascinating' discussion."

"And that sent you running here?" McCoy stretched lazily and swung his feet off the bed. He was wearing standard issue service pants, but his worn brown sweater dated back to civilian days. He groped on the deck for his boots.

"He was worried about you." Kirk had no doubt that his first officer had been conveying a new concern for McCoy's well-being.

"Worried?" asked McCoy. "What are you talking about? He's a Vulcan."

"He's also half Human." Kirk said out loud what neither of his two friends would ever voice themselves. "That Human side is quite fond of you, although the Vulcan half never lets him admit it."

"I guess that speaks well for 'Bones' McCoy," said

McCoy grudgingly as he rose to face the captain. "Not that it matters much anymore."

Kirk's eyes strayed over the altered cabin. The source of Spock's unease became clearer to him. He strolled over to the discarded pile of artifacts and hefted a carved stone head. "This was a gift from the High Teer Akaar of Capella IV. You lived for several months among his people. The present Teer is 'Leonard James Akaar'—named after the both of us. You delivered him, saved his life and that of his mother." He proffered the figure to McCoy for inspection. When the doctor made no move to accept it, Kirk carefully restored the statue to its usual prominence on a higher shelf.

The next item he picked up was a small rough rock. "Not much of a souvenir, but then Vulcan doesn't court the tourist trade." He held the dull red stone up to the light. "You saved my life on Vulcan. Not for the first time, either." He flipped the rock into the air.

Surprised into action, McCoy caught it before it fell to the deck. Almost as quickly, he tossed it back. "Look, Captain. I didn't ask for this." McCoy tapped lightly at his temple. " 'Bones' made the choice to leave and he doesn't show any signs of coming back."

"I don't believe that," said Kirk shaking his head. "I know you, McCoy . . ."

"Then tell me why I chose to forget you and this ship," said McCoy defiantly.

Kirk shrugged his hands in helplessness. "I can't answer that." He looked into the face of the man standing before him. A familiar face, yet now that of a stranger. "But your memory will return. You wouldn't choose to stay away."

"There's no place for me here," insisted McCoy. "This boy is going home to Georgia . . ."

"Dammit, McCoy, you can't leave the service. You can't leave the *Enterprise*." *You can't leave me.*

McCoy angrily shook his head. "Captain, once I get off of this ship, I'm never coming back."

The scream of the alert siren drowned out Kirk's retort. Red pulsing lights invaded the room. Uhura's voice cut through the wailing alarms. *"Red alert, red alert. Captain Kirk to the bridge."*

McCoy looked up in amazement. "Again? Don't you get tired of this?"

"Yes," said Kirk sourly, leaving the room at a dead run.

The image on the bridge viewscreen was deceptively untroubled. However, the long-range sensors were more sensitive. They detected a presence that could not be seen in the empty reaches of space.

"Our ghost has reappeared," explained Spock, vacating the command chair. He stood by its side as the captain sat down.

Kirk's face was still flushed with anger at being caught off the bridge a second time. "The Tennet Five battle-carrier?"

"Possibly," said Spock. "It is just inside sensor range, moving at a speed consistent with a sub-warp carrier. Its mass is also equivalent to such a vessel. Visual contact in twenty minutes; course intersection in one hour, twelve minutes."

"And we canna outrun it," said Scotty, stepping down from the engineering station. "Not with our power reserves so low."

"Then we fight," said Kirk. He checked the reactions of his two officers and sighed. "Any suggestions as to how we can win?"

"We do have the added resources of the *Falchion*."

Spock did not search for the warship on the viewscreen. Within seconds of the red alert signal, the Klingon ship had vanished behind its cloaking shield.

"Aye," agreed Scotty. "An' if we had a third ship, it might be an even match."

"If we can't beat them in a fair fight, we'll have to trick them." Kirk smiled broadly. "We'll give them a taste of their own medicine."

"What dose did ye have in mind?" asked Scotty.

Kirk leaned forward, studying the viewscreen before him, but his mind's eye was reviewing events of the past. "The Ravens in the Frenni ship could have attacked us at once, as soon as we lowered our shields, but they waited. They waited until we suspected a trap and recalled the shuttlecraft. If we hadn't suspected a trap, what would they have done?" He didn't wait for his officers to answer. "They would have taken over the shuttlecraft and tried to board us. The Ravens didn't want to destroy the *Enterprise*—they wanted to control her. So, perhaps the carrier crew can be lured into boarding our ship, instead of attacking it."

Scotty looked appalled at the suggestion, but Spock showed no surprise. Through long practice, Spock nimbly followed the quick twists of Kirk's mind. "And in order to board us, they would have to drop their shields."

"Aye! That they would!" The chief engineer began to smile just as broadly as Kirk.

Spock, however, withheld his approval and slipped easily into the role of devil's advocate. "If the Tennet Five crews consisted of only the second alien species, their motivations could be different."

Kirk gnawed at his thumb, then shook his head. "No, I don't think so." He looked up at the Vulcan. "I can't prove it, but I'm sure both Raven species are allied in the same cause. Another gamble, Mr. Spock."

"Then I hope our cards come up aces," said Scotty.

"A dice roll of seven, Mr. Scott." Spock quirked an eyebrow at the engineer's confusion. "Our current metaphor is craps."

"Whatever the game, Mr. Spock, 'tis a risky play."

"Mayday, Mayday. This is the U.S.S. *Enterprise*. Ship in distress." Uhura repeated the call over and over again, carefully edging her voice with an anxiety that was not entirely feigned.

Kirk concentrated on the crackle of static from the broadcast receiver. His eyes were riveted on the red, bullet-shaped carrier that grew like a blood stain on the viewscreen. If there was no answer soon, the bait would be taken without springing the trap. The *Enterprise*, adrift in space, was truly vulnerable. Her engines were shut down, leaving the weapons systems and deflectors without operating power.

"Its hull emblems are those of an Orion mercenary army," whispered Spock in his ear.

"More allies?" asked Kirk, wiping the sweat off his brow. Orion neutrality was more dependent on self-interest than good will.

Spock shrugged. "Or more victims of a Raven/Klingon alliance."

"Either way, that's th' battle carrier for th' Tennet Fives," said Scotty fiercely. "Look at all th' empty fighter berths."

A burst of noise cut through the static, halting Uhura's repetitious call. She instantly tuned the frequency. "Enterprise, *this is Captain Aeloran of the* Stellar Storm. *We read you.*" The words which echoed over the speaker were spoken in Federation Basic with a strong Orion accent.

With a wave of his hand, Kirk signaled a ragged cheer from the bridge crew and raised his own voice to answer the call. "*Stellar Storm*, this is Captain Kirk. Are we glad to see you!" He stepped down from his chair, channeling his tension into movement, keeping his voice balanced between a semblance of relief and weariness.

"*What happened, Captain Kirk? Your ship looks dead in space.*"

We may be soon. "We were attacked by Klingons, a small fighter force crossed over from their territory in the Belennii star system. We destroyed them, but not before they damn near killed us. Our engines are out of commission. No power left in weapons; our shields are gone." He waved a hand over the darkened bridge, entering into his part fully. "We're running life support systems from batteries."

"*What can we do to help?*" asked the disembodied voice.

Kirk laughed. "You'll be sorry you asked that. I've got a list a foot long of spare parts and supplies that we need to get going again. And all I can offer in payment is a Star Fleet credit voucher."

"*I don't mind,*" answered the Orion captain cheerfully. "*Federation credit is as good as gold.*"

Kirk hesitated. This voice sounded genuine enough to create doubt where there had been certainty. The same doubt had delayed his reaction to the Frenni merchant impostor by a fatal few seconds.

"Uhura?"

The lieutenant cut off ship-to-ship communications to answer him. "They are accepting our visual transmission but only returning audio."

Just like the *Serella*. More evidence that the Ravens were controlling the *Stellar Storm*, but still not absolute proof.

Uhura restored the ship-to-ship connection at Kirk's thumbs-up sign.

"I lied," announced Kirk to the *Stellar Storm*'s commander. "I do have one item on board that's good for trade—Saurian brandy. If you'd care to beam aboard, I'll open a bottle while I go over our requisition list."

"That's the best offer I've had since I left home!" crowed the voice. *"Give me your coordinates, and I'll be right there."* There was a momentary silence, then the voice returned. *"In fact, I'll bring some of my crew with me."*

"You do that," said Kirk. "We'll be waiting."

Uhura snapped off radio contact.

"Battle stations." Kirk's soft voice contrasted with the harsh meaning of the words. "Spock, prepare to run a sensor scan as soon as their shields drop."

The first officer turned from his science station. "Captain, if they detect the scanning . . ."

"They'll smell a trap and destroy this ship," said Kirk grimly. "Uhura, transmit transporter coordinates, then open a channel to the *Falchion*."

"Aye, captain." She followed his order without hesitation.

Scotty monitored the results. "Their shields are dropping."

The bridge fell silent. The only sounds came from the computers at the science station. The Vulcan officer's motions were controlled and deliberate and very, very fast.

Scotty looked up anxiously from the engineering panel. "Transporter room reports grid activation . . . Captain, if they succeed in beaming aboard . . ."

Kirk kept his eyes trained on his first officer while time stretched to the breaking point.

Then Spock uttered the vital word. "Ravens."

"Now, Sulu!" shouted Kirk.

The *Falchion* rippled into existence, blocking the

Enterprise's view, but providing the protection of its own deflectors. Simultaneously, the Klingon warship loosed a bright stream of phaser fire that cut through the metal hull covering the battle-carrier's impulse engines.

Seconds later the *Stellar Storm* no longer existed.

Chapter Seventeen

"SENSORS DO NOT detect organic remains, Captain."

Kirk stared past his science officer, eyes fixed on the computer station indicators. Their color confirmed the verbal report. "Run the check again, Mr. Spock."

The Vulcan's hesitation was slight, a brief betrayal of conflicting trains of thought. A second search was unnecessary and would waste ship's energy; logic dictated that he bring this fact to his captain's attention. Experience counseled that Kirk was in no mood to listen to logic. Spock tripped a switch for another sensor sweep.

Kirk stepped down from the duty station and stood by the side of his command chair. The helmsman and navigator toyed impatiently with the ship controls, eager to resume their course. Uhura was turned to her communications station, too intent on her radio monitoring to notice that Spock had initiated another, redundant, probe from his station.

The main viewscreen presented an empty, untroubled sector of space. No sign of the *Stellar Storm* remained; the explosion of its impulse engines had annihilated the entire ship. And its Raven crew. Which meant Kirk was no closer to finding an answer now than he had been after the first attack. His own orders had destroyed any possibility of learning more about the aliens.

The computer chattered its soft report. Kirk tensed for the translation.

"Negative, Captain. No organic remains."

"Very well, Mr. Spock." Kirk's voice was equally impassive. "Helm, prepare for impulse power."

"Aye, aye, Captain." DePaul and Benus sat up straight in their seats, hands poised over the controls. They had calculated and entered the course coordinates for Wagner Post several times over while Kirk lingered at the site of the *Stellar Storm*'s destruction.

"*Falchion* standing by." Uhura relayed the report from Sulu aboard the Klingon battlecruiser.

Kirk heard the too-quick responses from every duty station on the bridge. His officers had found the waiting tedious and were anxious to move on. "Full impulse power."

The crew fell into motion and the *Enterprise* shuddered into flight.

Kirk shuddered, too. *It's too damn cold in here.* His mind shied away from any other explanation for the chills. "Long range sensor scan, Spock?"

"Negative. No signs of activity within this sector."

"Confirmed by communications monitor," added Uhura.

"Let's hope it stays that way," said Kirk wearily. "We're still several days away from the trading post."

Uneventful days, he prayed. Time enough for the one event which could not be postponed any longer. He rose from the command chair. "Mr. Spock, I'll meet you in my cabin in an hour."

Kirk spent the hour staring at the contents of a small leather case. Command of a starship was a challenging and demanding calling; it could also be a high-stakes game of chance. Every mission required decisions that affected the lives of the ship's crew and of countless other beings. Most of the time, Kirk knew the answer, the necessary course of action. Every once in a while he had to guess. When he guessed right, he got a medal. Kirk had many medals. He treasured them not as symbols of glory but as markers for having made the right choice. How many risks could he take, how many chances, before he guessed wrong?

At the rescue of the *Serella*, his momentary hesitation had led to the crippling of the *Enterprise*. Despite that, Kirk had risked the *Enterprise* once again when facing the *Stellar Storm*. If the sensor scan had taken seconds longer, if it had been detected, the Ravens would have attacked again. This time they might have won.

A low whistle sounded over the intercom, a dirgelike tone which would reach every corner of the ship. The captain pulled his thoughts out of the past. He snapped the case shut and placed it back in a niche in the wall by his bed. A metal door slid over the opening, hiding the case from view. The uncertainties remained. He pushed them aside and concentrated on changing his clothes. When the door chime rang, Kirk was ready.

Spock entered the cabin with the air of formality which always accompanied his visits to Kirk's private quarters. He was past considering his presence an intrusion, but he still managed to convey a subtle sense of Vulcan ritual when he crossed the threshold. Now that formality was considerably heightened by the blue dress uniform he wore.

Kirk tugged at the sleeves of his own command-gold dress uniform. He had grown to loathe the suit because of its association with tiresome diplomatic affairs and Star Fleet courts-martial. And funerals.

"Lt. Uhura confirms that the chapel is prepared for the service," said Spock with appropriate solemnity, but then he would use the same somber voice to announce a wedding. "Ship's intercom will broadcast your address to the crewmembers on duty."

Kirk nodded absently at this recital of details, his mind still caught in a tangle of doubt and confusion. Neither officer had discussed Kirk's actions against the *Serella* or the *Stellar Storm*. Spock, the first officer, would not question a command decision unless asked for an opinion; Spock, the Vulcan, would probably see little value in debating a past action.

Certainly Kirk had no desire to bring his doubts into the open. To give voice to his fears would give them more substance. Only one man would have pressed the issue, before and after. What would McCoy have made of Kirk's actions? Would he have urged caution before firing or railed against the certain danger to the *Enterprise*?"

"I knew there were Ravens on that ship, even without the scan." Kirk was talking out loud before he could stop himself. "But I let them trick me once again. I should have destroyed them as soon as possible."

The captain's outburst did not surprise Spock. He spoke quickly, as if his response had been prepared before and held in check for just this moment. "At the risk of destroying an innocent Orion crew?"

"Instead, I risked my own crew."

Spock said nothing. There was nothing a Vulcan could say to refute Kirk's self-accusation. If he searched for the words a friend might use, he took too long to find them. Kirk had already left the room.

Diana Dyson could think of at least three good reasons why she should stop by McCoy's cabin. What disturbed her was the apparent need to justify that action to herself. Her tentative and reluctant introspection came to an abrupt halt inside the cabin. As she had expected, McCoy was immersed in his medical studies;

most unexpectedly, he was still in civilian dress. Dyson stared in dismay at McCoy's rumpled sweater.

"Why aren't you ready?"

McCoy pulled his attention away from the computer screen. "Ready for what?"

"The memorial service. It starts in ten minutes."

McCoy's eyes dropped back to the screen. "Oh, yeah, I heard something about it this morning. I don't have to go, do I?"

"For god's sake, you're a senior officer!" She sprinted past his desk into the bedroom and threw open the door to the closet. "Not to mention the man who signed a death certificate for every crewmember who was killed in the first attack." Her hands rummaged frantically inside the compartment.

"Oh." McCoy flicked off the power switch on the computer. "I guess that means I have to go."

Dyson emerged from the back room. She held out a shirt made of a soft, shiny blue fabric edged with gold. "Here, put this on."

McCoy looked as if she was offering him the body of a dead animal.

"And hurry!"

He rose to his feet, slowly unbending his lanky frame, then giving his spine a backward stretch. "Too bad my back doesn't think it's 23 years old." Dyson's lips pursed with obvious impatience. McCoy sighed heavily at her unspoken proddings, but he stripped off his sweater and threw it aside. "Dammit, it's cold in here." Giving an exaggerated shiver, he took the uniform shirt from her hands and tried to pull it over his head.

"No, not that way." Dyson tugged it off him and unfastened the front seam. She shoved the garment back at him.

"I hate funerals." McCoy put his arms through the

sleeves, one at a time, then laboriously started to reseal the shirt edges. "Never could see the point in deliberately choosing to be depressed and unhappy for near onto an hour. Two hours if you get an enthusiastic preacher." When he reached the neckline, his fingers fumbled clumsily with the seal. "Damn collar. Are you sure this is my size?"

"Oh, will you please shut up!"

McCoy was startled by the sudden attack.

"My roommate was one of the first casualties. This funeral is more than just a formality for me."

"Sorry." He was still fumbling with the last fastener.

"No, you're not the least bit sorry. You're barely being polite." She swatted his hands away from the shirt and roughly fastened the collar for him. "Well, four of the casualties were paramedics from your department."

Dyson stepped back to survey his appearance. "And you chose each one of those people. Hoffman, Russell, Wallace, Clark. Remember those names when the captain reads them. Be glad you can't mourn for them, because the man who was ship's surgeon nearly cried when he heard they were dead."

The stricken expression on McCoy's face stopped her tirade. She stamped down on a pang of guilt. "Come on or we'll be late."

He followed her without protest.

The chapel was little more than an empty hall with a nominal stage and podium at one end. Since Star Fleet did not wish to offend any creed or religion—and Star Fleet members were affiliated with an amazing variety of belief systems—the ship's designers had provided a bland, featureless room that appealed to no creed or religion. Only on those few occasions when the ship's crew filled the room to capacity did the unadorned walls reflect dignity and serenity.

Kirk stood erect behind the podium, waiting for the late arrivals to find a place in the crowd. No spaces were left on the long low benches arranged in the center of the room; most of the crew was standing along the perimeters, against the wall. Despite the large attendance, there was little noise beyond the rustle of moving bodies. As captain, his duty was to speak out into that heavy silence, to find words of comfort and reassurance for the friends and companions of those who had died. Captains were not allowed stage fright. Kirk smoothed flat the list of names he had to read, wiping the moisture from his palms onto the thin sheet of paper. The memorial service had been postponed twice due to battle action and each time the list had grown longer.

Kirk's glance traveled idly over the room while his mind wrestled with the wording of the approaching service. He saw a tightly huddled group of engineering crewmembers step apart to let Montgomery Scott into their midst. They pushed him down onto a bench and closed ranks around him. Bowed over with fatigue, his long face lined with sorrow, Scotty was unaware of the fiercely protective spirit which he inspired.

In contrast, the members of Spock's science division were scattered throughout the crowd. The loyalty of his department was less obvious, but ran as deep as that of engineering. The Vulcan challenged the minds and the intellect of the scientists—their emotions were strictly an off-duty concern. Yet, Spock was here, showing honor to the dead. He stood tall and austere, in the midst of humans, but not of them.

The quality of silence in the room altered, signaling a concensus that the service should begin. Kirk opened his mouth and words emerged. He couldn't hear them but the men and women seated before him listened intently. Even as one part of his mind found expression for the grief they were feeling and spoke it aloud, another part was silently observing the faces turned to his. Some, like Uhura, were easily moved to tears, declaring an open and unashamed testament to the love they bore for the fallen. Others released the tears grudgingly, with obvious effort, coaxed by his voice to share a common pain.

The words, sounding so faint and distant in his ears, did not stop here. They were carried out, beyond the confines of the room, to every corner of the ship, to everyone who had to stay at a duty post. Were those unseen faces transfigured as well? Kirk stood alone on the dais, unable to take in the comfort of his own speech.

The voice stopped. *Have I finished?* wondered Kirk. He looked down to the podium's tabletop and slowly read the list. A few of the names he uttered aloud wrung a stifled exclamation from someone who was just now hearing of the death.

At the end of that too-long roll call, Kirk allowed a time for personal meditation. He bowed his own head in silent prayer and tried to remember the dead, to conjure up the faces of those who were gone, but he found himself praying for the ones who were here now, that they might continue living.

Chapter Eighteen

Captain's Log, Stardate 5321.12:
We are less than a day away from Wagner Post, but even as we approach the haven of its dockyards, I am still unable to explain the attacks which have crippled my ship.

A PANORAMA OF stars stretched across the horizon. Their soft light illuminated the ground below, casting shadows from the trees, smoothing the grass into a blanket of furred velvet. A soft breeze rustled through the leaves with a gentle rhythm.

McCoy lay flat on his back, hands under his head, admiring his carefully calculated view. Ground shrubs hid the bottom rim of the viewport frame; the low-lying branches of a willow obscured the top edge. Deep space was magically transformed into a night sky. All he needed now was a blade of grass to chew on. He resisted the impulse to pluck a stalk of greenery.

"Now if only the stars would stop moving, I could almost believe this garden is in Georgia."

Dyson, sitting on a bench by the tree trunk, gave a small shudder. "Stars are supposed to move," she declared. "If they aren't moving, it means the station power supply has blown."

McCoy heaved a deep sigh, his fragile illusion shattered. He sat up to face her. "Humans were never meant to live in space—it destroys the soul."

"My soul is doing just fine, Doctor," said Dyson with a hint of asperity.

He shook his head. "This is no replacement for Earth." McCoy waved his arm at the lush greenery. "Synthetic breezes and recycled water. And not a single insect in the whole damn lot."

"You miss insects?" she asked skeptically.

"That's not the point," sidestepped McCoy. "It's not real."

Dyson shrugged her indifference. "You mean it's not Earth. No hurricanes, tornadoes, earthquakes, floods, drought . . ." She stopped before his exasperation turned to anger. "It sounds like a very dangerous place to live."

"It's also very beautiful." McCoy scrambled to his feet, absently brushing non-existent dirt from his sweater and pants. "With a wild beauty that you won't find in carefully manicured plots of grass. Here, life has to be nurtured and protected, coddled into growth. On Earth, life simply explodes from every square millimeter of air and ground."

The muted whistle of the ship's intercom effectively destroyed the last tatters of pastoral ambiance, turning the garden back into a section of the recreation deck.

"Spock to Dr. Dyson."

McCoy reached for her hand, pulling the woman to her feet. "You need a better union."

"Right. You tell Mr. Spock I've gone on strike." Brushing aside a feathery branch, Dyson revealed the intercom set neatly into a hollow of the willow trunk. She thumbed the answer switch. "Dyson here."

The science officer's crisply enunciated words echoed out. *"Cellular imaging scans on neurological tissue sample 21-Alpha will be completed in ten point two minutes. We will examine the results in Medical Lab 3A."* He cut the connection without awaiting her reply.

"What happens after you finish sample 21-Alpha?" asked McCoy, still holding her hand as they walked up the path leading to the turbo-lift.

She pulled out of his grasp. "Oh, then we analyze samples 21-Beta through Gamma."

"It all sounds deadly dull." They turned a final corner of the molded brick walkway. Bushes, trees, and rocky outcroppings gave way to the familiar lines and colors of the ship's deck and walls. The turbo-lift doors, framed by an incongruous trellis of ivy, snapped open. "Just what is it you're looking for?"

"Peace and quiet," answered Uhura, stepping out into the room as the two doctor's took her place in the turbo-lift. "If you see Captain Kirk, tell him I'm on Deck Twenty-eight."

McCoy puzzled over the lieutenant's words as they sped toward the upper levels. Dyson obviously found them humorous. "What's on Deck Twenty-eight?"

Dyson's smile faded at his question. "There is no Deck Twenty-eight, Len."

"Oh. Well, how was I to know that?" he grumbled, turning aside to escape her searching look. "I've got amnesia, Dr. Dyson. I'm not supposed to remember details like that."

"You're not even trying, are you?" The turbo doors swooshed open at Deck Seven, cutting short her accusation.

They walked in silence to the medical lab. It was empty and dark, but as they crossed the threshold, ceiling lights came to life and cast a dim glow over the long low counters which filled the center of the room.

McCoy was the first to speak. "Did the captain order you to spend your off-duty hours probing my pysche? Or are you bucking for a promotion?"

Dyson flinched away from his brittle sarcasm. Moving down an aisle, she snapped on the power for the equipment around her and trained her eyes on the fluttering sequence of colored lights that played across the control panels. "This is a medical matter involving a member of this ship's crew and I'm a ship's doctor. What do you expect me to do?"

"I expect you to help me get off this ship!" he shouted after her.

She turned back around to face him. "Len, you can't give up like this—you've got to fight this block."

"The hell I do!" He clenched his jaw, fought down his anger. When he spoke again his voice was softened. "Diana, I've got my life to live over again—to do it right this time." He stepped closer, pleading his case. "With a Star Fleet pension I can go back to Earth and set up a general practice at home, just as I've always planned. Somewhere along the way old Doc McCoy lost that dream, lost his family. I'm not going to let that happen to me."

"You can't pull yourself into separate pieces and stay sane," cried Dyson. "You're one individual, not two. And that person is a good man and a brilliant surgeon. Every man and woman on this ship would trust you with their lives. You may have joined Star Fleet to escape your mistakes, but you've become as much a part of the *Enterprise* as Captain Kirk and Mr. Spock. You mustn't throw all that away. You won't be allowed to throw it all away."

"So I'm just a temporary aberration, like some damaged clone cells. Wasn't it 'fascinating' to study young Len McCoy, but now it's time to stick him back where he came from; let him rot in the faded memory ingrams of your sainted chief surgeon." He grabbed her by the shoulders. His eyes locked with hers. "Is that what you really want?"

She dropped her gaze, breaking their contact. "Yes!

It's got to be yes." Her fists pushed against his chest, but he wouldn't release his hold on her. "Let me go, Len," she pleaded. "I'm losing all my objectivity as a doctor . . ."

"Doctor be damned! I'm fed up with being your patient. Is that all I am to you?" he demanded. "An interesting medical case?"

"You know very well that's not true," Diana shot back angrily. This time it was her gaze that held his. "You may be young, but you're not that much of an innocent."

"No," he answered in a husky voice. "No, I'm not." His hands loosened their grip but did not leave her shoulders. She closed her eyes, as if to ward off his approach, but she didn't pull away when he bent his face over hers.

"Which McCoy was that for?" he asked when the kiss had ended. "The young one or the old one?"

"I'm not sure." Her fingers traced the edge of his cheek. "I just know I've wanted to do that for a very long time."

"So the old man still had some charm left?" McCoy laughed gently. "But he never tried to kiss you, did he?"

Her body tensed once again and jerked out of his embrace. "No," she answered stiffly. "And when your memory returns, you'll probably be quite embarassed by this whole episode. Or you won't remember it even happened. Yet it's my professional responsibility to try to restore that memory. Even if I don't succeed, someone else will."

"Diana . . ." He tried to pull her back to him.

She stepped away from his reach. "So you see," she continued with a trace of bitterness. "Keeping my distance is not only an ethical issue, it's also a matter of personal survival. Some day, probably soon, your memory will come back, and when it does there won't be a place for me in your life."

"That's not true."

Dyson shook her head. "You see me as another resident, just like yourself. To Chief Surgeon McCoy I'm first and foremost a member of his medical department; strictly a professional associate. Not to mention that I'm several ranks below him and years younger in experience—two decades younger. We'll never be anything more than colleagues."

He searched for a way to deny what she said, but the words wouldn't come. "I'm sorry."

"Oh, not half as sorry as I am, Dr. McCoy."

Spock walked into the silence that stretched between them. One swift glance over the room raised a furrow on the science officer's brow. "Dr. Dyson, readjust the calibration on the holographic micro-scanner."

Dyson quickly turned her flushed face towards the offending machinery and busied herself with its controls. If the procedure took longer than usual, Spock appeared too absorbed in his own equipment preparations to notice. Erratic bursts of electronic noise were gradually transformed into a rhythmic chorus under his direction. Indicator lights settled into endlessly repeating patterns. Satisfied with the result, he spared a glance in McCoy's direction.

The doctor had edged into a corner of the room, far away from the door. Despite his best efforts, he had not yet become invisible.

Spock did not challenge McCoy's presence, he simply ignored it. He handed Dyson a holographic chip. "The dissection of the brain tissue samples from the second alien species has provided a new avenue of investigation."

The image which appeared on her scanner brought a

low whistle from the neurologist. "Very intriguing," she agreed. "The density of neural cells in the tissues of the left chamber's brain-lobe is significantly higher than that of the right lobe."

McCoy leaned over a counter, craning his head for a glimpse, but he could see nothing except a faintly luminous cloud hovering on the scanner stage. His curiosity was further frustrated as Dyson and Spock lapsed into the technical jargon of molecular neurobiology. As the intensity of their discussion increased, so did his restlessness.

Reasonably sure that the two scientists were too absorbed in their research to notice him, McCoy prowled quietly along the perimeter of the room. Sheets of flat film were tacked to the darkened surfaces of translucent wall panels. He idly scanned the row of dim images until one photo drew him closer. A flick of a switch brought the light panel to life, illuminating a shot of a decapitated head. McCoy studied the frame with great interest and a trace of amusement, but he waited for a prolonged lull in the exchange between the two officers before voicing his question. "Are these the aliens that attacked the ship?"

"Yes," answered Spock distractedly.

"Well, no wonder we're in such bad shape—they're pretty vicious creatures. Back in Atlanta, I used to have some pretty lively nightmares about them. I've even had a few bad dreams since I've been here."

Spock and Dyson turned to stare at him. Confused by their sudden attention, McCoy stammered an apology. "I'm sorry, I didn't mean to interrupt."

"What do you know of these aliens?" asked Spock, his tightly controlled mask revealing no more than mild curiosity.

McCoy shrugged. "Well, nothing in the way of scientific information. I heard about them from one of the patients in the Atlanta pysch ward. I spent hours listening to an old spacedog ranting on about his capture by hideous aliens." He waved at the photos. "These aliens."

He still had Spock's undivided attention, so he continued. "Sager was pulled from the wreck of a cargo freighter, half-starved and hysterical—the rest of the crew was missing. He explained their absence by a tale that seemed too outlandish to be true. The more likely explanation seemed to be that he had survived by resorting to cannibalism, and the guilt had driven him mad." McCoy smiled wryly in acknowledgement of the irony of the situation. "The medical staff assumed that he had imagined the aliens to relieve his guilt, and so did I, but his tales were so vivid that they stuck in my mind even after I left his case. Poor devil—I wonder how long it was before they realized he was sane?"

Spock arched a brow. "Unfortunately, he may still be in that pysch ward." He reached for the intercom switch on the wall. "Captain Kirk to Medical Lab 3A." Then, picking up a voice coder from the desk, the Vulcan beckoned McCoy to come closer. "Dr. McCoy, tell me what you remember of your patient's discourse."

Chapter Nineteen

"*. . . THE ALIEN PARALYZES its victim with just a scratch from its claws. Then it cracks the top of the skull open with its beak and plucks out the living brain, swallowing it whole, like picking a kernel from its shell. The body serves as food . . .*"

Spock stopped the tape at that point, aware that the human occupants of the briefing room were reacting rather emotionally to the narration. Engineer Scott was a shade paler than usual; Uhura's dark eyes had widened with alarm. Even Frazer and Dr. Dyson were subdued by the description.

Captain Kirk, presiding at the head of the conference table, had listened impassively until the break. "McCoy, you said this man was insane . . ."

"I said we *thought* he was insane," corrected McCoy. "But that was because he described an alien species nobody had ever seen before. However, since the aliens do exist, he could have been telling the truth."

Kirk nodded reluctantly. He didn't like what he had heard so far. "So which of the two alien species did he encounter?"

"There is only one alien," said Spock evenly. He started the tape again.

"*Once an alien has swallowed a brain, it begins to metamorphose, like a caterpillar without a cocoon. Its skin changes color from green to blue, its head crest*" *darkens. When the transformation is complete, it begins to speak in the voice of its victim."*

"I dinna believe it," cried out Scotty. "The man was probably space happy."

"No, it's theoretically possible," said Frazer excitedly. His scientific curiosity rapidly overcame his initial reaction of horror. "The physiological changes described imply a vast biochemical upheaval in the organism's system. The green Ravens—the larval stage—possess an organ at the base of the skull which is a powerhouse of amino acids. Their release could signal an organic processing of the structural RNA of the victim's brain. They could literally cut apart the old brain, while recording the connections."

Dyson shared his excitement. "The unusual concentration of neurons in the left chamber of the brain could serve as a blank template, awaiting the information. Once a pattern is set, the brain tissue gradually resumes a normal cell density."

"The result is two separate brains." Frazer jumped back into the explanation. "Normally, this would be dysfunctional, but not if the alien retains control over its secondary memories. There's a cluster of neurons at the branching of the brain stems that probably acts as a switching center between the two lobes."

Kirk listened to the theory without comment—three years in space had taught him a healthy respect for the fantastic—but he looked to his first officer for confirmation.

Spock added his consensus to the idea. "This process could account for many of the events which we have encountered. Granted, this is only supposition . . ."

"Go on, Spock," ordered Kirk impatiently.

The Vulcan could not be hurried. He settled into the physical posture which accompanied his theorizing—eyebrows drawn together, elbows propped on the table, hands steepled before him. "The Klingon crew of the *Falchion*, patrolling an especially isolated sector of space, may well have fallen victim to the Ravens. If the theory of brain absorption is correct, the aliens would then have had the knowledge to maneuver the commandeered battlecruiser into Frenni space . . ."

"Where they exchanged a very conspicuous Klingon warship for a neutral merchant liner and waited for the next passing ship to fall into their trap," said Kirk.

"Just like a hermit crab."

The captain swiveled his chair around in surprise. "What was that, Lt. Uhura?"

"The hermit crab moves from one seashell to another as it grows, always looking for a larger home," explained Uhura.

Spock's eyebrows raised in appreciative consideration. "An interesting analogy, with disturbing implications if this continual search for a larger ship also implies growth."

"But th' first attack on the *Enterprise* failed." Scotty puzzled over this added information. "And th' aliens were all killed. So where did th' battlecruiser and its fighters come from?"

"And how did they know we were here?" Kirk tried to pinpoint the source of a growing unease . . . "Damn!" His fist thumped down on the conference table. "The *Saucy Lady*. We only received an audio channel transmission from the freighter which passed on the Frenni distress call. The captain *said* his ship didn't go near the caravan, but if he was lying, if his ship went to the aid of the *Selessan* . . ."

"Then we were actually speaking to Captain Neil's Raven persona, and the crew of his ship may have taken over Wagner Post by now," finished Spock. He turned to the engineer. "In all likelihood that is the origin of the sub-warp carrier and its fighters."

"Aye, and that's where we're headed now," Scotty pointed out.

"We've got to fight them," said Kirk decisively. "Every ship that docks at that station will be vulnerable to attack. The Ravens could spread throughout this sector." His gaze traveled over the officers seated around the table. A plan began to form in his mind.

"When the carrier crew fails to send back a report, the station Ravens will be prepared for the arrival of the *Enterprise,* but they won't be expecting the *Falchion,* and thanks to the Klingons cloaking device they won't see it either. That's our key. The *Enterprise* will be the bait, drawing their firepower and their attention away from the *Falchion's* approach. A landing party will beam aboard the station to take control of communications and docking facilities." Even as he spoke, Kirk was selecting crew members for the foray.

"And if the landing party fails in that attempt?" asked Spock.

"Then the *Falchion* must destroy the station," said Kirk without hesitation.

Spock nodded his agreement and understanding. If he experienced regret at the proposed annihilation of T'rall's construction, he did not reveal it. "Captain, I . . ."

"Yes, Mr. Spock," said Kirk. "You were my first choice for the landing party." He then looked to his communications officer. "I'm only accepting volunteers for this mission."

Uhura met his grim look with a wide smile. Her throaty voice answered him without hesitation. "I've been looking forward to shore leave, Captain."

"Aye, 'tis a welcome chance t' stretch our legs," agreed Scotty amiably.

"Not you, Mr. Scott." Kirk overrode the engineer's

protests. "The *Enterprise* engines will need your supervision. As will the bridge."

Spock's lean frame stiffened. "Captain, on our last Star Base docking, Admiral Bolles was most emphatic about ending your participation in landing party forays."

"Yes, well, if I survive she can't fault me and if I'm killed her censure can't hurt me." Kirk's grin had no effect on the Vulcan's stony features.

"Jim, you mustn't go. More than your death is at stake. If our theory on the nature of these aliens is correct, we cannot risk the chance of your capture. The enemy would gain the expertise of a Federation starship captain."

"And what of my first officer?" demanded Kirk.

"There are certain techniques of Vulcan mental discipline which would effectively disable my mind."

The clash of will between the two officers was fought without words and was over in seconds. With the briefest flicker of his eyes, Kirk acknowledged the truth of Spock's argument. "You'll also need a security force. Keep it small to lower the chances of detection. Stealth will do you more good than phaser power."

McCoy spoke up for the first time since his voice-tape recording had ended. "Captain, there's a strong possibility that there are still people alive at the trading post. Station personnel would be killed for their knowledge, but civilians were probably paralysed and stored for . . . future use. They'll be in need of medical aid and the paralysis antidote which Lieutenant Frazer synthesized."

"Good point, Bones," said Kirk absently. He did a double-take. The concern was typical of his chief medical officer, and for a moment he had hoped . . . but McCoy winced at the nickname. "Thank you, Dr.

McCoy, I'll ask for volunteers among the medical team."

"That won't be necessary, Captain." The doctor's tongue flicked over dry lips. "I'm volunteering to go as a paramedic."

"Len!" cried Dyson. "You can't be serious. You've never set foot on a space colony before." She turned to the captain. "I'd be a much more suitable choice. I know the workings of a space station and . . ."

McCoy gave a stubborn shake of his head. "At the moment I'm your resident expert on the Ravens—you can't leave me here. Besides, it's not that much safer on the *Enterprise*. If this attempt doesn't succeed, the aliens will destroy your ship next."

Spock entered the fray on Dyson's side. "I have a complete record of your knowledge in this matter, Dr. McCoy. Your presence is not required."

"You have a complete record of what I've remembered so far," countered McCoy. "But there's no telling what I might recall later. You can't take the risk of missing any details about their behavior." He turned to Kirk. "And any critter that eats my brain would probably have my amnesia, too, so you don't have to worry about my giving away Federation secrets."

"Do you agree with that, Dr. Dyson?" Kirk demanded.

Dyson remained silent for a moment, then gave a grudging answer. "I can't say for certain . . . but, it's possible."

Spock was less reluctant. "Under those circumstances, Dr. McCoy would be a logical choice for the landing party. At present he is probably the most technically ignorant member of the crew."

Kirk automatically braced himself for McCoy's outburst. It never came. This man accepted Spock's evaluation without comment. Once again Kirk missed his friend, with a stabbing pain that surprised him in its intensity. He shoved the feeling aside. "Dr. McCoy, you'll accompany the landing party."

Standing up from the conference table, Kirk brought the meeting to a close. "We reach Wagner Post in twelve hours. To your stations."

McCoy hefted the neatly assembled medical kit which Nurse Chapel had handed him. "How did you know . . ."

"Let's just say I had a hunch." She slid the frosted door of the wall cabinet to a close. "Based on long experience with doctors in general, and you in particular."

"But I didn't expect to volunteer for this mission," protested McCoy. Chapel and Dyson exchanged a knowing look that only increased his chagrin. "Since when does Star Fleet hire doctors with an instinct for self-annihilation?" He opened the kit and sorted through its contents. "No wonder I became chief medical officer. Promotion due to a high rate of casualties."

"Not true," corrected Chapel as she headed out of the office. "You replaced Dr. Boyce, who is quite happily retired."

"Now that's a man with a good sense of timing," McCoy called after the nurse. Finished with his kit inspection, he snapped the bundle shut.

"It was your choice to go." Dyson leaned back on the edge of the office desk, watching him clip and unclip the heavy pouch to his belt, searching for the proper point of balance for its weight.

McCoy nodded. "Yeah, but aren't you going to try to talk me out of it?"

"Would it do any good?" she asked.

His eyes narrowed at her show of detachment. "No, probably not, but I still wish someone would try."

The door to the chief surgeon's office whisked open again. Dr. Cortejo walked into the room and stopped short at the sight of its unexpected occupants. His irritation at their presence was obvious and he made only a token effort to hide it. "Dr. Dyson, since you have been transferred to the Science department, there is no need for you to report to sick bay."

She jumped off the desk. "No, sir. I was . . ."

Cortejo did not wait for an explanation. "And since you are no longer on the active duty list, Dr. McCoy, your presence here is also unnecessary."

McCoy's brows arched at the brusque dismissal. A flush of anger warmed his face.

"On the contrary, Dr. Cortejo." The precise voice of First Officer Spock rang out from behind the acting chief medical officer. "It is your presence which is unnecessary." Spock walked into the room and placed a stack of tape cassettes on the desk. "Dr. McCoy and I have a great deal of work to do before our departure and his office will suit our purpose admirably."

He leaned over the intercom. "Lt. Uhura and security team A report to Dr. McCoy's office for briefing."

When the Vulcan looked around again, both Cortejo and Dyson were gone.

Six hours later Spock handed McCoy a communicator. "You have become separated from the landing party. What communications channel would you use to contact them?"

"I wouldn't," answered McCoy wearily. The security team had left the office two hours before and he felt like a slow student kept after school. "The exchange would give away both our positions." The doctor flipped open the cover with a flick of the wrist. "But I'd activate the communicator grid so that I could be traced by the landing party."

"Assuming all landing party members except yourself are dead, what would be your next action?"

"Other than prayer?"

Lt. Uhura smiled at the doctor's dismay over the proposed scenario, but it was obvious that Spock expected an answer.

McCoy frowned in thought. "Well, I could head for the connecting spoke that carries the ventilation pipes. Once I worked my way in deep enough to hold off my capture for a few minutes, I'd try to contact the *Falchion*." He twirled a dial on the face of the communicator and showed Spock the setting. "With luck, Mr. Sulu would beam me aboard before the Ravens ate me for supper."

Spock nodded his approval. "And if you were captured nevertheless?"

McCoy tossed the communicator back onto the table between them. "I'm a doctor, Mr. Spock. The next step would be easy for me."

The Vulcan's eyebrows traveled upwards. "A drastic measure."

"I have a good imagination, sir. After hearing Sager's stories, I'd prefer a quick escape."

Uhura shook her head in disagreement. "You say that now, but when you're actually faced with danger, you'll find that it's not that easy to give up." She glanced aside at Spock, expecting the first officer to interject a comment concerning the illogic of Human emotion. Instead, he nodded in agreement.

Discomfited by Uhura's bemused expression, Spock brought the examination to an end. "There is much more you should know, but there is not sufficient time to conduct a thorough orientation. Humans possess a limited capacity for absorbing new information."

"Amen to that," agreed McCoy, rubbing his reddened eyes. His head was whirling with the details Spock had force-fed him for the last few hours.

Spock inserted a tape into the computer terminal. "You and Lt. Uhura are dismissed until 0700 hours. I suggest you use the time to sleep." He turned back to the computer screen and was immediately absorbed in its data.

McCoy waited until he and the lieutenant had reached the safety of an outside corridor before speaking. "Diana must have been pulling my leg about fighting with Spock. I'd rather wrassle a Bengal tiger than cross that man."

Uhura answered him with a velvety laugh that echoed softly down the dimmed passageway. "It was an even match, Dr. McCoy." She laughed again at the confused mixture of emotions on his face. "Take it as a compliment."

They parted company on Deck Five, but McCoy walked past his quarters and did not stop until he reached a cabin on Deck Six. He tapped lightly on the door, a quiet sound that would only be heard if the room's occupant were still awake.

The door opened and he stepped inside.

Diana Dyson walked out of the back section of the cabin. She was wrapped in the warm folds of a long, thick robe; her hair fell loosely over her shoulders. Her face showed signs of fatigue, but her eyes were bright with controlled tension. "Len, you should be asleep by now."

"So should you."

"No, I can't sleep." Dyson tucked a stray lock of hair behind her ear. "Nervous about tomorrow?"

"Who, me?" McCoy wiped his palms on his trousers. "I'm scared silly. My heart's beating so loudly I can hardly hear myself think."

"Have you changed your mind?"

McCoy considered the question for a moment. "No. I've got to go. Bits and pieces of what Sager talked about keep surfacing. Words and phrases that didn't make much sense—they still don't—but they could be useful."

Her softly-spoken concern was replaced by a clinical crispness. "Len, you must realize that this knowledge was part of the trigger for the fugue. You weren't just running away from your wife's remarriage—you were trying to recover information that was vital to the safety of this ship."

"All right." He crossed his arms. "Maybe that was the case, but I still have the amnesia."

Dyson burrowed deeper into her robe. "This mission isn't over yet."

"Yeah, and when it is over the whole matter may be academic. My muddled brains will be walking around inside some blue-skinned . . ." He stopped when Dyson turned away. "Sorry."

She shrugged but still did not face him.

McCoy's eyes traced the curve of her back. The soft cabin lights edged her dark brown hair with a golden aura. "I'd better leave," he said abruptly.

"Please, don't." She turned around. "Not just yet. I could use the company, too." She waved her hand around the empty quarters. "I'm still not used to being alone here."

McCoy gave a shaky laugh. "Diana, you'll have a lot more company than you bargained for if I stay here much longer."

"Oh." A pale pink touched her cheeks. "And I thought you were a gentleman."

"That's why I offered to leave." She didn't answer, so he spoke again. "I'll go now . . . if you want me to." When her silence continued, he stepped away from the doorway and took her into his arms.

After the long kiss, he pulled back but did not let go of her. One hand caressed her upturned face. "Diana, I . . ."

"No, please." She laid a finger against his lips to still the words. "Don't say anything . . . not until you come back." She smiled, to take the edge off her words. "We'll have plenty of time for talking then."

He bent down to kiss her again.

Chapter Twenty

"YOU PUT HUMAN beings in that unholy device?" McCoy came to a dead stop at the threshold of the transporter room. The platform which had held Uhura was now empty. She, and a stack of cargo containers, had dissolved in a glittering cloud. McCoy turned a look of horror on the chief engineer who had effected their departure.

"Dinna look at me as if I'm Jack the Ripper," said Scotty indignantly. "We've got th' best safety record this side of Star Base 5." The engineer reset the levers of the control panel and three more crewmen stepped forward to take their place on the circular grids.

McCoy edged back a step as the high hum of the transporter beams emptied the chamber once more.

Spock, data tablet in hand, checked three names off his crew list and double-checked his equipment list. Then, and only then, did he look up. McCoy had not moved from the doorway. "It is your turn to board the *Falchion*. Take your position on the transporter platform." This latter statement took on a strong declarative tone in view of McCoy's mutinous reluctance to move any further into the room.

The doctor marched forward at Spock's command, but only for a few steps. "Are you sure this thing is safe?" asked McCoy.

"Yes," said Spock impatiently, but he stopped at the

last moment. The intended retort was never uttered. "The last twenty years have brought about a high degree of sophistication and reliability in matter transportation. Malfunctions are rare."

McCoy followed the Vulcan up the low steps of the transporter platform. "Maybe, but you can't tell me I ever willingly went through that matter-mixer."

Scotty responded to the doctor's words with a deep chortle.

"You did in fact use the transporter," said Spock as they assumed their positions on the circular grids. "Though no one could ever have accused you of being enthusiastic about the process."

"Glad to know I didn't lose all common sense in my old age," muttered McCoy before he dissolved in a shower of particle beams.

Lt. Palmer touched hand to ear. "Captain, Mr. Scott reports that the last of the landing party has beamed aboard the *Falchion.*"

Kirk waved an acknowledgement to the communications officer. "That's it, Sulu. We begin radio silence from this point on."

"*Yes, sir.* Falchion *out.*" Within seconds the image of a Klingon battlecruiser on the bridge's viewscreen faded into nonexistence.

Lt. Kyle checked the instruments on the science station panel. "All sensor readings on the *Falchion* are gone, sir. Cloaking device operational."

"Maintain course, Mr. Leslie. Full impulse power," ordered Kirk.

"Aye, Captain," answered the helmsman.

Ensign Benus scanned the navigation coordinates. "We'll reach Wagner Post in one hour and thirteen minutes."

Kirk's fingers drummed uneasily on the side of the command chair. Bridge duty had always rotated among a hand-picked group of crewmembers, so none of the voices or faces at the duty stations was unknown to him, but the *Falchion* had carried away the best and most familiar of that select crew all at once.

He glanced to his left and right and frowned at the empty space around him. McCoy and Spock often acted as if each side of his chair was an official post they should fill. Their absence exacerbated the changes on the bridge. "Frazer, come over here."

"Sir?" The Martian scientist looked up from the bioscience station.

"I still have some questions about the Ravens." Kirk motioned Frazer to stand to the left of the command chair.

"Eets like swimming through borscht," explained Chekov, having found a useful metaphor for describing the shortcomings of the navigation screen while under the effects of the cloaking device.

"That is hardly a scientific assessment," said Spock as he leaned over the ensign's shoulder.

"Vhatever," answered Chekov recklessly. Time away from the *Enterprise,* and Spock's repressing influence, had seriously undermined his habitual struggle to maintain the dignity and solemn demeanor appropriate to a starship officer. "It makes my job very difficult. The cloaking device needs much improvement."

"Ensign, are you suggesting that you would approve of greater technological advancement for the Klingons?" Spock judged that he could spare sufficient time to instill a renewed sense of discipline in the ensign.

"No, sir! Certainly not." Sulu and Aziz let Chekov flounder on his own. Older, and wiser, they had snapped back to shipboard demeanor as soon as the landing party boarded the *Falchion*. "I vas simply . . . that is to say, I . . ."

Spock continued. "Intelligence reports, and our own experience in conflicts with the Empire, have indicated that Klingon crews can operate a battlecruiser with considerable efficiency while cloaked."

"Yes, Mr. Spock." Chekov tried to salvage the situation with an about face. "Eet was only difficult at first, vhen I vas new to the *Falchion*. Now I am quite good at reading the sensors." Too late, he realized that his words were a rather arrogant boast.

"We shall see, Ensign."

The dry retort confirmed Chekov's worst fears. Now he would be held accountable to an impossibly high standard. The ensign lapsed into a worried silence, his concentration focused on the snowy navigation panel.

The Vulcan decided that this exchange had resulted in the desired effect and turned his attention to Sulu.

"Coordinates set for Wagner Post," said the helmsman.

"Ahead warp factor four, Mr. Sulu."

"Aye, Mr. Spock." Sulu kept his comments to a safe minimum as he eased the Klingon ship into warp drive.

"Just don't bump Scotty's tail end," cautioned a muffled voice from behind them. Juan Cruz's head was enmeshed in the folds of his red security shirt. His flailing elbows brought grunts of protest from Archer and Rivera, who had already exchanged their ship's uniforms for copies of the purple jumpsuits worn by the Wagner Post maintenance crews.

Uhura stepped up onto the captain's throne, out of the crowded cockpit, and took a deep breath. "Forget a better cloaking device, the Klingons need a bigger bridge." She leaned over the edge of the platform to hand the first officer a neatly folded change of clothing. "Purple is definitely not your color, Mr. Spock, but purple is all I've got."

Spock accepted the bundle without comment. Over the years, the Vulcan had learned to recognize, if not completely understand, the role humor played in releasing tension among his Human companions. He allowed the banter of the crew to flow around him unimpeded.

"Since we're maintenance workers, these must be our wrenches." Archer began unpacking pistol phasers from a cargo box and handing them out to the other members of the landing party. He was left with one extra. "Dr. McCoy?"

McCoy eyed the weapon with distaste. He made no move to take it. "I'm not a gunslinger."

Uhura jumped back down into the crew pit. "You'll be a corpse if you aren't properly armed." Taking the phaser from Archer, she hung it onto the doctor's utility belt.

"Ma'am, if my life depends on firing that thing, you might as well bury me now. I couldn't hit the broad side of a barn."

"Why would you wish to?" asked Spock.

"Sir?"

"That was a Vulcan joke, Dr. McCoy," Uhura explained.

Spock corrected her immediately. "Lieutenant, Vulcans do not recognize the concept of humor."

Uhura's smile only confused McCoy more.

"Mr. Spock, we're entering the trading post scanning range." Sulu's words silenced the room.

The clearsteel dome of Wagner Post glittered like a jewel dropped into a black pond. Its four rings were golden ripples, spreading away from the faceted center. Sparkling droplets marked the presence of ships moored to its outermost docking ring. T'rall's creation appeared calm and peaceful.

"Sensor data?" asked Kirk as he studied the trading post image on the bridge viewscreen.

"Indeterminate life forms, Captain," answered Lt. Kyle. "We're still too far away to identify specific biological profiles." He adjusted controls on the science station panel and heaved an audible sigh. "Even if we get closer, I can't do much better. The patchwork repairs on the computer systems are affecting all my readings."

"I can't attack this station on a hunch." Kirk's fist hammered an insistent rhythm on the arm of his chair. "I've got to *know* that the Ravens have taken over."

"Captain, I've established contact with the Wagner Post communications officer," announced Lt. Palmer from her station. "Hailing frequencies open."

"Welcome, Captain Kirk," came Timmo's soft, whispering greeting. *"Stand by for Post Manager Friel."*

"For god's sake, Kirk, your ship is a wreck," boomed the station commander. *"I only hope the Klingons are in worse shape."*

"The Klingons are dead," answered Kirk. Strictly speaking, it was the truth, even though it was not his doing; but then Friel probably knew that already. However, the *Enterprise* damage report Kirk gave her was an exaggeration, although not nearly as much of one as he would have liked.

"Then you'll be laid up in our dockyards for weeks," said Friel with the calculating tone of a woman whose profit margin was dependent on ship repairs. *"I'll clear anchor space for you right now."*

Kirk lowered his voice. "Well, Frazer?"

The lieutenant shook his head. "I can't tell from the

210

voice. The Ravens are perfect mimics, right down to the character quirks of their victims."

The captain looked back over his shoulder. "Palmer, request visual contact with the communications center." Their refusal would serve as confirmation of the takeover.

"Enterprise, *prepare for docking instructions.*" The view of deep space was exchanged for the visage of the cobalt-blue Andorian Kirk had seen on his last visit to the station.

Kirk stared in amazement at the technician. "Good God, I was ready to fire on that station . . ."

"It's a trap," declared Frazer emphatically. "He's being coerced, or possibly drugged."

"How can you tell?" Kirk saw nothing out of the ordinary in the alien's stolid demeanor.

"The set of the antennae," explained Frazer. His finger traced the cant of the delicate appendages. "They're tilted back along the skull, a position reserved for exchanges between family members. With outsiders the antennae are held upright to optimize hearing."

"Captain, the pilot droids are approaching," warned Leslie.

"Yellow Alert," ordered Kirk. "Benus, lock phasers on droids."

"Phasers locked." At the captain's command she fired. "All droids destroyed."

"Visual contact with Wagner Post has been severed," announced Palmer as the main screen filled with meaningless squiggles.

Kyle raised his voice. "Engine activity increasing in all dockyard vessels . . ."

"Well, that's the diversion I wanted," said Kirk. He signaled the helm. "180 degrees about and full impulse power. Let's get the hell out of here."

* * *

The landing party materialized in the center of the crystal dome.

Chekov had declared the area empty after a hasty sensor scan and, as he'd predicted, there was no one present to witness their sudden appearance. As soon as the transporter beam faded, Spock activated his tricorder, sweeping the unit across the darkened portals encircling them. "No Ravens in the immediate vicinity." He checked another indicator. "The communications center lies there." His index finger pointed in one direction, then abruptly shifted several degrees to the right. "But we shall approach from connecting shaft Delta."

Uhura silently motioned the three security guards forward to the designated corridor, one of eight spokes in the wheel-shaped station structure.

"Doctor," said Spock very softly. "There is indeed a solid floor beneath your feet."

"Yes, I know that," replied McCoy calmly, though his eyes remained shut. "I can feel it."

"Then I suggest you accept the evidence of your tactile senses. Otherwise, I shall be forced to leave you here."

"No, that won't be necessary, sir." McCoy opened his eyes and gulped audibly. By carefully keeping his line of sight centered on the back of Spock's head, McCoy walked over the transparent deck, over the limitless reaches of space yawning beneath his feet. He breathed a silent prayer of thanks when he finally reached a surface that was solid to the eyes as well as the feet.

Moving in single file, the landing party stalked quietly through the long corridor. The translucent lighting panels set flush into the ceiling were dimmed, limiting vision, but the passage appeared deserted.

At the juncture with the first station ring, the team members gathered into a bunch. Spock crouched by the corner, phaser drawn, listening intently. He peered around the edge to check out the wider passageway which crossed the spoke, then turned back to Uhura. "The crew quarters are located on this ring," he observed. The section was obviously deserted.

"Looks like the Ravens have gobbled the crew up," muttered McCoy.

Rivera reached a hand toward his tricorder, but the Vulcan stopped him from activating its sensors. "We shall have to rely on our own senses. Continued operation of the tricorder will give away our position."

Lieutenant Uhura nodded. "Besides, the captain's diversion seems to have worked. They're probably all chasing after the *Enterprise.*"

She kept the lead as the landing party resumed its single-file progression toward the next ring intersection; McCoy trailed last. His initial fear had been subsumed by the effort of moving quietly and quickly through a claustrophobic world of cold hard metal. The weapon in his hand was heavy and uncomfortable and, if he wasn't attentive, it displayed a disconcerting tendency to aim itself at Spock's back. The soft echo of his own boots hitting the deck only increased McCoy's disorientation . . . He turned to look behind.

"Spock!"

The Vulcan whirled about. He took immediate aim at the Raven as its weapon sprayed red beams of light over McCoy and continued sweeping across the corridor. Yet, even as the rays arced towards him, Spock did not return fire. He delayed an extra fraction of a second, changing the setting of his phaser before pulling its trigger. The two opposing beams crossed paths, flared into brightness, then faded. The Raven dropped. Spock remained standing.

He rushed to where the doctor slumped against a wall. "Dr. McCoy, are you injured?"

After a moment's silence, McCoy took a shuddering breath and stood upright. "No, Mr. Spock." He rubbed the side of his temple. "I just . . . felt a little dizzy, but it's passed." He met the science officer's piercing gaze. "Really, sir, I'm okay now."

"You did not fire your phaser."

McCoy looked blankly at the weapon in his hand. "No, I guess I froze." He winced again. "I told you I make a lousy soldier."

Spock studied the blue-skinned alien, its heavy body sprawled face down, stunned into unconsciousness. The shattered remains of its toy rifle, crushed by the fall of the massive chest, littered the deck. "Your hesitation was not unreasonable. I'll explain later." He grabbed McCoy's elbow and propelled him along the corridor to catch up with the rest of the landing party.

At their approach, Uhura ducked her head back from an inspection of the juncture of the corridor and the second station ring. "All clear, Mr. Spock. The communications center is to our right, three doors down."

Spock snapped his phaser to firing position. "Proceed with extreme caution."

The landing party stepped into the empty passageway of the ring, moving along its gently curving wall. Spock's acute hearing gave him only a split-second warning of the trap. It was not enough time in which to react.

Doors on either side of them sprang open. Blue forms jumped out from the shadowed portals, moving quickly to block both ends of the passage, cutting off any retreat. The *Enterprise* crew was surrounded by armed Ravens.

One tall, strongly muscled alien strutted forward from the others. It was dressed in the tattered remains of a Klingon uniform. "We have been expecting you, Earthling worms."

Chapter Twenty-One

THE RAVEN COMMANDER spat onto the deck. "So, Esserass and Aeloran failed to capture the *Enterprise*. Typical Federation incompetence. If the Queen had allowed me to leave, I would have led the attack myself, ensuring victory. Instead, your ship has limped from battle to battle until this foolish attempt to infiltrate the home nest." It thumped a fist against its chest. Its black crest bristled. "I'm a Klingon warrior— your shallow tricks cannot fool me."

At their leader's signal, several of the blue-skinned aliens stepped forward to relieve the landing party of its weapons. "Gently, gently," it urged. "Do not scratch them . . . just yet." The blood-red eyes of the Raven commander ran over the Humans, studying their faces. "I see only followers here." It stopped briefly before the Vulcan, but shrugged away in disgust. "Second in command, but not the leader. So, your captain lacks the courage to carry through his own knavery. It matters little in the long run. Even now, my forces are pursuing the *Enterprise*. Your captain will be killed in battle and his ship taken from him."

"Commander Kyron!" With a scrabble of clawed feet against the metal deck, a Raven messenger ran up to the group. It spoke with the breathless voice of a young Andorian. "Report from Manager Friel. Sensors can't locate the enemy vessel which activated the transporter beams."

"Incompetents!" Kyron's persona took a half-hearted swipe at the bearer of the news. "They didn't materialize out of thin air." It turned to Spock. "Where is the craft which brought you here?" It did not expect an answer and none was given. "Your silence is admirable, but it will not last long. Very soon, you will tell me all your secrets, all I need to know to conquer this entire sector. Just as Esserass knew how to lure Captain Neil to his doom; just as Neil knew how to trick Manager Friel."

A wave of its arm set the landing party into a forced march out of the communications area and back into the connecting corridor. They were pushed and prodded past the darkened third ring where trading-store display windows had been shattered and their goods plundered. In contrast, the larger fourth ring was alive with light and activity. Ravens walked purposefully through the curving passageways, dutifully following the maintenance routine of their victims.

The first larval form of the Raven did not appear until the group had traveled nearly a quarter mile through the docking ring. The green-skinned alien was burdened with an odd assortment of cartons containing sealed food pouches, vitamin supplement capsules, and boxed liquids. It carried the supplies through a wide doorway ahead.

"The Queen grows hungry," commented Kyron. "She has been producing many green hatchlings." The commander paused briefly when they reached the open portal of the cargo bay.

Deep in the shadows, a massive blue-black form lay quivering on the deck, dwarfing the shuttlecraft beside it. The round slug-like body of the alien bore no head or limbs. It rested mute and immobile as green-skinned Ravens scurried about the distended bulk, stroking and petting its surface.

The mass shifted at the approach of the hatchling carrying its load of goods. A gaping pink orifice took form at the near end of the shapeless creature; a soft sucking cry issued forth. One by one, the green Raven tossed each of the packaged items into the mouth.

"Our Queen," announced Kyron's persona. "Quite a vision of regal splendor. I long to introduce her to certain members of the Imperial High Council." The Raven fixed Spock with its round eyes; its rough Klingon voice took on an air of arrogance. "The Queen impels us to conquest, but I have planned the details of our victories. She is linked to our minds and controls our will, yet she has no real intelligence. Not so different from those I once served."

With a roar of laughter the Klingon commander resumed the march along the docking ring. Its soft chuckling continued until the group reached a cargo storage room. The security doors were unlocked, opened wide to allow easy access to the interior. The deck had been cleared of shipping crates; in their place, the bodies of over a dozen paralyzed humanoids had been flung into a careless pile.

The commander kicked one of the unmoving forms. "These civilians have no technical knowledge to offer us. They await their proper use as food for the Queen. Fortunately, the hatchlings can live for years before their transformation, waiting for a proper victim." It looked over the landing party members. "But now we have many brains to offer our young. The hatchlings will not have to wait."

Kyron walked over to Archer. "Who shall be first? You, perhaps?" It scraped the man's neck with its claws, marking four lines of oozing blood. Archer fell to the deck. "But do not worry that you will be ignored," the Raven assured Rivera and Cruz. "Eventually, you two will also join the ranks of the Queen's defenders." It spread its arms out to embrace the two security guards, sinking the needle-sharp tips of its talons into their shoulders. Like Archer, they collapsed.

The commander did not bother to taunt Uhura. "To think the Emperor made peace with an army of women and children." It pointed to the still bodies of the civilians. "Stand away, so there will be no danger that you are chosen for our purposes. You will serve for food when we grow hungry, but we want no part of your inferior spirit."

It approached McCoy next. One long finger stabbed at the doctor's medical pouch. "What do you carry there?" The alien trailed the claw up the front of McCoy's jumpsuit until it reached the neckline. The scaled hand curled; its claws tickled McCoy's chin, but did not break the skin. "Hmmm?"

The doctor held his head very still. "Medical supplies."

The alien hissed. "A doctor?"

McCoy could not nod, but he blinked his eyes in assent.

The clawed hand dropped away. "Typical Federation corruption. We will not sully our fighting force with one who panders to the weaknesses of mind and body." It pointed to where Uhura stood. "Go, there, with the woman."

Finally, it turned to Spock. "You, however, are not weak." A hand lashed out, leaving a fine line of green across the Vulcan's cheek.

Spock remained standing. "I appear to be immune to the paralyzing effects of your venom." He did not mention that the scratch had numbed the right side of his face and that a deeper cut would probably have the desired effect.

The alien hissed again. "Very well, you shall watch. And if you are chosen, the hatchling shall feed on you without the pain-killing effects of these." It fluttered its claws in Spock's face. "You shall feel your skull cracked open."

It pointed to one of the armed Ravens. "Jaeger, bring a hatchling here, so that it may feed on the knowledge of our prisoners."

"Yes, my lord." The Raven executed a Klingon martial salute and left the room. It soon returned accompanied by a green alien.

The tips of the hatchling's beak rasped together as it caught sight of the motionless bodies on the floor. With a low clucking sound it bent down and grabbed one of the security guards. Oblivious to McCoy and Uhura's horrified cries, it brought the head of its victim up to its powerful beak. The sharp tips took hold at the top of the man's forehead and at the base of the neck, piercing the skin. The pressure increased.

Kyron's persona listened appreciatively to the loud snap of cracking bone. "It must be done quickly, while the body is still living, because the memory traces deteriorate quickly."

The crown of the skull split open, revealing the soft tissue of the brain inside. With a swift thrust of its beak, the Raven plucked the organ from the skeletal shell and swallowed it whole. The body slithered from its grasp onto the deck. Juan Cruz was dead. Smears of blood and clear liquid trickled from the empty cavity above his forehead.

The hatchling let loose a high-pitched cry as its limbs first trembled then locked into rigidity. The bulging sac on its neck swelled in size, growing like an inflated balloon that threatened to engulf the alien's head. A brilliant blue color transfused the distended skin, then spread quickly over the hatchling's body. The limp pale down on its head bristled upright and darkened to black.

The swelling subsided gradually, but even before it had disappeared entirely, the newly transformed Raven began to move again. Its eyes widened. Its beak opened and closed. It stared unblinkingly at the captive landing party. Then the voice of the dead Cruz issued from its throat. "Commander, the cloaked *Falchion* beamed us aboard the station while the *Enterprise* created a diversion." It pointed to Spock. "The crew is waiting for his instructions."

"The *Falchion?* My ship?" roared the former Klingon warrior. "They found my battlecruiser?"

The Cruz persona continued its revelations. "The *Enterprise* is leading the station ships into a trap. Captain Kirk planned to lie about the damage to his ship—he still has enough power to wipe out our forces."

"This treachery shall be avenged!" raged the alien commander. "Jaeger, take these soldiers to the dockyards. Kath will need reinforcements in his combat against the *Enterprise*. Go!"

Kyron pulled one of the commandeered phasers off its belt and handed it to the alien Cruz. The transformed Raven trained the weapon on its former superior officer without hesitation while the Kyron persona confronted Spock. "You shall be next—your signal can recall the *Falchion* and your Vulcan brain will ensure the defeat of this Federation starship."

"You will never have the use of it," said Spock. "I can send my mind into itself, beyond recovery." Silently, he began the first steps of that process.

The alien watched the Vulcan's skin turn pale in response to his bio-control. "Enough! You are a dishonorable race, but a truthful one. In this event, I will kill you outright. Not such a great loss—your brain would probably taste vile."

The Raven aimed its disrupter at Spock's chest. A talon curled around the trigger.

Uhura's scream was precisely timed. The alien's weapon jerked in her direction, but the cutting beam went wild as McCoy's weight landed on its back. The hiss of a hypospray was lost amidst the bellowing yell of the commander. One sweep of its powerful arm dislodged the doctor and flung him across the room and against a wall. Yet even as McCoy fell to the deck, Kyron crumpled as well.

In the same instant, Spock aimed a series of rapid karate chops at the Cruz persona by his side. One blow loosened the alien's hold on its weapon; subsequent punches had minimal effect on the alien's rock-solid physique, but they served to distract its attention from Uhura. The lieutenant picked up the discarded phaser. One blast on heavy stun stopped "Cruz" from ripping out Spock's neck. The second blast rendered the Raven unconscious.

Spock gave the spreading green bruises on his hands a cursory glance, then dismissed both them and the accompanying pain from his mind. "Thank you, Lt. Uhura."

"Any time, Mr. Spock." She stood guard over the aliens while the Vulcan moved quickly to where McCoy had landed.

"McCoy?"

The doctor pulled himself upright with a groan. "I'm fine, sir." He moved again and winced. "Well, I've been better."

"My commendations," said Spock, helping McCoy to his feet. "You succeeded in stunning the alien."

"Oh, I think I did better than that," McCoy boasted.

One hand touched the nape of his own neck. "One night Sager grabbed me and laid a plastic butter knife against the back of my neck. 'Cut them free right here,' he said, then laughed and let me go. Evidently, he had used a knife to cut that portion of an alien's spinal cord."

Spock quickly grasped the effects of McCoy's action. "How long will the alien nervous system be inoperative?"

"Damned if I know," the doctor answered. "That neural paralyzer is meant for use on Humans."

Spock raised one brow. "We shall have to rely on your injection. I do not think the commander would welcome a knife wound at our hands." He pointed to the Raven commander who was crawling groggily to its knees.

Uhura dropped into a crouch, her phaser aimed at the rising alien. Only Spock's signal stayed her fire.

The Raven shook itself. Clawed hands reached up to its beaked face. A stream of glutteral Klingon oaths issued forth from its throat. "Vipers that dare take my ship! My crew! I shall rend them until they are unfit to feed ship mites!"

Spock approached the alien. "Commander Kyron, we shall endeavor to help you to that end."

"I need no help from weakling Humans to avenge this insult," roared Kyron's mind, freed from its alien control. It staggered to its feet.

"I am a Vulcan," corrected Spock testily. "And I assure you I can be of assistance."

"Mr. Spock," called out Uhura. Her phaser had switched its aim to the Raven who had consumed Cruz's brain. The prone body was beginning to twitch. "This one is also regaining consciousness."

"Uhura, set another stun . . ."

"Kill it!" demanded Kyron looking down at the

guard. "Once awake, its agitation will disturb the Queen." When Uhura did not obey the order immediately, the commander reached for its disrupter.

"No, wait," called out McCoy. "We can save his mind, too." He pulled another hypo from his medkit and knelt by the Raven's body. The tip of the slim metal chamber made contact with the right branch of the divided spinal cord and hissed as its contents were ejected.

The Raven gave a low moan. Its blood-red eyes blinked; one hand reached up to touch the bristling crest atop its head, then moved down to the beak on its face. The beak opened and Cruz began to scream. Kyron stepped forward. One savage blow of its fist stilled the cries. "Human scum. Only Klingons have the true spirit of a conquering race."

Spock's firm grip on McCoy's shoulder kept the doctor from lunging at the commander. "Dr. McCoy, attend to the welfare of the landing party and the civilians. Lt. Uhura will assist you in reviving them."

McCoy scowled, but he reset the dials on the hypo and pulled ampules of the paralysis antidote out of his medkit. While he and Uhura brought Archer and Rivera back to consciousness, Spock and Kyron discussed strategy.

"We have little time in which to act," warned Kyron. "Soon the Queen will sense my defection and her forces will organize against us."

Spock pulled a communicator out of a pocket. "Fortunately, we have the resources of the *Falchion* . . ."

"We?" cried Kyron. Its taloned hand grasped the front of Spock's jumpsuit and shook him fiercely. "*My* ship." Abruptly, Kyron released its hold. "Even the Queen's influence could not make me destroy it. Now it has become a hidden dagger with which to strike her down." The alien threw back its beaked head and laughed.

Spock tugged his suit back into order. "We must devise a plan . . ."

"Silence!" roared Kyron. "I know what must be done." It snatched the communicator out of Spock's hand. "I will go to the Queen's chamber and transmit my coordinates to the *Falchion*. Your crew will beam a photon mine to my location. The explosion will destroy the Queen who impels these monsters. Then even you and your weakling Human companions can deal with her minions."

"There will be little time for you to escape," observed Spock.

"There will be *no* time for an escape," said Kyron scornfully. "What does that matter if I destroy these walking excretions? Far better to die in the glory of battle than to live in this blasphemous shell." It thumped its blue-skinned chest.

Spock nodded gravely. "Very well. I will arrange the attack. However, the explosion will destroy the outer ring of the station. Since we cannot beam aboard the *Falchion* without giving away its existence, we must relocate to another section."

McCoy was kneeling by the side of a man still limp from the numbing effects of the Raven poison. "I need more time! These people can't be moved yet." He waved a hand at the eight civilians who were slowly regaining their coordination. Uhura and Rivera had helped most of them into sitting positions against the wall. Archer was administering stimulants, but they were still weak and disoriented.

"Why save defective refuse?" spat Kyron. "Each moment we delay increases our risk of detection. Call your crew, Vulcan. I go now." Pushing Spock aside with a sweep of its arm, Kyron marched out of the room.

"We must leave before the explosion," announced Spock to the landing party crew. "As soon as this ring loses pressure the damaged area will be sealed off from the rest of the structure." Uhura and the security guards began urging their charges to their feet.

Spock yanked a communicator from McCoy's belt. He flipped the top back and set the frequency. His exchange with the *Falchion* crew was terse and brief, giving Sulu no chance for questions or arguments and the Ravens no chance to trace the origin of the transmission. As soon as the contact was severed, Spock checked the progress of the evacuation. The room was clear except for McCoy and a half dozen unmoving bodies. "We must leave *now*, doctor, or we shall all be killed."

The doctor ran his scanner over the robed form of a Tellarite merchant. "The other five are dead, but I'm getting a weak pulse from this one." He administered a hasty injection.

Spock grabbed the Tellarite's arms and pulled him up, hoisting the bulky body onto his shoulder. "Run," the Vulcan instructed McCoy, and set the pace for their escape out of the room.

McCoy and Spock caught up with the others as they headed for the nearest corridor leading off the docking ring. The civilians were moving more quickly now. After an initial confusion they had absorbed a sense of urgency from the landing party. Spock's furry burden was recovered sufficiently to walk on his own feet, though he mumbled groggy oaths at having been awakened from his sleep.

Archer was the first to reach the safety of the corridor. He inspected the controls of the vacuum safety doors of the portal as Uhura and Rivera herded the civilians across its threshold. McCoy and Spock, covering the tail end of the procession, were still several yards away when the communicator on the first officer's belt gave a warning beep.

"Kyron has reached the Queen's chamber—45 seconds until detonation," announced Spock calmly. He prodded the Tellarite merchant into a faster waddle.

"What's your hurry, Mr. Spock?"

The first officer whirled around at the mocking words. A blue-skinned Raven stood in the middle of the passageway. It held a phaser.

Spock froze in place. "Good evening, Manager Friel."

"The Queen will be most unhappy if you leave us so soon." The Raven glanced at the small group standing behind the Vulcan. "All of you will return now."

"The Queen wants me unharmed, for the information I possess. I will come peaceably if you let the others go," offered Spock.

"You aren't in any position to bargain," laughed Friel's persona.

"Is this the way you treat your paying customers?" Spock nodded towards the Tellarite merchant. "It seems a poor way of doing business."

When the Raven hesitated, Spock continued. "The Queen doesn't understand the essentials of good management, as you do." Spock casually waved McCoy and the Tellarite toward the entrance to the corridor. "Why disturb business clients with the internal concerns of the station's operation?"

The alien did not answer, but it made no move to stop the escape of the doctor and the merchant as they ducked past the corridor portal. Spock was left standing alone in the ring passageway.

The Raven beckoned him forward with a wave of the phaser. "No more delays, Mr. Spock." A searing white light blossomed behind the alien, etching a fiery halo around its body. "You will come with . . ."

The words were lost in the roar of heated air that blew through the length of the fourth ring. An explosive wind jerked the Raven high off the deck; a rain of sharp-edged metal sliced through its body. Spock—lifted by the same driving force—writhed in midair, striving to turn his back to the fire and the cutting fragments. He felt the jolt of shrapnel burying into his chest, the shock of his body slamming against a wall.

He blacked out before he felt the pain.

Chapter Twenty-Two

"SURRENDER YOUR SHIP or die!"

"No reply, Lt. Palmer." Kirk leaned forward in the bridge command chair, studying the viewscreen and the ships massed upon it. At half impulse power, the *Enterprise* was just staying ahead of the motley assortment of trading vessels, passenger liners, and scoutships.

"The Vegan tradeship is probably the most powerful," said Lt. Kyle, pointing to the source of the radio transmission. "It's a renovated assault craft, but the basic arsenal seems intact. Combined with the two Andorian scouts, it could do some damage."

"We can't take *any* damage," warned Scotty, looking up from the engineering station.

"What's the maximum speed for an assault craft?" asked Kirk.

"Three-quarter impulse power," said Kyle, consulting the computer. "The scouts are a bit slower."

"And what about the rest of the . . . fleet?" Kirk knew his disdain for the trading post forces could be dangerous. In its weakened state, the *Enterprise* was no match for the rag-tag band if they attacked all at once.

Kyle took a minute to evaluate the capabilities of the remaining ships. "Most are going to do little better than half impulse power."

"Then we can outrun the bunch of them," snorted

Scotty. He was making no attempt to hide his contempt.

"If we outrun them," said Kirk thoughtfully, "they'll just return to the station. We need to destroy them. The trick will be getting the forces to spread out so we can take them one at a time."

"This is Lord Kath, Captain Kirk. Spare yourself and your crew an agonizing death—submit now to my authority!"

"No reply, Captain?" inquired Palmer.

"No reply." Kirk swiveled to face the science station. "Kyle, run an intelligence check on this Lord Kath. What do we know about him?" The captain waited impatiently for the answer. Spock's ability to directly interpret computer language had made his responses almost immediate.

"There is no *Lord* Kath," said Kyle at last. "Not on the *Falchion* and not anywhere in the Klingon military. However, there is a record of a communications officer named Kath."

The news was met with scattered laughter from around the bridge. Kirk grinned broadly. "So we're fighting a crewmember with delusions of grandeur." And little tactical skill. "Lt. Palmer, open ship-to-ship."

"Hailing frequencies open, sir."

"Hear me, 'Lord' Kath." Kirk dripped scorn on the title. "This is Captain James T. Kirk of the U.S.S. *Enterprise*. I won't surrender my ship to the dregs from a Klingon cockpit. I wait to hear from a true Klingon warrior . . ."

The roar of outrage from the communications officer baffled the translators. On the main viewscreen, the image of the Vegan assault craft pulled ahead of the Wagner forces.

"That was even easier than I expected," mused Kirk.

"Mr. Leslie, increase speed to three-quarter impulse power. Keep that Vegan ship on our tail, but make it work to stay there."

Within minutes the attack force had lost the tight structure of a single formation. Instead, the Vegan flagship headed a long string of vessels, each moving according to its maximum speed. Kirk studied the line until he judged the distance between ships to be sufficient.

"Let's give the over-eager Kath just what he's been waiting for. Cut speed, Mr. Leslie," he ordered the helm.

The *Enterprise* came to a dead halt in space.

"Not yet, Benus," Kirk cautioned the ensign against firing phasers prematurely. "Let the lead ship get closer . . . closer . . ."

Palmer's fingers touched the metal spiral in her ear. "Another transmission from 'Lord' Kath."

The guttural Klingon voice, its anger barely under control, resumed its warnings. *"You are a fool, Captain Kirk. We know your shields are gone and your weapon power is depleted. Now your engines have failed."*

"Take careful aim," ordered Kirk. "We can't afford to waste any phaser power."

"Locked on target, Captain. One blast should do it."

"Fire!"

The bridge lights dimmed as ship's power surged to the weapons.

"I shall rejoice to see your brain torn from . . ." The threat was never completed. A single beam of phaser fire reduced the assault craft to blazing rubble. Seconds later the flames flickered out in the cold vacuum of space.

A cheer rang out from the bridge crew. Even Kirk could not resist a fierce smile at the victory. He preferred a fair fight to trickery of this kind, but in the final analysis he preferred to win. "Well done, Benus." He allowed the crew an extra minute of rowdiness, then pulled them back to order. "This war isn't over yet. Helm, one hundred and eighty degrees about. Full impulse power."

The *Enterprise* swung around in a graceful arc, gaining speed as she faced her attackers, overtaking them one by one, and dealing well-placed phaser blasts.

"*Enterprise* 8, Ravens 0," crowed Leslie as the ensign picked off another passenger liner. "Four more to go . . ."

"Captain!" Lt. Kyle's anxious voice cut through the air. "Sensor scans show another attack force coming from the trading post. Tight V-formation, four Class Two scouts led by a Tellarite escort."

"Damn." Kirk knew the power of an escort vessel. The Tellarites used the heavily shielded ships to guard their mining operations, especially the illegal ventures. "The Ravens know I lied. Somehow they've been warned that the *Enterprise* is strong enough to offer resistance." Which meant that the landing party had been captured.

"Open hailing frequencies." If the tactic worked once . . .

Palmer shook her head. "They are not accepting radio transmissions, Captain."

So this commander was not to be tricked into spreading his forces too thin. "Scotty . . ."

"Ye can have shields or ye can have phasers, but ye can't have both. An' if we crack another dilithium crystal, ye won't have either."

Fight and be killed—or turn tail and run. Kirk had never run from a fight before. "Kyle, what's our best time to reach the nearest Federation outpost."

"On impulse power, over four months."

The second attack force was now close enough to

appear on the viewscreen. Kirk studied the growing image. Using the trading post as their center of operations, the Ravens could do a lot of damage in four months. They could spread throughout the entire sector, follow trade routes to a dozen colonized planets. "Cut engines, Mr. Leslie. Let them come to us. All power to phasers, Mr. Scott."

The starship phasers began firing as soon as the Raven ships were in range. "Three scouts destroyed, one crippled," counted out Kyle. "But the escort is getting close enough to return fire . . ."

"Phaser power drained." Benus pushed futilely at the weapons control panel. "Recharge in two minutes."

The *Enterprise* rocked under the impact of an energy bolt.

"Shields buckling, Captain!" cried Scotty. "The next one will blast right through us."

Kirk tensed for the next, and final, attack. It never came. The Tellarite ship hung in space, unmoving. "Ship to ship, Palmer."

"Still no response from the Ravens," answered Palmer.

"Phasers recharged, Captain." Benus's fingers hovered over the weapons control panel. "Target still in range."

"Hold your fire, ensign." Kirk turned to the science station. "What do you make of it, Mr. Kyle?"

"Long-range sensor scans indicate an explosion at the trading post. Given the strength of the energy reading, the station has experienced substantial damage."

"He's done it!" exulted Kirk. "Spock found a way to hit them hard."

Even as he spoke, the Tellarite ship began to retreat. Leslie monitored its direction. "The escort flight coordinates are for Tellarite space, not Wagner Trading Post."

"Let them go," said Kirk. "At impulse speed, they'll be in deep space for months. We can pick them up later. Right now the landing party will need reinforcements. Helm, plot a course back to the trading post. Scotty, what's our best speed for getting there?"

The query moved Scotty to an immediate concern for his engines. "You're askin' for speed when it's all I can do t' keep the ship from fallin' apart? This last battle round with the Ravens has probably ripped all my patches t' shreds. By rights, we shouldna move from this spot for at least five hours."

"Five hours." Kirk looked askance at his chief engineer, yet before he could challenge the estimate he was interrupted by Lt. Palmer.

"Captain, I'm receiving sub-space radio transmissions from a Federation starship. The U.S.S. *Lexington* has entered this sector."

"Just after the nick o' time," snorted Scotty.

Kirk turned back to the disgruntled engineer. "On the contrary, Mr. Scott. I'm sure the *Lexington* will be glad to take us in tow to Wagner Post."

"Nay, Captain," cried Scotty indignantly. "We'll be movin' before they're near us."

"I'm sure we will, Mr. Scott," said Kirk with a straight face.

The main viewscreen flickered to reveal the solid figure of Commodore Robert Wesley. "Enterprise, *Star Base 10 received your message drone. We are ready to provide all necessary assistance.*"

Kirk settled back in the command chair and assumed a look of nonchalance. "Sorry, Bob. The excitement is all over."

"Then I missed quite a show," said the captain of the *Lexington* as he surveyed the damaged *Enterprise* on

his own viewscreen. *"Jim, you do get yourself into the biggest messes . . ."*

"But I also get myself out of them," insisted Kirk. *On my own.* "Stand by for transmission of my ship's log—it will fill you in on our current tactical situation. We can still use some back-up at our destination." The two commanders established a rendezvous time at the Wagner station. With an operative warp drive, the *Lexington* would travel half the length of the sector in the time it took the *Enterprise* to limp its way back to the trading post.

Lt. Kyle looked up from his sensors as communications between the ships came to an end. "Captain, I'm getting a reading for another ship, approaching from the direction of the trading post."

"It's the *Falchion*," announced Palmer as she played the controls of her communications board. "Transmissions are erratic . . . too much interference from ion debris in the area of the explosion." She strained to listen. "Just one word, Captain—casualties."

Chapter Twenty-Three

Medical Log Update: Landing party reports death of Security Chief Juan Cruz and critical injuries to Commander Spock—prognosis unavailable at this time. However, *Enterprise* crew has sustained minimal casualties in last battle action . . .

DR. CORTEJO'S LOG entry was drowned out by the rumble of running footsteps and shouting voices. He stepped out of the chief surgeon's office in time to observe McCoy and two paramedics race into sick bay, propelling a suspension stretcher ahead of them.

The waiting emergency staff burst into action. A doctor snatched the medical field scanner out of McCoy's hand and shouted out its readings while Nurse Chapel issued a stream of instructions to her nurses. The overlay of voices appeared chaotic, but Cortejo unraveled the strands without difficulty. With calm, unhurried motions he began preparing for surgery.

Dyson came up from behind McCoy and cast a quick look at the muddy patches which spread across the front of his jumpsuit. "Is any of that blood yours?" she asked as the paramedics lifted Spock's body off the stretcher onto a diagnostic bed.

McCoy shook his head. "No, just his."

The Vulcan's face and hands were smeared with black smudges and streaks of bright green; his chest was soaked with blood, staining his suit to the same dark colors splattered on McCoy's clothing.

"Glad to hear it," she said crisply. "Now get out of the way."

McCoy stepped back from the bed to allow Dyson to take his place, stepped back again to allow the paramedics to leave, then was shoved even farther aside by a nurse wheeling in medical equipment. By the time Captain Kirk barreled into sick bay, the doctor was standing in a far corner of the room, towel in hand, methodically wiping himself clean of Vulcan blood. Kirk automatically headed toward McCoy.

"Sulu filled me in on the tactical details of the attack on the aliens. What happened to Spock?"

"He was standing in the docking ring when the mine detonated," explained McCoy, dabbing ineffectually at his ruined clothing. "It's pure luck he's still alive. An alien body shielded him from the direct effects of the explosion and the force of the blast threw him into our corridor just before the airlock doors snapped shut. He's badly injured—burns, shrapnel wounds, several bone fractures and internal bleeding of the major organs."

Kirk scowled at the recital. "But he'll live."

McCoy recognized Kirk's adamant statement as a question. The doctor averted his eyes. "I'm sorry, Captain, I really couldn't say. I'm not familiar with Vulcan physiology." He finished wiping his hands and laid the bloodied towel aside. "The civilians at the trading post still need medical care. I'd like to return there with the security force . . ."

"The hell you will!" A passing nurse was startled by the savage exclamation; McCoy's face turned stony. Kirk quickly dropped his voice, but it was still tight with repressed anger. "Dr. McCoy, your place is here in sick bay . . ."

"I'll go, Captain." Dr. Dyson had threaded her way out of the crowd hovering around the medical bed which held the first officer. "My work here is done." She followed Kirk's glance back to the diagnostic panel which monitored Spock's readings. "Dr. Cortejo will operate as soon as Mr. Spock's vital signs stabilize."

Kirk gained control over his temper. He spoke calmly. "What is his condition?"

Unlike McCoy, Dyson faced the captain squarely. "Not very good. The internal injuries are quite severe and he's lost large quantities of blood. He'll lose even more during the surgery. Since there's no match for Mr. Spock's blood type on board, we're limited to the accumulated stock of his own donations. The crucial issue will be repairing the torn tissue before the supply is exhausted. However, if Dr. Cortejo can . . ."

"Thank you, Dr. Dyson." Kirk grimaced at the mention of the surgeon's name, turning his face away from McCoy. "You'd better hurry if you're going to the trading post. The first security team has already beamed aboard the *Falchion*."

Kirk abruptly walked away from the two doctors. He circled the knot of people still grouped around Spock, but did not stop there. Instead, he followed Nurse Chapel as she rushed out of the emergency room. When Kirk crossed the threshold of the hematology lab, Chapel was standing by an open storage unit inspecting its contents. All but one of its racks held sacks of bright red liquid; the last one displayed packets of emerald green.

"Can he do it?" Kirk demanded.

Chapel looked up in surprise. "Sir?"

"Cortejo. Can he do the surgery on Spock?"

"He's an excellent surgeon." The nurse dropped her eyes down to her data tablet. "He seems to feel that . . ."

"I don't give a damn what he thinks," snapped Kirk. "I'm asking for *your* opinion."

She met his gaze with difficulty. "No, I don't think he's qualified. He's never operated on a Vulcan before."

"Neither had McCoy when he performed heart surgery on Ambassador Sarek."

"Mr. Spock's injuries are more extensive this time." Chapel's voice quavered briefly. "And Dr. Cortejo hasn't studied Vulcan anatomy as thoroughly as Dr. McCoy . . ." She shook her head, unwilling to go on.

"Thank you, Nurse Chapel."

She returned to her inventory with an expression of fixed concentration.

"That one," instructed Dyson, pointing to the top of the small alcove in which she and McCoy were standing. The field expedition supplies were stored on shelves that stretched from the deck to the ceiling, forming a partial buffer from the noise and commotion of the sick bay emergency ward.

McCoy reached up and pulled down the metal case she had chosen. "I don't see why I have to stay here," he complained as she took the case from him. "I'll only get in the way of doctors who know what they're doing. At least I can be of some use as a paramedic at the trading post."

Dyson popped open the locks of the medical pack and began an inspection of its contents. "You're wasting your breath, Len. An order is an order."

He was not deterred from his protests. "*I* didn't enlist. That other McCoy joined this outfit, so why should I have to follow orders?"

"Just try leaving this ship. Captain Kirk will have 'that other' Dr. McCoy thrown in the brig but *you'll* be one who gets the leg irons. And a court-martial."

"I'll plead diminished capacity. You can be the star witness and testify that I haven't got the brains to be a ship's doctor." McCoy frowned when he realized that Dyson had stopped listening to him. "I might not see you again for days."

That brought her attention back. The corners of her mouth twitched. "You've seen quite enough of me already."

McCoy flushed a bright red but he affected a look of wide-eyed innocence even as his gaze flickered down from her face. "I'm the ship's chief medical officer. It's my duty to keep a close watch on the crew."

Dyson choked down her laughter. "Oh, suddenly you're back in Star Fleet. Well, listen here Lt. Commander McCoy . . ."

The rest of her reply was cut short by Kirk's sudden appearance. "I'm on my way, Captain." She hastily locked the field case and tugged it off the table.

"I'd better help . . ." McCoy moved forward to accompany her, but Kirk's hand shot out. Its iron grip on the doctor's arm stopped him from leaving.

"We have some business to discuss in your office," said Kirk as a sober-faced Dyson escaped from the alcove.

"It's not my office, Captain." McCoy yanked his arm free of the captain's hold, but Dyson had already left the room.

"Let me rephrase that statement," said Kirk in a low voice. "You can walk into that room, or I can drag you there myself."

McCoy stared back at Kirk in surprise. Whatever emotion he read in the captain's face muted his own response to a quiet, "Yes, sir." He remained silent until they reached the privacy of the chief surgeon's office and Kirk issued his next order.

"You've got to operate on Spock."

"What?" exclaimed McCoy, half-laughing. "Are you out of your mind? I don't have the surgical skill to operate on a Human, much less a Vulcan. I'm barely qualified to *assist* Cortejo . . ."

"That's not true." The stiff posture of a starship commander melted away. Kirk stepped closer, arms raised to urge his appeal. "You've got the knowledge, McCoy—somewhere. Reach for it, use it."

McCoy shook his head. "You don't know what you're asking of me, Captain."

"I don't care," said Kirk fiercely. "It's your duty as a doctor, as my ship's surgeon . . ."

"No!" McCoy pulled back in horror. "You can't just order me to cut open a living being. I've never done that before."

"You've done it a hundred times," Kirk thundered. "Goddammit, Bones, Spock is dying!" The words had no effect on the man standing before him.

McCoy shrugged impassively. "I'm not your 'Bones.' I can't remember and I can't help him."

"Can't?" asked the captain bitterly. "No, I think you *won't* remember. You're quite happy to forget the last twenty-five years. They frighten you because they weren't tidy and predictable—they were messy and full of nasty surprises. You're still a boy—a boy who wants to go through life without making mistakes, the bad mistakes that can't be set right again. To admit the mistakes means facing your own weaknesses . . ."

"Stop it!" shouted McCoy.

". . . and finding your strengths." Kirk's tone turned flat and harsh. "Listen to me, Leonard McCoy. *You* may not care what happens to Spock, but somewhere inside of you is a man who would stop at nothing to save his friend's life, to save any life, no matter what the personal cost. It was that quality that made him the best medical officer in Star Fleet. If you don't have that same passion for the value of life, you'll never be half the doctor he was. Or half the man."

Kirk fixed his eyes on the doctor's pale face. "Can you really let Spock die so easily?"

McCoy flinched away from Kirk's gaze, then slowly shook his head. "The first time I lost a patient, I kicked a hole through a wardroom door . . . cost me a week's salary to pay for the repairs. The other doctors told me I'd get used to it."

"You stopped kicking doors," said Kirk, "but you never got used to death."

McCoy stood silent for a moment, staring past the captain at a private vision. Then his eyes blinked as if to clear it away. "That's as good an epitaph as any doctor could ask for." McCoy took a deep breath and squared his shoulders. "I can't promise anything, Captain Kirk —except that I'll try."

Kirk's surge of relief was chilled by McCoy's next words. "You'll have to show me the way to surgery."

When the captain stormed onto the bridge, his yeoman waved a data tablet in his direction as a token gesture only. The past two weeks of battle action had created a staggering backload of damage and repair reports which Kirk had persistently pushed aside with contempt. To her surprise, this time he seized the offering as if it were a lifeline. He scanned the report with a deepening frown, then scrawled his initials on the form.

"This requisition is twelve days old, Yeoman," Kirk observed with grave displeasure. "Why haven't I gotten it before?" He didn't wait for an answer. "Bring me the updates," he ordered curtly. "Bring me everything you've got."

He settled down into the command chair and began a determined attack on the reports.

When Cortejo cracked open Spock's shattered chest, McCoy fought the urge to race out of surgery. He just managed to keep from getting sick. Pale-faced and sweating lightly, he watched Cortejo and Nurse Chapel engage the bio-support system, lacing its lines and tubes around the major organs inside the exposed body cavity.

Over the course of his first year at Atlanta General Hospital, McCoy had established an uneasy mastery over the horror of seeing a body so brutally violated. Emergency room cases were generous with blood and gore and demanded immediate action; queasiness was a luxury that could cost a patient's life. Walking into this room behind Spock's stretcher, he had mentally prepared himself for the coming scene, but without making allowances for the alien nature of the patient. McCoy's composure disintegrated under a barrage of colors and shapes and smells that were all *wrong*.

"Don't feel compelled to watch," said Cortejo acidly. "Captain Kirk may feel better having you in this room, but I have no intention of allowing you to assist during this operation."

McCoy took a deep breath and moved two steps closer to the surgical table. "As a doctor, I welcome the chance to observe new medical procedures." He forced himself to gaze past the blue light of the sterile field. The interior of the Vulcan's chest was awash with a muddy green liquid. McCoy swallowed, yet did not look away. "But I know my limitations. I'm here to learn, not practice."

"This is not a teaching hospital . . ."

"Bio-support engaged," murmured Chapel as she started the unit's controls.

". . . so don't expect a medical school lecture." The surgeon plunged his hands into the body cavity. The fingertips disappeared into the pool of blood, feeling their way across the tissues beneath. They stopped suddenly. "Suction here."

Chapel directed a clear length of tubing to the site. The transparent tubing turned green and within seconds a severed blood vessel was exposed as the liquid it pumped out was drained away at a slightly faster rate. Silently, without instructions, the nurse slipped the necessary clamps into place.

Cortejo's scalpel beam sprang to life, trimming off the jagged edges of the vessel. A suture beam rejoined the ends. When the clamps were released, the vessel remained whole. Yet the sea of blood still did not recede.

A high-pitched *bleep* from the support equipment brought a frown to Chapel's face. "Blood volume has dropped to 68%."

"Maintain present transfusion rate."

"What is a Vulcan's loss capacity?" asked McCoy.

"Theoretically, a Vulcan should be able to tolerate another 10% loss."

"But Mr. Spock is not a full Vulcan," added Chapel, quietly but distinctly. She addressed this statement to McCoy, but she uttered it for Cortejo's benefit. "He probably can't withstand more than another seven or eight percent loss of blood volume."

Cortejo did not acknowledge her comment, but the nurse knew he had heard and noted the information. Without slowing his hand movements, the surgeon launched into a lecture. "Given the expected duration of the surgical session, our constricting parameter is the limited blood supply. Increasing the transfusion rate while the patient is still hemorrhaging will rapidly deplete the supply. Furthermore, until I can repair more of the bleeding sites, the added volume will just get in my way." He exchanged the suture gun for a scalpel with a dextrous sleight of hand that almost escaped detection.

McCoy followed Cortejo's surgical technique with increasing fascination. The man's hands moved with a steady assurance, wielding the scalpel to pare away dying tissue, then deftly sealing the wounds with the suture beam. Though the form and function of this body was foreign to him, McCoy could still discern the pattern of the surgeon's movements, and appreciate the rapid mental judgements which balanced the severity of one damaged site against another without pausing for deliberation.

The return of the high-pitched alarm pulled McCoy's attention back to the bio-support unit and the two empty blood packets now stacked by its side.

"Volume down to 62%," announced Chapel grimly.

"Prepare to increase transfusion rate." Cortejo continued his unhurried conversation while his fingers flew even faster. "I've always enjoyed the challenge of truly demanding surgery. Dr. McCoy, this is an excellent opportunity for you to observe just such a situation."

"Wagner Post to Enterprise. *Come in,* Enterprise." Uhura's voice crackled over the loudspeaker, barely fighting its way through the static of the dissipating ion clouds. Palmer's best efforts did little to clear the channel.

"Uhura, can you provide me with visual contact?" asked Kirk as he gazed uneasily at the blank screen above the communications post.

"Sorry, Captain, but the video transmitter was blown away, along with about a third of the docking ring. It's taken me hours just to get audio channels functional."

Kirk accepted her statement with a resigned sigh, but he suspected it would be a long time before his confidence in radio contact would be completely restored. He leaned closer to the panel, as if his proximity to the board would increase its efficiency. "What's your status on the station?"

"All clear. The hatchlings were destroyed with the Queen and the surviving Ravens have been placed under sedation."

"Sedation?" cried Kirk. "I want those aliens under confinement! With a 24-hour guard."

"I agree, Captain." Dr. Dyson's voice answered him. *"But for medical reasons rather than security. Once the Queen was destroyed, the 'borrowed' persona of each Raven's victim gained dominance, and the resulting emotional trauma was fairly severe. Most of them were having hysterics, so I've placed them under heavy sedation to prevent a mass suicide."*

"Most?"

"One . . . man—a Captain Neil—doesn't seem to care what he looks like so long as his ship is okay. He may be useful in helping the others learn to adjust to their situation, but for the moment, I've got my hands full just trying to keep them under while I treat the civilian survivors. I could use some help. Make that a lot of help."

"That won't be a problem, Dr. Dyson. The *Lexington* will arrive at Wagner Post in a little over three hours."

"Well, it's about time!"

"My sentiments exactly," said Kirk with a weary smile. His smile faded at her next words.

"Captain, what is Mr. Spock's condition?"

"I don't know yet. Cortejo and McCoy have been in surgery for over five hours."

Uhura's repair work must have come apart, because

the communications link with Dyson was abruptly severed.

"This is our last packet of T-Negative." Chapel slipped the green pouch into the bio-support system without interrupting the flow of blood through the web of tubing.

"Drainage recovery?" asked Cortejo as he carefully explored the exposed organs for an injury still highlighted on the surgical monitor.

"Levels have dropped to 3% of infused volume."

"And what is the significance of that fact, Dr. McCoy?" The surgeon gently worked his fingers around the edges of the left lung. A small rip in the spongy tissue was easily repaired with a regen probe. Another light died on the life systems panel.

"The patient's condition is improving," answered McCoy. As he spoke, he studied Cortejo's subtle wrist motion in wielding the surgical tools. Every movement was precisely calculated, and sheared of time-wasting excess. "His system is retaining the administered transfusion, which indicates the internal bleeding is under control."

The surgeon nodded. "We must be ready to close soon. This blood unit will just be sufficient for replenishing the patient's minimum blood volume." He pulled his hands out of the open chest and exchanged his probe for a newly recharged scalpel resting on McCoy's palm. "There is only one more cut . . ."

Cortejo aimed the instrument tip at a blackened patch of tissue and released a final burst of the thin cutting beam. A thick orange fluid welled up from the site and a new light flared into life on the surgical monitor.

For the first time in five hours, Cortejo's hand faltered.

McCoy looked across the sterile field at Chapel. "Nurse, have you got any idea what . . ."

"I'm in charge of this operation," snapped Cortejo.

"What is it, then? What happened?" McCoy asked.

"I don't know. It's not Human . . ." The fluid continued to ooze from the wound. "Suture," the surgeon demanded, throwing the scalpel aside. He razed the site with the new beam but it did not staunch the flow.

"Vital signs dropping," announced Chapel tersely. "Blood packet at 50% of unit volume."

Cortejo repeated his suture work, but the second pass had no effect. The life system indicators continued their descent.

McCoy stared first at the open wound, then at Cortejo, whose hands had stopped moving.

Spock was dying.

Kirk was pacing the sick bay deck when the two doctors emerged from surgery. A grim-faced Cortejo walked away without speaking. McCoy leaned wearily against the wall, ignoring the captain's barrage of questions. He peeled off his surgical gloves with maddening deliberation. He unfastened the clasps of his gown and tugged at its neckline. He stretched. Only then did McCoy speak.

"He's out of immediate danger."

"What does that mean?" demanded Kirk as relief and worry clashed.

"It means that barring post-operative complications, Spock is doing just dandy." McCoy rubbed the back of his neck. "Damn crazy-quilt physiology! Vulcan this and Human that, plus elements his genetic code dreamed up out of thin air. Every time I take him apart, I wonder if I can put him back together again."

A moment passed before the full impact of the words

hit the captain. "Bones?" he whispered, then grabbed the surgeon's shoulders and shook him. "Bones!"

"Lay off, Jim," said McCoy irritably. "I told you I can't be more specific than that. Have some consideration for a tired man—I've been in surgery for days . . ." His face contracted as if in pain.

"What happened in there?" demanded Kirk.

Passing a hand over his eyes, McCoy frowned in thought. After a few seconds he looked up into Kirk's face, confusion deepening the lines of his brow. "How did Spock get hurt, Jim? He wasn't wounded in the attack . . ." McCoy's gaze turned inward—he continued as if talking to himself. "And he was in my room, talking a blue streak about memory circuits and back-up chips, while I knocked down some absolutely vile Red Nova."

"What do you remember after that?" urged Kirk.

"In surgery . . . I thought we'd lose Spock when his liver ruptured." McCoy was talking with some effort. "I had to do some fancy suture work to patch the tissue together."

"So you finished the surgery," said Kirk softly.

"But why was Cortejo operating?" demanded McCoy with renewed alarm. "He may be a good surgeon, but he hasn't had enough experience with Vulcans to handle an operation that complicated—this was no time to start."

The doctor shook his head as if clearing away a distracting fog. "I don't even remember entering sick bay . . ." McCoy suddenly looked horror-stricken. "Jim, I can't have gone into surgery drunk. Nothing would excuse that, not even . . ." He stopped short. "Nothing," he reiterated grimly.

"Don't worry, Bones." Kirk savored the sound of the name. "You weren't drunk, just sleepwalking." He smiled at McCoy's incomprehension. "I'll fill you in on the details over a glass of that Red Nova. We can drink to Spock's health."

And to the memory of one Leonard McCoy, civilian, who gave up his life in the line of duty.

Epilogue

"BONES . . ."

"Yeah, Jim," answered McCoy absently as he scanned the over-long requisition list displayed on his desk computer. An alarming number of medical report tapes were stacked by its side. Acting chief Cortejo had exhibited little interest in the more mundane duties accompanying his temporary promotion.

"Have you ever given any thought to quitting the service?" asked Kirk with forced nonchalance as he inspected the wrapped parcel with his name written on the front.

A startled McCoy looked up from the terminal screen. "Is that a not-so-subtle hint that your chief medical officer should retire?"

"No, not at all." Kirk's fingers broke the seal and began peeling away the paper. "I just thought maybe you preferred the idea of a practice back home, in a small town . . ."

"But I've got my practice right here, Jim," said McCoy with a puzzled smile. "With this starship crew. Besides, I'm a surgeon—a damn good one—and I wouldn't get much chance for surgery in the boondocks. Not to mention the use of a better research lab than you'll find anywhere in Georgia."

"Just checking." Kirk ripped through the last layer of

wrapping. He stared down at the contents of the package. "Bones!"

The doctor grinned broadly at his friend's reaction. "I meant to give it to you sooner, but what with one thing and another . . ."

Kirk raised the Tyrellian knife up to the light, delighting in the glints of the blue and green that flashed off the blade. "You went back for it." A sudden thought pulled his attention back to the doctor. "How much did you have to pay?"

"None of your business," said McCoy firmly. "I'll settle for the difference with Spock," he added under his breath.

The knife spun into the air, hung suspended for an instant, then tumbled back downwards. The handle landed in Kirk's palm with a satisfying slap.

"Just don't cut yourself," grumbled McCoy as he calculated the amount of unfinished business still ahead of him. "I've got enough work to do as it is."

"That reminds me. You're due for a ship deck-klutz award. Injury due to inattention to ship-wide . . ."

"I knew it! I'm never going to live this down."

"Just wait until Spock gets ahold of you." The captain laughed to see McCoy wince. The Vulcan could be quite caustic when given a chance. Kirk carefully wrapped the antique weapon again and tucked the bundle under his arm. "Drop by my cabin when you're done."

"You can expect me next month," sighed McCoy as Kirk strolled out of the office.

Seconds later the door whisked open again for Christine Chapel. Her hands were filled with even more record tapes. Ignoring McCoy's warning growl, she detailed each cassette as it was added to the existing pile. "Personnel duty log. Surgical operations summary. Walk-in patient log. Critical-care patient updates . . ."

"Didn't Cortejo handle any of this?" McCoy cried out as the stack teetered dangerously.

Chapel began a second stack. "Patient discharge log. Case review: tape one. Case review: tape two." She handed this last cassette to him directly—"You're in that one"—then continued as before. "Case review: tape three. Medical lab supply inventory. Medical equipment maintenance log." A resounding click heralded the end of her load. "Welcome back, Dr. McCoy."

"I wish I'd never left." He eyed the record tape in his hand. "Speaking of amnesia, where the hell is Dr. Dyson? I've been trying to reach her all morning."

"Oh, somewhere in the Research section," murmured Chapel vaguely. "She's been working with Frazer on the final report on the Raven research project."

"I'm gone for two weeks and this place falls to pieces." McCoy jammed the cassette into his terminal. "Spock steals half my staff for his science department, Gonzalo spoils an entire batch of stokaline . . ." When he looked up again, Chapel had reached the door. "Find Dr. Dyson and send her in here," he yelled after the nurse.

Nearly two hours passed before the buzzer to his office announced a visitor. "Come in," he called out absently.

A woman in science blue stepped across the threshold. "You wanted to see me, sir?"

McCoy beckoned her inside, but kept his eyes fixed on the terminal. "No wonder Gonzalo botched that synthesis; he's been covering for Tajiri on the duty log.

Good thing that boy is in Star Fleet—he'd make a lousy forger as a civilian."

He snapped off the screen image and turned his attention to the neurologist. "Have a seat, Dr. Dyson."

"Thank you," she said without moving. "But I haven't got much time, sir."

McCoy cocked an eyebrow at her impatience. "Mr. Spock will be in sick bay for another few days. If I were you, I'd take advantage of the lull to take it easy."

"Yes, sir."

"That wasn't a suggestion, it was an order," he said gruffly. "I'm not a soft touch, like Cortejo." He was rewarded by Dyson's involuntary smile. Now if she would only relax. "Nurse Chapel informs me that you were a great help during my 'extended leave.' Unfortunately, I can't thank you for any specifics . . ."

"That's quite all right, Dr. McCoy. You proved to be a rather interesting case." Her brittle smile resurfaced briefly. "Just be glad I'm not doing a journal article on you."

He grinned ruefully. "I feel like I've woken up from a night on the town. The kind where you figure you had a good time because you can't remember what happened."

After a pause, he continued with some embarassment. "And if I did anything foolish, nobody would tell me."

She shrugged. "Your drawl was a bit thicker, but mostly you kept to your studies—you made it up to the third year in current medical school curriculum."

"Good Lord," McCoy groaned. "My first vacation in years and I spend it trudging through medical textbooks. What a waste."

Dyson stole a glance at the door. "If you'll excuse me, Dr. McCoy, I've got a lot of work . . ."

"All right, Dyson. You're dismissed."

"Thank you, sir," she said, wheeling away.

McCoy noted her hasty departure with bemusement. *Still a bit green, but promising medical material.*

He turned back to his work.

THE EXPLOSIVE NEW
STAR TREK ®
HARDCOVER

PROBE

by
Margaret Wander Bonanno

Pocket Books is proud to present PROBE, an epic length novel that continues the story of the movie STAR TREK IV.

PROBE reveals the secrets behind the mysterious probe that almost destroyed Earth—and whose reappearance now sends Captain Kirk, Mr. Spock, and their shipmates hurtling into unparalleled danger…and unsurpassed discovery.

The Romulan Praetor is dead, and with his passing, the Empire he ruled is in chaos. Now on a small planet in the heart of the Neutral Zone, representatives of the United Federation of Planets and the Empire have gathered to discuss initiating an era of true peace. But the talks are disrupted by a sudden defection—and as accusations of betrayal and treachery swirl around the conference table, news of the probe's reappearance in Romulan space arrives. And the *Enterprise* crew find themselves headed for a final confrontation with not only the probe—but the Romulan Empire.

Available In Hardcover
from Pocket Books

POCKET
B O O K S